A Case for Dr. Palindrome

Colin Brezicki

For Catherine Rose

One

"You go off into your own little world, Paul, and I think one day you might not come back."

Linda's comment that morning still rankled. Okay, so he had forgotten to put out the recycling bins—no big deal, he thought, a little put out himself. Now, turning into his driveway, with Vaughn Williams' *Lark Ascending* drawing him even further into his own little world, he reached for his house keys, somehow knowing they wouldn't be there.

And yes, the tray was empty.

So he was on a roll now—recycling bins and house keys the latest casualties of his own-little-worldliness—and the day not half over.

Could he maybe draw some comfort from having suspected the keys wouldn't be there? Might that count as a last fingernail hold on being *compos mentis*?

He saw them on the hall table that morning when he came down for the newspaper. So he forgot to pick them up when he left for school—distracted perhaps by Linda's remark about going off into his own little world.

In the driveway now he leaned back to listen to Nigel Kennedy's violin follow the lark on its final rhapsodic rise into a clear sky beyond distraction, beyond recycling bins and house keys—beyond silence.

Somewhere beyond that was his own little world, but whatever Linda believed, it wasn't a place he could get to anymore.

When the music finished he switched off the radio, but kept the engine and A/C running; he was in no hurry to step into the steamy sauna outside.

It was only June and already the stifling heat of high summer hung over Niagara. Early that morning a clear blue sky had emerged from a milky dawn, and a bright splash of sun rinsed the new magnolia leaves outside his study window; but by noon, the sky had glazed into a translucent dome and trapped the hot, fetid air over the city. The day was already wilting, with the fierce hollow of afternoon still ahead.

The house offered no refuge because he had no way of getting in, a consequence of being absent-minded.

"Just so you know, I'm very here-and-now minded," he said aloud to no one in particular, and felt better for it.

Taking an occasional leave of absence from a world inhabited by everyone else was reasonable enough, he thought. Whenever the marauding thought hordes pinioned his brain he was rendered incapable of focusing, or responding to people when they spoke to him. Once the hordes had done with the looting and pillaging of his mind they left him drained and disoriented.

And here he'd spoken out loud to himself. Again. He was doing it more often now, but maybe that wasn't so strange. At least what he said to himself was logical and clear.

So he spoke his thoughts. What of that? He only really communicated with himself anymore so why not do it out loud? Characters in plays spoke dramatic monologues—all those soliloquys in Shakespeare—nothing unusual there. Quite normal in fact. Not just normal but necessary at times. How do we know what we think until we hear what we're saying? Someone said that recently at a seminar. Said it out loud and didn't just think it. In other words—or any words—thoughts aren't real till they're spoken.

So why should he not speak out snippets of his own thoughts in his minivan—or in his classroom, where more and more these days he might as well be talking to himself—and not worry that he was taking leave of his senses?

Then he remembered the wild-haired vagrant he saw outside the courthouse the other day, a crazy man ranting and waving his arms and dividing a sea of pedestrians who had suddenly become *very* preoccupied with their own thoughts. No doubt the man's soliloquy made perfect sense to him.

Paul first spoke aloud to himself, he remembered now, in a confessional booth when he was ten. He'd gone well into the whole spiel of bless me father and how long it had been since his last confession and these were his sins, all declaimed loudly enough for the priest to hear him on the other side of the grille, when he suddenly realized there *was* no priest. The booth was empty because he had got the wrong day. A forgivable mistake, he reckoned now, but he had confessed his sins—the ones he was prepared to admit to—out loud to himself.

When all was said—aloud or otherwise—he would have to watch this development in what wife and daughter now suspected to be a loosening of rivets in a once securely bolted mind.

Dad, you have to go back to counseling.

Seriously Paul, think about it. One session with Dr. Hannah was never enough.

But, *seriously*, one visit was more than enough. "I have wherefore I know not forgot my keys!" he announced to his dashboard now because he could, and for the time being be okay with that. No Dr. Hannah around to tell him he needed therapy for doing so.

The homes on the opposite side of the street, set back behind trim lawns and ornamental shrubbery, their doors closed and blinds drawn against the murderous sun, displayed an indifference to his plight. Inscrutable, in the way houses are.

He always saw facial expressions in house fronts—he started doing it as a child—maybe an early warning of the rivet loosening to come.

When he first gazed up at his stepfather's large gabled house on Maple Street in Toronto he remembered seeing a face in pain. It was the startled expression of a woman he had earlier observed in the dentist's chair when his mother took him downtown to meet his brand new father in the brand new clinic where he fixed people's teeth. Following his mother down a corridor he passed an open door and paused to look inside. He saw the woman stretched out on a chair, staring up at the ceiling. A man in a pale green top and trousers with very long legs was bending over her, holding a drill between thumb and finger. Her mouth gaped wide and her eyebrows shot up when he lowered the whining drill into her face.

His new father's house was that face—its verandah wide open, the blue-eyed glass above, the gables arched in surprise. His new father had lived there alone, but it had rooms galore, his mother told him, more than enough for all of them—Jennifer and himself, their mother, Aunt Helen and their new father who fixed peoples' teeth. All of them together in a house with a Rapunzel tower attached, and fish scales all around it, and a huge chestnut tree in front that turned black and menacing in winter.

Now, a lifetime later, Viktor Crane was once again the sole inhabitant of his house on Maple Street, only packed away this time under layers of ice bags deep inside his own basement freezer where he had resided for the past ten years.

Ten years and still Paul had found no way to dispose of him. Like old Mrs. Harrison who lived opposite and had kept her husband's ashes on the hall table until she figured out what she should do with them, which she never did as far as Paul knew. When she was moved out to the nursing home she most likely took them with her.

So thought Bradley Caldwell, the insufferable know-all who had recently purchased the old woman's property and now lived right across the street from the frozen remains of Viktor Crane.

Caldwell was insufferable because he was nosey and because he had called Paul *Paul* without so much as a by your leave when they first met. Mrs. Harrison must have told him Paul's name, along with everything else she had told him. Now the man persisted in asking questions about the Crane house. How long had it been empty? Why was it empty at all when Paul could *make a killing* by selling it? More than once Paul came close to telling him to stay on his side of the street and mind his own business. But he thought better of it. No point in antagonizing him.

Caldwell would have to be watched—though that was a challenge with Paul struggling to live his own life sixty miles away in Heritage, in the house he inhabited with wife and daughter when he wasn't *off in his own little world*. But a house he could neither inhabit nor even get into right now because he had no key.

He checked his watch. He had to find a way to kill time until Linda came home.

She worked till five at Summerfield and Day. An accountant and very precise with numbers, she left work at five on the dot and, traffic permitting, pulled into the driveway forty minutes later. But that wouldn't be happening for another three hours.

Rachel would have finished Yoga class and gone straight to her afternoon shift at 'Body and Soul'. Not at school anymore because she'd had quite enough of that.

Without his keys he had no choice but to wait outside. He couldn't possibly sit in the minivan running the A/C all afternoon. Idling an engine for three hours would only add to the greenhouse gases that had already overheated the planet. He supposed he could drive back into town and spend the afternoon marking exam papers in the air-conditioned public library, but city crews were resurfacing half the streets in Heritage and he was reluctant to face the delays again.

What to do? If he had a cell phone he could call Rachel at work, get her to call a cab and give the driver her house key. But giving a cabbie the key to your house maybe wasn't a good idea.

Anyway he couldn't phone Rachel because he didn't have a cell. Not as in he had left it somewhere, which would be par for the course, but as in he didn't own one. Another point of contention with his family. They told him a cell would make his life simpler. But his life was simpler without one. If he had a cell people could contact him at any time, come crashing into his little world along with the thought hordes and bind him fast to the ground like Gulliver. He didn't mention Gulliver or the thought hordes to Linda and Rachel, because if he had they'd have looked that certain way at each other again.

He wondered if he should make that second appointment with Dr. Hannah, the shrink with hypnotic powers who had made Paul say things without realizing he was saying them during that one session. He didn't mention Dr. Hannah's hypnotic powers to Linda, or that he referred to him as Dr. Palindrome, because it was she who had recommended him and she'd think Paul hadn't taken seriously his introductory session with a distinguished clinical psychologist whose name just happened to be spelt the same both ways.

The meeting had not begun well.

"Good evening, Mr. Throne. Please take a seat."

"Thorne."

"I'm so sorry, I have Throne here. Paul Throne. It must be a typo. I'll have it corrected. Please take a chair."

"Thanks. I was *thrown* there for a moment." He waited but the man either missed the remark or more likely didn't think it was all that funny. In any case the session went downhill from there.

Dr. Hannah had opened up a whole new can of worms—like there weren't more than enough open already—because in getting Paul to say things he didn't know he was saying or remembered saying when he finished, the therapist had made him even *less* certain of his mental state. It was for sure a whole new can of worms to know that he had let all sorts of things come tumbling out of his mouth while he was in some kind of induced coma.

At least when he talked to himself and not to a

therapist, he was completely aware of what he was saying and could clearly recall afterwards everything he had said.

No, he couldn't risk another visit. Whatever he had already told Dr. Hannah that filled all those pages of his spiral notebook there was plenty more where that came from, and his new propensity to spill his guts without being aware he was doing it made a return visit out of the question.

He would be stark raving mad to consider it, he thought now, and smiled.

He could manage things on his own without having to see Dr. Hannah again. The school year was nearly done and he would soon have time to take care of things. It was long past due. Ten years in a freezer was ludicrous. He should have his head examined. And how had he got away with it? How was it that in all that time no one had inquired about the sudden disappearance of Viktor Crane? His luck couldn't hold out forever.

Especially now with Bradley Caldwell living right there and already curious about the vacant house. Paul should have installed an alarm system last summer. He should have done it years ago. Right away in fact, when everything happened. But he never got around to that either.

Linda would have got around to it. She wasted no time installing an alarm in their own house after a rash of break-ins in Heritage's south end. But she would have nothing to do with the Crane house. Not since she learned never to ask questions whose answers she didn't want to hear. That was Linda. She had even stopped asking him when he was going to sell the property.

As the automatic garage door rumbled open he

looked up at his house once more. It stared past him, closed off, impenetrably secured thanks to Linda's efficiency, and with the air conditioner going full blast, again thanks to Linda, bollock-freezing inside.

A year ago he might have forced open the connecting door from inside the garage to the hallway, but not now with the coded alarm system installed.

The only person he knew well enough to share the code and a key with was Magnus who taught with him at Centennial, but Magnus lived in the north end, too far away and not worth the bother. It would take an hour to drive there and back, with the traffic and road construction. Besides Magnus would invite him in and Paul would have to decline, which, along with his obvious agitation over his forgotten key and lost time, would prompt Magnus to ask him if all was okay. All was far from okay and had been that way for as long as he could remember. Magnus was his friend but Paul didn't want to have that conversation right now.

He didn't know his neighbours well enough to entrust them with a key. The Greek family on the right had just moved in and the retired couple on the left kept pretty much to themselves. Same with the family across the street—in twenty years of living opposite they had never talked. Okay, once he had gone over with a letter that was mistakenly delivered to his own mailbox and attempted to engage the sullen teen that answered the door. But after taking the letter and mumbling something, the boy closed the door in his face.

Could Dr. Hannah imagine that? Not once in twenty years had two families living a mere twenty meters apart made any real contact. What a neighbourhood. No wonder he talked to himself.

Cars were one problem. People went straight from their front doors to their vehicles in the driveway or, like Paul and Linda they drove straight out of their garages with a click of the remote and took off down the street.

Then there was winter. For five months everyone stayed indoors. You might wave at a neighbour as you snow-blowed the driveway after a blizzard. Perhaps the word was *snow-blew.* In any case no one stopped to talk because it was freezing and everyone was busy snow-blowing. Even if you didn't mind the cold and wanted to chat you couldn't because snow-blowers were loud. *Unspeakably* loud. So winter became a long separation.

Summer wasn't much better. People hired landscapers to look after the yards while everyone stayed indoors with the air conditioning on and minded their own business. What a bloody climate.

Still, there was an upside to neighbours who minded their own business. Bradley Caldwell should mind his own business instead of being so eager to mind Paul's.

"I see the guy reading your meter, Paul. How come you keep the hydro going when there's no one living in the house?"

He first noticed the man standing on his own porch back in February when he pulled up at the curb, but made no eye contact with him. He stepped out of his car and went directly down the side of the house so he could enter by the back door.

But sometime later, in March, when he pulled up outside the house, Caldwell crossed the street to introduce himself. He addressed Paul by his first name, therefore making it unnecessary for Paul to introduce *himself,* and then asked him about his frequent visits to the empty house.

"I just maintain the property Mr. Caldwell, check on things inside, you know, leaks, that sort of thing." He didn't mention that he checked the freezer too, always a priority. Thankfully it was a Westinghouse. Very reliable. *They built them to last in those days Mr. Caldwell but you can never be too careful when you've got a family member stuffed inside.*

"Why don't you sell, Paul? The market's at peak. Now's the time. And *this* neighbourhood? The Beaches? Are you kidding me? Outa sight. I was lucky to get in when I did." He was interested in the history of the old street he said. "Got to be lots of stories," he said, arching an eyebrow at Paul in a way that made him wonder if Caldwell had a particular story in mind.

Inside the garage now he switched off the engine and stepped out of the minivan. He looked around to see what options were open for him to kill time. He could cut the lawns front and back, but really it was too hot and the grass was already going dormant. Anyway he felt stupid sitting on the tractor mower that Linda had landed him with one birthday—for a front lawn the size of a small golf green, and a back with too many flowerbeds, birdfeeders and shrubs to allow him to get up a decent head of steam even though the mower was the junior model which forced his knees out at the sides and made him look silly as well as feel stupid.

He could sweep up the husks of spider-sucked bluebottles from their window-sill graveyard, re-read the yellowing *Globe and Mails* piled high in one of the recycling bins that he had neglected to put out, or hose down the minivan for the second time that hot and rainless month. The possibilities were endless.

He looked at the old beer fridge in the corner. He

should defrost it; the thickening ice deposit made it difficult to shut the freezer compartment properly.

It was a blessing, he reminded himself a dozen times a week as he had done for the past ten years, that the old reliable Westinghouse in the basement of the late Viktor Crane's house in Toronto, whose history had become a source of great fascination for the inquisitive Mr. Caldwell, was self-defrosting.

He took two bottles of water from the fridge and grabbed his briefcase. He would pass the time by marking that morning's exam papers.

He left the garage open for Linda and walked around the side of the house to the back.

The blossoming crab apples were already sagging in the fierce heat. He hung his jacket on the back of the patio chair, removed his tie and undid the top button of his shirt. Twisting the cap off one of the bottles he took a swig. You paid more for a liter of water now than you did for a liter of gas. Who would have imagined that twenty years ago? It didn't stop there. "I paid more for my son's running shoes than I did for my first car," a colleague recently said.

He took another swallow from the bottle. In this humidity what he needed was a gulp of air.

In the trees at the bottom of the yard a cardinal piped in treble, like someone doing scales on a recorder.

The piping sound was smothered by a car crawling past the front of the house with its speakers thumping like depth charges. The stereo system probably cost more than the car. More than a pair of running shoes. The driver would be deaf by the time he was thirty. Probably half-deaf now like Paul. Except that Paul's impairment happened years ago when old Frenchie blew up the mountain at Great Bear Mine. No one wore ear-protectors back then and so he was half deaf now because he was on the mountain the day Frenchie primed a bench with double the prescribed explosive and blew himself away.

One day he feared he would go completely deaf and live inside a soundproof bubble where he wouldn't hear even what he spoke out loud to himself and so it would be just like thinking.

Now everyone wore ear-protectors, even the college student who flagged the one-way-only traffic where the town was installing new storm drains. At the end of his shift the young man would go home, remove his ear-protectors, turn on his stereo and make shit of his brains with heavy metal from his juiced-up woofers.

Or maybe not. Perhaps the young man listened to Mozart with the volume low. Linda told him he always assumed the worst. But the worst was always the way he thought when the thought hordes charged into his head like demented Huns.

He must try to be more positive. Now a noun. *Positivity,* Linda called it when she admonished him to have more of it, like sprinkling bran on his cereal. The word made him think of power walkers on the street, punching the air like boxers and grinning fiercely through it all. Give me positivity or give me death, he imagined them thinking to themselves.

The cardinal flew off to a neighbour's yard. He opened his briefcase and took out the sheaf of exam booklets.

Senior Literature.

Section A. *Hamlet* by William Shakespeare.

Section B. *The Birthday Party* by Harold Pinter.

Together they sounded like a Danish children's story. Some of his students might fare better if the curriculum offered literature coated in fairy tale frosting. *The Berenstein Bears Picnic at Wuthering Heights. The Dubliners Meet the Pied Piper. King Lear and the Giant Peach.*

He opened the first exam booklet. Tessa Barnes.

At least Tessa Barnes couldn't start an exam as she did a term essay, with a dictionary definition. Students who had no idea what to say in a term essay always began with a dictionary definition.

Discuss Fatalism in *Hamlet.*

Fatalism. A belief that all events are predetermined and inevitable; a submissive attitude to events as being inevitable.

They would pin a tail on any word in the question and go straight to the dictionary. *Poem. A composition in verse rather than prose.* It was always a false start. A spinning of wheels. The poem still had to be discussed, the essay to be written.

But dictionaries weren't allowed in a year-end exam, and so Tessa Barnes would be out of luck.

He summoned his positivity, but suspected the paper would be a crock.

If Hamlet spent less time thinking about what he was supposed to do and more time just getting on and doing it he would of been a much happier man. He could of killed Claudius and been reunited with his mother, then he would of become king which would of been great for Denmark and for him. He was a lot like Edipus who more or less did the same thing. You could say Hamlet and

Edipus had the exact same Achilles Heel.

"Could you really? Christ in a blender, Tess," he said aloud, using her own pet profanity. He pushed the booklet aside and sat back in his chair. Maybe dictionaries should be allowed in examinations. Along with a guide to the conditional. Would *have* and could *have*. Basic grammar was a losing battle with students who didn't read and didn't care anymore that they didn't.

Tessa Barnes sat in the front row, flashed her wide green eyes and pretended to listen while she sucked on a long strand of crimson-streaked hair or played with her bracelet. His teaching of *Hamlet* was clearly lost on her. He wanted the class to see that Hamlet was real because he was conflicted—his urge to kill his stepfather was countered by what he knew to be perfectly valid reasons not to. And so we connect with him, he explained—we who likewise dither over decisions large and small. But for Tessa Barnes and her strand of crimson hair or string of pink gum coiled around her little finger the play was just a meaningless void between act one and the last scene where shit finally happens.

Waiting for Hamlet by William Shakespeare.

He picked up the exam booklet again. She had provided a patronizing storyline to demonstrate that most of the play was unnecessary.

Hamlet is the prince of Denmark. When the play opens his father is dead and his mother remarries his uncle Claudius only a short time later. A ghost appears who is Hamlet's father also named Hamlet (okay so that's weird). GHOST Hamlet tells SON Hamlet that Claudius killed him so Claudius could become king and marry Gertrude, ghost Hamlet's widow and son Hamlet's mother. So now that son Hamlet knows Claudius killed his father why doesn't he just kill him back? But no. He lays on a whole bunch of sylliq...sellilequeys...speaches! to tell us what he's thinking. Does any of this really matter? In the end he does what he should of done right away. Kill his stepfather. Yay! Meantime his two school friends get hoisted by their own petard, his squeeze drowns herself, and her father and brother also peg out. As does Gertrude and then finally Hamlet himself. All of which could of been avoided if he just killed his stepfather at the beginning and got on with his life.

The way they did in a good TV drama full of sirens and emergency rooms and eleventh hour cocaine busts, the crisis solved in exactly sixty minutes including time-outs for our sponsors. What was the point of all this thinking?

He tried to get them to see that, like Hamlet's, our lives are a muddle. The thought hordes are always on the horizon, ready to invade, loot and pillage the moment we lower our guard and ask *Why*? Hamlet tries to make sense of his life and makes a dog's breakfast of it instead, same as we do.

He tried to explain that the decisions we consciously make are trivial in the grand scheme—what dressing to have on a salad, what clothes to wear, what car to buy, carry an umbrella or chance the rain.

Life-changing decisions on the other hand seem not to be made at all. To kill or not to kill. To be or not to be. They happen anyway. The road not taken is the one we don't see until we've passed it, and the one we take is the road we're already on. Hamlet didn't have GPS and neither do we. We play it by ear and follow our noses. It is what it is, we say, when all's said and done. *There's a divinity that shapes our ends,* is how Hamlet put it.

Paul never *decided* to become a priest, nor did he decide at the end of a humiliatingly brief stint with the Pentecostal Fathers of Mount St. Michael *not* to become one.

Life decided those things.

He didn't decide to be a teacher. Father McGrath planted the idea in his head when Paul was politely let go from Mount St. Michael; and when Johnny Fonseca, the young Portuguese labourer at Great Bear Mine, randomly asked him for English lessons after work one evening, he became a teacher.

He didn't decide to love Linda. That was never a decision. He was already in love with her before he met her that New Year's at Chris Turnbull's party. Anyway who actually *decides* to fall in love?

Or fall out of it.

They didn't decide to have a child nor did they decide not to. They made love one night or more likely one weekend morning when they weren't too tired or had to rush off to work, and so Rachel was conceived. Then she was born and some time after that he and Linda did not decide, in the sense of sitting down one day and drawing up a list of the pros and cons, to stop making love. They just didn't anymore.

He didn't decide to help his stepfather die. He agreed to do it without realizing that's what the old man was talking about when he asked him. He loathed and despised the cretinous old bastard, and so his mind always wandered whenever the man spoke. So he was already thinking about Linda being proposed to by Trevor at the very moment the cretinous old bastard was telling Paul he wanted him to *manage things*. It was only when the time finally came for him to manage things that he realized he meant *help him to die.* He was eager enough to oblige until the moment came when he had to well and truly manage things because his stepfather's detailed instructions turned out not to be worth the paper they were typed on.

It unsettled him now to realize he had spent more than half his allotted lifespan not really deciding anything for himself.

He returned to the essay. Had Tessa actually read the play apart from them all reading it together in class, she included, in a coil-the-gum-twirl-the-crimson-strand sort of way? On her own she likely read one of the student guides on the Internet. *Hamlet for Idiots.*

The philosopher Augustus Comte read nothing, on purpose, so he would think only original thoughts. Tessa Barnes read nothing so she could think no thoughts at all. An enviable state to be in, he thought.

Linda would upbraid him for his lack of positivity and remind him again to make that second appointment with Dr. Hannah.

He wondered if Dr. Hannah had read *Hamlet.* Enough material there for an entire symposium, he would reckon.

He took another swig from his bottle to slake the thirst that heat and negativity had brought on.

A second car drove past. Not Linda. Not yet.

Inside the house he was locked out of, on his laptop, there would be another e-mail from Bradley Caldwell who was interested in the history of old streets, and one address in particular that had a story to tell.

Hey there neighbour havent heard from you in a while. just wondering when I can come and look around your stepfathers house. dying to see the old furniture and the moldings. I think I have someone who's interested in buying. let me know. bradley.

That was yesterday. He sent his first one in March, the day after he introduced himself. *Hi Paul.* After that the messages became increasingly, increasingly what? *Importunate.* A lost word. Like *feckless*—another apt word for Caldwell who was feckless and importunate.

The man was up to something. Why else would he bother about an old house on a leafy street in the Beaches? Was it a deliberate blind for him to say the house had historical interest? With all the new houses that had sprung up on the street over the past thirty years the Crane house had become a museum. Frozen in time was how he put it. The fucker. Another good word for him. Importunate feckless fucker. And now he had a buyer for the house. Well, the house wasn't for sale. Period. That's all she wrote.

He gave Tessa Barnes a C for her failing *Hamlet* essay. She wanted to study kinesiology. What did *Hamlet* matter? Help the girl on her way and stop being so negative. Linda was right. He took things way too seriously, seeking out his own little world and absenting himself from everyone else's. He flipped open a second booklet.

Jason Dowling. The handwriting was practically indecipherable.

He put down the booklet and looked at his watch. Four o'clock and he had marked just one paper. At least when he was done with this lot there would be no marking for a couple of months.

He took a gulp of water and re-opened the booklet.

Sorry to say this Mr. Thorne but I think Hamlet's an asshole. There's so much good in this world and all he can do is dis the planet for being a foul contagion of vapours and be a prick to poor Ophelia. Just sayin' here before I answer the question.

He dropped his pen and sighed. What had come over these kids? Had the heat melted their brains? Dehydrated them maybe? The brain cells were always the first to go, he read that somewhere. More likely some of them were just bagging an exam that didn't really count. They all had their university acceptances tucked away and exams were a thing of the past anyway. Now worth a negligible fraction of the year's work. But still, Hamlet *an asshole*? Seriously?

He had spoken to Jason about his penchant for expletives. He didn't use the word penchant because Jason wouldn't know what the hell a penchant was. Paul once believed that the young man was finally coming around, but here he was in his last ever high school exam unloading on Hamlet for having a bad attitude. He had backed the Prince of Denmark into a corner and was kicking the crap out of him.

He took out his newspaper that was folded at the cryptic crossword begun that morning. He had completed half of it while he was proctoring the exam. Working on the crossword always put him in a better mood.

This could be a pledge by the Spanish (5). An easy one. *Vowel. Vow* was pledge and *el* was Spanish for 'the'. So, *vowel.* The letter *a* was a vowel. 'This could be *a*'. Pledge alongside Spanish for the. He liked the way every detail in the clue was accounted for. Nothing left over.

A phone rang somewhere. Inside the house? He couldn't be sure. Sometimes he heard ringing inside his head. He couldn't trust what he heard any more. If it was the phone inside the house then there was nothing he could do.

What was the politically correct term now for being half-deaf? *Hearing impaired* seemed to be the best they could come up with. Or maybe *aurally reduced.* Frenchie's explosion at Great Bear set off a screaming fire alarm in Paul's head that eventually settled into a steady dial tone. Now he couldn't make out conversation whenever there was background noise. For some reason people still found hearing loss amusing. Like aging. Two subjects you could still joke about in an otherwise joyless age of austere correctness. *Did you hear the one about the old deaf guy? No, sorry, I'm auricularly challenged.*

The phone in the kitchen *was* ringing. And now it had stopped. Linda had set the answering device to kick in after five rings. Five rings gave her time to drop what she was doing and pounce on the receiver. Paul was never that keen to pick it up but there were few calls for him anyway. Linda and Rachel both had cells now so the days of their landline were numbered.

Hi. We're not available so please leave your name, number and the time of your call and we'll get back to you as soon as possible. Have a fantastic day.

What exactly did she mean by having *a fantastic day*? Winning the lottery? Peace on earth? Or just uninterrupted bliss? Not much to ask was it? Of course it was just an expression, as meaningless as *literally* or *awesome*, but for Linda it actually meant something because she believed that fantastic days could happen if you let them. "It's all a matter of attitude," she said to him once. "You wake up in the morning and you make up your mind there and then that you will have a fantastic day and nothing can stop you." He'd seen her do it. Breathing and stretching first thing then getting out of bed to face the day like a gymnast lining up the next apparatus. So when she passed on her positivity to everyone who phoned, whatever personal dilemmas and disorders they might be suffering at that very moment, she meant it. *Have a fantastic day—you can do this!*

There are more things in heaven and earth Dr. Palindrome than are dreamt of in my wife's positivity.

Sitting under the wilting crab apple with half-baked *Hamlet* essays in the serious torpor of an Ontario June, he felt as though the afternoon had drawn in breath and held it. Under his shirt a tickle of perspiration ran cold down his skin.

The steaming tropical temperatures had come early this year and with air conditioners putting more strain on the electricity grid than furnaces did in winter he worried about brownouts.

There had been an outage in the Beaches area during a thunderstorm last summer. Luckily he was in the Crane house at the time and the power was out for only a couple of hours. But he had added another layer of ice bags to be safe, putting more strata between himself and the buried remains, which he hoped he would never have to look at again. At least until he figured out what to do with them, a problem still without a solution. But all that would change now he had time to manage things.

When he found the solution he would have to manage it better than he did ten years ago when he created the problem in the first place.

Two

He had prepared everything—the medications, morphine, vitamins, the killing pills and bottled water—nothing to do now but wait.

The procedure looked simple enough. Crane had typed the instructions on cream vellum in standard 12-point on his old Underwood. Paul knew them now almost by heart. Those solid Underwood keys had hammered every detail onto the fresh black ribbon into his brain.

He had imagined how much simpler it would be to slide a stiletto up through his stepfather's eyeball into the spongy mass of his temporal lobe as he slept, but that would be murder and there would be consequences. It was better to follow to the letter the old man's meticulous instructions.

Crane slept deeply through the nights like he was already in his coffin. During the day he drifted in and out of consciousness to suck nourishing fluids through a plastic spout. Paul reminded himself that he was a caregiver really. Someone to provide the nutrition and hygiene that would actually prolong survival. Crane would take care of his own death when the time came. And then Paul would just watch.

As caregiver he had obligations. His stepfather's incontinence made doing laundry a necessity on the days when Paul could be there. The old man's shit was a wet green paste like a baby's. Paul gave him regular sponge baths to keep him free of infection and continued to feed him to make him strong. Strong enough to die, to be sure, but technically he was doing only what the old man needed to hang on as comfortably as possible until he was ready to administer his own death.

Linda didn't ask Paul about his more frequent visits to Toronto. She kept herself busy with work and attending to Rachel's bouts of depression. Not asking about his extended absences helped her to block out the conversation she had with Paul that evening a week ago.

Rachel was asleep, and they were finishing the bottle of wine they had opened at dinner. They had taken their glasses out to the deck to enjoy a balmy late spring evening under the fairy lights they had put up for Rachel.

"You have to be kidding me. It's murder Paul. Do you get it? It's murder."

He should never have brought it up. But he wanted her to know. Nothing to do with being truthful—it was part of the larger lie. He wanted her to be his accomplice, to say to him it was okay. Implicate her by telling her the truth.

He had kept things from her before. When he came over from England to propose to her that time he said nothing about going to his stepfather's house and signing death papers. At that time she didn't even know he had a stepfather. Paul never spoke of him. Even now, years later, she hadn't met the man. He didn't come to the wedding, a quiet one in any case, and so she knew of him only as someone who was once married to Paul's mother and now lived with Huntington's disease in a house in the Beaches area. He had home care and wanted no visitors. She never asked to meet him.

She stared at him now under the fairy lights, and shook her head.

He could think of nothing else but to say it again. "My stepfather is ready to die and he wants me to help him. I agreed to do it." He repeated the words exactly as he had said them the first time. Like they were from a script, words written by someone else. But they were his.

She put down her glass. "When Paul? When did you agree to this?"

He looked beyond the fairy lights across the dark lawns to the glow of houses on the next street. He hadn't expected her to ask when. When wasn't important. "I promised, that's all."

"No Paul. It's your *promise* that doesn't matter. If you can't tell me when, then how am I supposed to believe you even promised? So when did this happen?"

He couldn't tell her that he made the pact with his stepfather on the same day he asked her to marry him. The two events had to be kept separate. So he said nothing.

"Did you agree to it on the phone? Or by letter? Somehow I don't think so. So when did you see him to make this insane pact?" Her voice was steady as she worked through the possibilities. Linda was a problem solver, she dealt with ledgers and amortizations, checks and balances, payrolls and preferred stock—things you don't get excited about. Emotion confuses the thinking, clouds the judgment. "You told me once that you saw him that time you went home to sort out your mother's stuff, your own father's records, and you saw him when you went back after your mine accident and he had sold everything to a second hand store. Was that when?"

"What matters is I wasn't thinking. About what he was saying, I mean. I wasn't thinking at all. Not really. I didn't know what I was agreeing to or even thinking about."

"So what's he going to do now, fucking *sue* you if you

don't go through with it? You owe him nothing, whatever you think you promised. You can't do it. I won't let you even think about doing it."

It was the first time he had ever heard her use that word. Fucking. It shocked him because she never swore. It was like the gloves were off now. He remembered his sister saying the word to their stepfather when she was twelve. That had shocked him too because he was eight. It was the same now.

"I'm past thinking about it. Whatever *it* turns out to be. Listen, it isn't a crime unless I actually do something. He just wants me to be there. He'll do it all himself in the end. He's got it all down on paper. He researched the steps. Typed them out. It's all there in black and white."

Her face went gray, like she'd been injected with cement. But he carried on.

"It's only a real crime if I actually do something. Listen. In some countries it's legal, a humanitarian act even. If I flew him to Amsterdam or Zurich then just like that it would be okay. Of course there are conditions. The patient must be mentally competent. The request must be made of the patient's own free will and must be ongoing, not impulsive or wavering. The patient must be experiencing unbearable suffering. There must be no realistic chance of successful treatment. Check, check, check on all counts here, right? But I can't just take him off to Amsterdam or Brussels and sign some papers. He can't travel for one thing. He's hardly alive *now*. Death would be a blessing."

"Paul, that's not for you to say. You can't decide these things for yourself. It's not right. It's more than not right...." She searched for the word, shaking her head. "It's obscene. That's what it is. Obscene. Tell me you're not doing this."

"It's not about right or wrong Linda. No one knows what's right and what's wrong here. Half the time a doctor turns a blind eye or cranks up the morphine when he knows it's over any way or there's a living will and who knows what gets switched off or on? Look at abortion." He had run out of script now and was saying whatever came into his head. "Yesterday it's not okay but today we're fine with it. Ottawa passes a law tomorrow saying that it's okay to help someone out of their misery and all of a sudden what was wrong yesterday is legal today. Yesterday you can't marry someone of the same sex, but today you can. So much for right and wrong. It changes all the time."

She stared at him. She had heard him, but his words were spoken in a foreign language. Her voice was quiet again. "I can see you want to do this, Paul, and nothing will stop you. But if you do it—I won't know how to know you anymore."

She looked at him from somewhere far away. From a distant and safe shore. Then she picked up her glass and went into the house.

Oh Linda, her name very nearly an anagram of denial, though very nearly didn't cut it in a crossword. Every last letter of the clue had to fit in a crossword. Daniel would work in a crossword. His own middle name. Paul Daniel Thorne. The perfect cryptic clue. *Lion's den occupant scrambled to show denial (6).* Daniel.

He regretted saying anything to her. She would go up to Rachel's room now and kiss their sleeping daughter one more time before getting ready for bed herself. Tomorrow would be another day in a world that she understood and where everything was accountable. She had already begun to put distance between herself and this conversation. In time she would forget that it ever happened. Learn how to not think about it. He knew she could do that. It was a gift he wished he had.

But it had become his business to think. Endlessly. At first he wondered if Linda was right, that he should just let it go. He owed the old man nothing, and at his rate of decline he'd soon be dead on his own. The worst he could do was die. Let him slip away. What was the big deal?

He could show up, say in a couple of weeks, call 911 and report a home death by natural causes. Bring in the coroner and it would all be a cakewalk.

But it wouldn't be a cakewalk, would it? The police would investigate. Why was no one around when the old man was dangerously ill? Where were the doctors? The homecare? Why was Dr. Crane not in hospital? Paul was executor—the verbal irony was almost funny—his signature was on all the papers, he would be charged with criminal negligence at the very least.

All things considered, it was safer to be with Crane in his hour of need whenever precisely that might be, and make sure it was his final one.

He didn't particularly like that he looked forward to being there. Or that, for all of Linda's revulsion, and the lawyer Gilpin's discouraging lecture on legalities, he wouldn't want to be anywhere else.

Eventually the time came. The hour of need. He entered the house after being home for a couple of days and thought it really was over. The old man lay crumpled on his bed like a dried leaf. His blistered mouth was open, and his dribble pooled on the pillow. His cold bluish hands wrinkled to the touch like raw chicken skin.

But he still had a pulse. His breath stank like the grave but it was breath. A little disappointed but relieved as well, Paul let him sleep while he read over the checklist. When Crane woke up his face winced with pain and soon his body was writhing with stomach cramp. A blockage meant tumors. His eyes opened wider, imploring Paul to act. The sores in his mouth had erupted and spread and prevented him now from speaking.

Enough already. Soon he would be unable to swallow the pills and that would be tragic. It was getting past time.

He opened the bathroom cabinet and took out the bottles one by one, the salves and lotions for allergic reactions, the vitamins to give him the strength to die, the painkillers, analgesics to calm the stomach and drugs to keep the hormones balanced. There were narcotics that would knock out a giant, to be taken when fear might keep him awake. A bottle would do the job by itself, but Crane had been very specific about what was to kill him. He didn't trust the narcotics to succeed on their own. More than a few gave him a reaction and he couldn't keep them down.

There were three bottles of the Seconal that would put him away. Paul opened one and emptied the fluorescent orange capsules into his hand. They looked like Pez and there were fifty of them. Overkill he thought, but the Underwood had clacked out fifty as the precise dosage to be on the safe side.

The safe side. Jesus.

He prepared a snack to help the old man keep things down. The instructions stipulated warm tea, no milk and no sugar, with two mashed up slices of whole wheat bread, no butter, made into a kind of soup. He took it upstairs and fed it to him. Crane sucked it down then sank back into a sleep.

Paul had emptied the freezer a week ago. He was surprised at the mundane things that he had to do. The common task, the trivial round. It was like taking out the garbage. Death by routine. He wished for it all to be done and wondered again how he felt nothing beyond a touch of pride that the freezer was his own idea.

Now it was time to wake up the old man and give him the medication in the correct sequence. The vitamin pills, tablets for his bladder, capsules for his blood pressure and lozenges for his heart. All coloured like Pez.

Propped up against his pillows his stepfather looked at him from somewhere far away and seemed to mumble something through his flaked lips and blistered mouth. Maybe that he was tired of swallowing these bloody pills.

It took ten minutes to give him the vitamins he required to be strong enough to die. No time for weakness. He had to go the distance. No bailing. No jumping ship. No weaseling.

But the blistered, sphinctral mouth refused the pills, and Paul had to coax them in as he would with a sick cat, spread the flaked lips, insert a pill, squeeze and hold the mouth shut, then stroke the loose, scrotal throat until he swallowed. He gave him water through the plastic tube and waited.

Crane's eyes shot out a sudden look of panic. What was he was afraid of now? Dying? Or not dying? He hoped it was the vitamins kicking in. After a few minutes Paul gave him the anti-emetics and stayed by him to ensure they didn't come back up. Anti-emetics a near anagram of anti-Semitic. Just one of the cretinous bastard's claims to ignominy. His gang of neo-Nazis beat the crap out of the Jews in Christie Pits all those years ago; Paul had found the yellowed news clippings in the desk with its intricate network of drawers. Crane had accused Paul's mother of being a whore. And that business in Jennifer's bedroom when she was twelve. Everything. The whole suppurating cesspool of his life. He should never have been born.

He took out the bright orange tablets and placed them one at a time in the old man's hand. And one at a time his patient gulped them down. His sudden energy was surprising. Paul refilled the plastic drinking cup with bottled water. Crane had stipulated non-carbonated mineral water and not tap water to help him die. No contaminants to make him ill. When he swallowed the fifty pills like Paul Newman in *Cool Hand Luke* who forced down all those hardboiled eggs he fell back against his pillows, his bony chest heaving from the exertion. His face was calm now and he closed his eyes. On his thin blue scabby lips was there the trace of a smile?

This was a moment Paul hadn't prepared for. How to say goodbye to someone whose death he'd wished for all his life. A gentle squeeze of the hand? An embrace? A prayer perhaps? A whispered *Fuck you*?

He stood and went to the door. He turned and saw the colour drain from the face on the bed, a pallor descend in the way that low afternoon sunlight becomes dusk. He closed the door and went downstairs.

He sat in the living room. Ten years before this, he had waited in a hospital room for Rachel to come into the world. There was nothing to be done, then as now, but wait and hope it would all work out.

He went over the details once more, just for the record.

Viktor Crane acquired the lethal medication though Paul didn't ask how. Dr. Crane was a dentist and had access to pharmaceuticals, and who knew how long ago he acquired them in preparation for this moment? All that was his doing.

He put each of the fifty orange tablets into his own mouth and swallowed them one by one like Cool Hand Luke. Paul put them within reach, but who would know that if it came to it? No matter. Not now. He had teased down the old man's throat only the vitamins and the medication for his blood pressure to keep him alive. He had given him bottled water to drink, refilling the drinking cup with its thin spout through which his patient could suck the non-carbonated hydrating liquid that was completely free of contaminants. A human being could survive for weeks on water only. He had given him things to keep him alive. No crime in that. The old man took the orange pills himself. He put them into his own mouth and gulped them down like a druggie.

Even John Gilpin the lawyer would concede there was no wrongdoing here. His annoying fountain pen would stay well below that line he had drawn on the paper, well below the criminal point of no return. But Paul would not be consulting the lawyer again to check.

After a couple of hours he figured Crane would be in a deep coma, his body well on its way to shutting down. He climbed the stairs and quietly made his way down the hall. No noise to waken the dead. But when he got to the door he heard an odd slurping sound coming from inside the bedroom, like a toilet running. He pushed open the door.

What he saw made him angry. *Fucking hell.*

The old man, thin and white as a fetus, was sitting up in his bed and leaning over a stream of fresh vomit. With one hand he was scooping the orangey soup back into his mouth in quick, jerky movements, and sucking it all down again. Then his tiny body shook as he retched the same vomit back onto his sheets. He fell back against the pillows and stared up at Paul. His body heaved and tears trickled down his face. He waved a vomit-streaked hand in a gesture of hopelessness and his eyes begged Paul to do something. Anything.

Administer a blow to the head with a blunt instrument? The telephone receiver by his bed perhaps? Drive a knife into his heart? Wrap strong hands around the thin, scrotal throat and push his Adam's apple out through the back of his neck?

He ran downstairs to the kitchen. From a cupboard under the sink he grabbed a handful of plastic garbage bags.

He took the stairs two at a time on his way up. Inside the room again he approached the bed where the old man was scooping vomit back into his mouth again.

Nothing else to be done. The old hands-on approach.

He stuffed one plastic bag inside another and pulled them over the contorted face. The body started to jerk and twist. He climbed onto the bed and forced the old man onto his stomach, so he could push his bagged face into the pillow. Twisting the bag-grips tightly around the neck he lowered his full weight onto the heaving body, feeling the wet from the vomit-soaked sheets seep through his own pants. With one hand he held the bag-grips as tightly as he could, and with the other he forced the head down into the pillow. He needed all his weight to fight the violent throes. The old man pitched and bucked beneath him. He had no idea how long he kept his grip on the tie-loops around the throat while he forced the head deeper into the pillows. Five minutes maybe? A lifetime?

At last the convulsions diminished, and then the body went still.

He continued to press down with all his weight, gripping the tie-loops at the throat and breathing hard after the surprising struggle. After some more minutes he relaxed his hold and straightened up.

Then the smell hit him. The old man's bowels had loosened in death and the sharp stench of liquid feces knifed into his nostrils. His stomach churned and when the saliva gathered in his mouth he slid off the bed and rushed to the bathroom. He leaned over the toilet while his stomach heaved and spasmed, but nothing came up. He spat a stream of fresh saliva into the bowl. His face running with perspiration, he reached for a water bottle and drained it. When his stomach settled he returned to the bedroom.

Crane was surely dead. There was no movement now. Limbs splayed out, he lay as though he had fallen from the ceiling, or had newly been sodomized and now lay crumpled in a post-coital sleep. Paul slid the bags up over the head and turned him over. The face was twisted, the mouth gaped as if for a teeth cleaning, the eyes open but not seeing.

He wanted to go to another room and lie down, but there were things to be done. He pulled the body to the edge of the bed and lowered it onto the floor. He stripped off the pajamas and stared at the wrinkled fetus stained with its own shit and vomit. He stared in disbelief as the dead man's penis rose briefly in a half-erection, a final priapic salute from the afterlife.

He bundled up the soiled blankets and the soaked bed linen and stuffed them into two black garbage bags, carried them downstairs and set them down outside the back door. Then he opened windows. It was evening, and what the weathermen now called a jet stream had brought in cooler air and a fresh breeze. August nights in southern Ontario could be chilly, he thought with an odd relief.

Upstairs again he sprayed air freshener around the room to cover the smell of his stepfather's parting shot. When he was a kid, there was that joke about Beethoven's *final movement*, a steaming pile of shit on top of a grand piano. He filled a basin with hot water and began to sponge down the smeared grey corpse on the floor, taking quick gulps of water whenever his stomach heaved.

He wrapped the body in a clean sheet and strained to lift it off the floor. It was heavier than he expected. A dead weight. Its arms and legs seemed longer than they should have been. On the way to the basement he had to stop twice, once at the bottom of the stairs to steady the body against the railing, and again in the kitchen to rest it on the counter, so that he could reach over and open the basement door. It had blown shut from those welcome drafts coming through the windows.

In the basement he raised the lid of the freezer and removed most of the ice bags he had purchased the day before. He laid out an even bed with the remaining bags and lowered the swaddled corpse onto them. Then he packed the rest of the ice bags around the body and piled more layers on top. When the body was completely buried, he closed the freezer lid and spun the dial of the combination lock.

No prayers for a soul already kicking his heels at heaven, and as damned and black as the hell whereto it goes. Here lies Viktor Crane, a real stiff.

He went upstairs to the bathroom and filled a garbage bag with the bottles from the medicine cabinet.

Two hours later he had four garbage bags stacked against the bedroom wall. Another three stood outside the back door. He had double-bagged and filled them with the vomit-stained sheets and feces-smeared pajamas. They would have to go first, before the rats emerged from the alleyways and gnawed their way through to the shit and the puke. He loaded them into the back of his station wagon which was parked well up the driveway, so that old Mrs. Harrison who still lived opposite and spent her days seated at her front window wouldn't see the little boy she had watched grow up over the years now disposing of his stepfather's filthy bedclothes having suffocating him.

He drove to the strip-mall. On one of his trips into the city he had marked two dumpsters in the service lane behind a strip mall, and now in the gloomy passage away from the mall lights he swung the bags into one of the dumpsters and lowered the lid. He drove back to the house and collected the remaining bags of medicine bottles, damp towels and empty water containers.

It occurred to him now that he could still retrieve the body, put it into a garbage bag and drive to another mall somewhere, where he could dispose of it forever. But a body in a dumpster might be discovered before it became landfill. A garbage bag containing a body couldn't possibly look like anything else. And with his luck it would end up in plain view at the very top of whatever pile it was dumped on, or else it would slither down the mound of unloaded garbage bags, so the landfill attendant would notice it and remark to himself that the bag sliding down the mound looked like it might contain a body, and think it a good idea to call the police. DNA tests on the bag and the body inside would identify traces of Paul Thorne, and a police car would eventually pull up outside his home, or he would be hauled out of his classroom in the middle of a lesson, and that would be end of story. So it was the freezer until further notice.

He would leave the old man's wardrobe and other personal effects until later in the week. Goodwill or Cerebral Palsy would be happy to take them. Paul would tell neighbours if they asked, *that he had been flown out to Victoria to spend his last days with relatives*. Crane had left instructions for him to say that. What relatives though? A niece? A cousin? It didn't matter. No one would ask. No one would miss him, or really give a shit. But he was ready with the story in case someone asked. Mrs. Harrison would be sure to ask, so he would pre-empt the question and just tell her, when the time was right.

When he had finished cleaning up the bedroom and disposed of all the bags, he didn't feel like driving home. He wasn't yet prepared for re-entry. Decontamination was in order. He drove out of the city and checked into a motel near Oakville. He showered, standing under the hot needles for a good five minutes. Afterwards he lay on his bed watching a late movie on the television, trying to make sleep come, but all he could think of was Gilpin the lawyer's final caution. "It's not like putting out a light, Mr. Thorne." Understatement of the year, that was.

Eventually he switched off the TV and his bedside lamp. Sometime later the glowing numbers on the clock by his bed showed 3:27, the last time he looked before falling asleep.

He woke up just before checkout, grabbed a coffee at a drive-thru and drove home. He said nothing to Linda, and she didn't ask. That afternoon he began to strip away the old paint from the window shutters on the upper storey.

Two days later he drove back to Maple Street to check that the freezer light was on and to see if he had left any traces of a messy and unassisted murder in the first degree. All looked normal. His new normal now.

He went across the street to tell Mrs. Harrison that Dr. Crane had been flown out to Victoria to die. She thought he said *today*, but no he said, it wasn't today, it was two days ago that he flew out to Victoria *to die*. She was losing her hearing too, along with just about everything else. But who was he to talk about hearing impairment?

When Rachel came home from summer camp at the end of the week, she and her mother spent a lot of time together shopping for school and watching movies in the evening. Paul kept himself busy painting the windows frames apple white and the faux shutters forest green. Rachel chose the colours. He was happy with her choice. And happy to be busy.

A *Globe* weekend edition that summer published a feature about a girl whose body had been dredged up from a peat bog in the Netherlands. She had drowned in the bog hundreds of years ago, and archaeologists had just recovered her mummified remains. They called her the Yde Girl, Yde being the Dutch village where the bog was located. Using CT scans, scientists were able to construct a model of her skull, her face and her hair, replicating her appearance when she was alive. The photograph of the reconstructed face showed her eyes staring out like a zombie's.

Three

He wondered who was trying to get hold of him. The phone had rung twice inside the house.

It couldn't have been Caldwell. There was no way Caldwell had his private number.

A telemarketer maybe. They also addressed you importunately, like an old friend. *Hello Paul. This is Anita from Mothers Against Drunk Driving. How are you today?* He wanted to reply, "Go away. Don't call me Paul. I don't know you. We've never met." But of course he never did. It was more like "Yes I'll donate twenty dollars. Thank you for calling."

Hello, this is DAM—Mothers Against Dyslexia.

Linda was right. His attitude sucked. But DAM was Rachel's joke. She shared his sardonic humour, and sometimes his moodiness, which worried him a little. She had once been more like her mother. Buoyant was the word that came to mind when he thought of Linda, as she was when Rachel was once like her. Effervescent even. Before she became depressed.

He took another expensive swig of bottled water and resumed decoding the rest of Jason Dowling's essay.

Inside, the phone rang a third time. Linda? *Have a fantastic day.* He finished Dowling's exam, put the booklet to one side and shuffled through the pile, pulling out two or three that might put him in a better mood. He opened the first, took a last slug from the bottle and began marking in earnest.

An hour later he heard Linda's car pull into the driveway. There followed the familiar sounds of her brisk disembarkation. Driver door opening and slamming shut, passenger door opening for her to grab her purse and briefcase, then slamming, the trunk opening and, allowing a moment for the removal of grocery bags, slamming shut. Wife and daughter closed all doors with conviction.

Now it was too late to walk round to the front and help her. Preoccupied with the slamming doors and picturing her unload the car, had rooted him to the spot.

Moments later she slid open the glass door and stepped out onto the deck. Backlit by the late afternoon sun, in a patterned summer dress, her sunglasses perched on top of her head and bobbed hair rejuvenated with blond highlights, she looked pretty.

"Hi." She slid the door shut behind her. "Is everything okay? I called three times but you didn't answer. I left messages for you to call me back."

So she had told herself three times to have a fantastic day. But she didn't look like that was happening right now.

"I'm sorry. I forgot to take my keys this morning. I couldn't get into the house so I've been sitting out here marking papers." Now she was giving him an odd look, like he had mustard on his chin. "Something wrong?"

"The spare key is in the garage. In the empty paint can. It was your idea to keep one there. You forgot?"

So he could have let himself in and marked exams in the bracing climate of his air-conditioned study. Instead he had sat outside all afternoon in the heat. He hoped she wouldn't tell him he'd gone off into his own little world again.

She didn't. "There's something else." She pulled out a chair and sat down opposite, lowering her sunglasses to shield her eyes from the glare. “Rachel is moving in with Dan. She called me this afternoon.”

She rested her forehead on the upraised back of her hand, fingers spread out in a gesture of personal distress that struck him as a little melodramatic. He reached across the table and took her other hand so as not to disturb the elegant tableau of her disquietude. He didn’t know what to say. This was turning out to be a pretty crappy day all round.

Dan was thirty-one, an engineering student at McMaster. Rachel met him one night at a club where he played guitar in a band. She phoned home late to say she was hanging out with a friend and she might stay the night, but everything was cool.

Dan drove her home the next morning in his rusting Hyundai Accent, the name like an Eastern dialect. He accompanied her to the front door, leaving his engine idling uncertainly and the driver door open. For a quick getaway if things got awkward, Paul mused. It was an awkward moment for sure. Dan had been with their daughter all night, but he seemed unused to talking to people he didn’t know anyway. He wore jeans and a t-shirt with a faded Bob Marley print in Rastafarian red, green and yellow. He looked a bit like Marley himself, apart from being white. As in Caucasian—in colour he was more sallow. His attempt at a Marley beard looked like pubic hair—thin, curly, dark and growing patchily in random areas of his face. But he had deep brown eyes and, having driven Rachel home first thing in the morning, he had come to the front door to explain things.

“Sorry for keeping her out, Sir, but we kind of got it together after the gig. Not what you’re thinking though.” It’s exactly what Paul was thinking. “We just hung out at my place." Then an earnest look. "It got late so I gave her my spare room."

"It's all good Dad." She gave him her broad, lip-ringed smile, but her ice blue eyes were challenging him. "Dan doesn't drink if that's what's worrying you. He could have driven me home last night but we just ended up talking, like *for-ever*."

Paul hadn't really been worried. He trusted Rachel's instincts. While a lightning strike or a drunk driver or an attack of viral meningitis wouldn't come up on her radar—she liked to say she had things on her radar—young men with dishonourable intentions were a prominent blip. Dan didn't look dishonourable. He just looked like he needed more sleep. The hollows around his eyes were the colour of used tea bags.

He wondered if Dan might be studying sociology. He had that bland earnestness about him. He had moved out of his own home ten years earlier, Rachel told them afterwards; he didn't get on with his father who was something on Bay Street.

And it turned out he himself was in engineering, not sociology.

Paul made another mental note to stop judging people on a first meeting. Linda was right about that too.

Rachel's sleepovers at Dan's had become more frequent during the year, and at some point she no doubt moved from guest room to his bedroom. Now the relocation was complete and, like pretty well everything else she did, irreversible.

There was never any going back—give up school, move in with Dan. And now head off to Malawi.

She first mentioned Youth Without Borders several

months ago. Operation Malawi. An irrigation project with funding from External Affairs. They planned to save up and go next year, once Dan qualified as an engineer. All good intentions for sure. Better than dashed hopes by a long chalk.

Sitting now, holding the hand of a woman he thought he no longer loved and learning that his daughter had defected to the apartment of her lover, he wasn't sure what he felt, beyond a little lost. Nothing surprised him anymore. Rachel's move to Dan's apartment seemed inevitable now that it had happened. Before it happened he didn't expect it but now it struck him as always going to happen. That was the way with hindsight and the receding road in the mirror. Her move was inevitable. There were no real surprises with inevitable. Character was inevitable. Like gravity.

He looked across the patio table at his wife shielding her eyes from the late afternoon sun reflecting off the glass door. We should have seen this coming love. Our daughter all grown up around us, like your clematis.

When he was at school Malawi was labeled Nyasaland in his geography book. It became an independent state in 1964, half a century ago, the same year that his sister moved out to live with her boyfriend in what was now called the Annex, whereas back then it was just downtown. Nyasaland, Malawi. Downtown, the Annex. Jennifer was nineteen when she moved out. Like Rachel now.

What goes 'round.

Linda leaned across the table, and he realized she must have been talking while he was thinking and not listening. "Paul, did you hear me? Did you listen to anything I said just now? She's our daughter and she's just moving in with this guy. We are not going to let that happen."

He tried to pretend he'd been listening. "She's nineteen."

"That's all you're going to say? She's nineteen! Your solution to this problem is to tell me how old our daughter is? Aren't you concerned? How can you be blasé about your child, who is all of nineteen as you have now kindly reminded me, moving in with this random guy she hardly knows? And he's thirty-one Paul, if you've forgotten. A bit older and he could be her father."

He shot her a quick give-me-a-break look. "Listen. If she were going to university she'd be living in a house with three guys she just met. Or in a residence sharing a bathroom with twenty people she didn't know at all. She knows Dan and she chose him. He's not some random guy. He's harmless. I think he's even okay. In any case she wouldn't move in with him if she didn't feel he was right."

She shook her head in the way she sometimes did to clear her mind rather than to disagree. "All that aside, they're coming for dinner tonight. I insisted. We're going to talk this through." She examined her fingernails one by one, like she was counting them. Her nails were perfect, natural, never painted and evenly filed along the top and there were ten of them.

"Dan won't say much. You know that."

She shrugged. Whatever. It was Rachel who mattered.

"And Rachel won't be talked out of it. You know that too." He knew she knew that. But again, she could deny what she knew. More like putting what she knew on hold, hoping it might change so she wouldn't have to accept it. *Give me that old positivity.*

She let go of his hand. "I'm going in to prepare dinner. Do you need to clean the barbecue?"

"No. I did it on Sunday. It's ready to go."

"Okay. I'll start preparing. Carry on with your marking. I'll let you know when it's time to cook."

She got up and stepped into the house. She wanted to be on her own, he knew. She slid the patio door shut and disappeared into the kitchen leaving him to stare at his reflection in the bright glass.

"My father -- methinks I see my father –"

"Where, my lord?"

"In my mind's eye, Horatio."

"I saw him once; he was a goodly kind."

"He was a man, take him for all in all.
I shall not look upon his like again."

*

"Your father, my dear Paul, was a wonderful man and you're getting to look just like him."

Aunt Helen told him that on his high school graduation day. She helped him twist a pair of his late father's gold links through the stiff French cuffs of his new white shirt, stood back and said, "There, you're getting to look just like him. Your own dear father, and my dear brother." Then she wiped away a tear.

The last time he saw her, in the restaurant where they had Easter brunch after she broke her hip, the time he came back from England to propose to Linda with whom he was already in love before he met her, Aunt Helen said to him again as though he were still a teen, "Your father, my dear Paul, was a wonderful man and now you look just like him." He was thirty then, a year younger than his father when he died, so maybe she'd been tracking the resemblance all along.

Jennifer was five when their father died. She adored him and, later, told Paul all about him, because being only a year old when he died, Paul had no memory of him. She told him the stories their father had read to her in bed, when he would do all the voices. He sang silly songs like *The Wheels on the Bus* and *There's a hole in the bucket, dear Liza, dear Liza.*

He especially loved to hear her tell about the little balloon man. How she came in the front door once with Aunt Helen and got the surprise of her life. A tiny man in funny clothes was dancing in the hallway. He was an odd little man, only as tall as the umbrella stand with a smiling round face and funny little concertina arms and legs. He wore a little top hat on his blue head that bounced about as he danced, and he held a silver-tipped cane in his hand. In his tiny tuxedo and bow tie he looked like Jiminy Cricket. He tap-danced on the spot, and his tiny black shoes clicked like June beetles on the hardwood floor.

"Look, Jen, you have a little friend," Aunt Helen said, standing behind her at the front door. "Go and say hello." He was such a cute little fellow, but when Jennifer stepped forward he stopped dancing and tilted his head to one side. She stood still and he danced again, his head and top hat bobbing all over the place. Eventually she got close enough so that she could put out her hand to him. He danced more slowly then, and smiled at her. He would be a dear little friend.

Then she spotted the thread. Her eyes traced it across the room and saw her father crouched down behind the archway. He had the end of the thread in his fingers and grinned at her. She squealed, and ran to him. He picked her up and gave her a hug, laughing the whole time. Aunt Helen had to sit plunk herself down on the sofa and dab at her eyes with her hankie.

A bit later, when she heard her mother coming in from the doctor's, she picked up the end of the thread and ducked behind the archway where her father had hidden. But when she made the little man dance she pulled too hard, snapped the thread and watched him collapse on the floor. Everyone laughed again, including her mother now for she had just come in through the door and had no idea what was going on until she saw everyone laughing at the little balloon man crumpled in a heap.

They lived in a small corner house on Wellington Street, a detached two-bedroom with a shared driveway. Paul had only ever seen photographs, and so he asked Jennifer once, when he was in high school and she was then living downtown with her boyfriend, to show him the actual house. They went to the neighbourhood together, but the house was now a convenience store.

The park and the baseball diamond were still there. Jennifer told him that in the long summer evenings their father would take the family out for a walk after dinner, Paul in his carriage and Jennifer pushing him through the honeysuckle dusk. They would stroll down to that same little park at the end of Wellington Street and watch the local teams play softball under the lights.

Hartman Thorne was a civil engineer who worked for Toronto Hydro-Electric. Occasionally his work took him away to cities like Ottawa and Montreal, and once even to Halifax. Aunt Helen was fond of saying, "He knew his pipes", and he traveled to these cities to give important people advice about upgrading their water and sewage systems. When he went away on those trips, Jennifer missed him. She said that when her father away her mother would move quietly about the house and close doors softly, like someone was asleep.

When Paul was born, and no one was sure if he would make it through, their father was careful to explain to her why her new brother was still in the hospital and why he would not be coming home just yet. He could make anything seem like it was the way it was supposed to be, she told him.

Atrial Septal Defect (n). *A medical condition. Commonly called "hole in the heart".*

She said she was shocked at the sight of her infant brother when she was taken to visit him the first time. He was tiny and lobster red inside a transparent tent. Thin plastic tubes protruded from under the black and brown stickers attached to his chest and head. On the way home she told her father that her baby brother looked like a broken Martian (she watched a lot of Warner Brothers cartoons in those days) but he reassured her that her baby brother was safe and sound in his little transparent tent, and he would be just fine.

Scanning machines had detected his heart murmurs while he was still in the womb. But the doctors were hopeful. With proper care and an avoidance of extreme physical exertion or emotional distress the hole would close naturally by the time he was twelve. But a severe emotional upset or physical trauma in the early years could cause rapid pathological rhythm and unconsciousness. He would have to be taken to emergency to prevent coma and possible death. Barring all that, by his early teens he would lead a perfectly normal life they said. Her father told her that her new brother came from God not Mars, and what was broken would soon be mended. Everything would work out he said. And he was right, mostly.

A year after Paul was born it was their father who died. He had just bought a new car, a Kaiser Henry J., and was excited about taking it on its first long trip. He had to drive to Windsor to meet with city contractors, and when his meetings were done he planned to head over the bridge to Detroit and catch a rare Tigers' night game. He had always been a Tigers fan.

He planned to stay over and drive home in the morning, but when the game finished he changed his mind and headed back straightaway. It was a Friday night and so maybe he decided to get home and have the whole weekend with his family.

Aunt Helen's album had a photograph of their father leaning against his Kaiser Henry J. on the day he set off for Windsor. Opposite the photo she had inserted the clipping from the *Kitchener Herald.*

Paris, Ont. July 6 – A Toronto man drowned on Thursday night when his car skidded off Highway 2 in a thunderstorm and plunged down an embankment into the swollen waters of the Grand River near this quiet rural town in south-central Ontario.

Hartman Thorne, aged 31, of 22 Wellington Street, Toronto, was pronounced dead at the scene after rescue workers pulled his body from the half-submerged vehicle.

There were no eyewitnesses but O.P.P. Sergeant Jim Davidson blamed poor visibility and a wet road surface for the accident. "Conditions were very hazardous at the time. The victim lost control of his car in the heavy rain, drove through the guardrail and down the bank." Alcohol and speed were not factors in the accident, he said.

Motorists who use the stretch of Highway 2 west of Paris have complained for years about the severe bend and inadequate guardrail protection just before the highway goes over the Grand River. Mr. Thorne was traveling eastbound to Toronto when he drove off the road.

He leaves his wife Sarah, a daughter Jennifer aged five, and year-old son Paul.

Years later in the university library Paul thought to look up the details of the baseball game his father had attended at Wirtz Stadium in Detroit. He found the newspaper box scores on microfilm. The Tigers had played a doubleheader against the Yankees that day. Detroit won the afternoon game 5-3 despite a double and a home run by Yogi Berra, but he had to miss that one. He arrived at the stadium in time for the second game after his meetings, and had to watch the Yankees beat the home-side Tigers 8-7. New York jumped into a 5-0 lead in the first inning and were up 7-2 in the eighth. By then many of the 45,919 people who attended the game had considered it well out of reach, and left the stadium. If his father had left with them he would have beaten the storm on his way home. But it was like him to stay to the end. *It ain't over till it's over.* Detroit came back with two runs in the eighth and three more in the ninth, but still fell one short. It was an exciting finish and no doubt his father felt rewarded for having stuck it out.

The funeral was well attended. “He was a respected man,” Aunt Helen told him. It was after her brother’s death that she began to put on weight, Jennifer said.

And their mother began to lose it.

When Jennifer learned that her father had died in a car accident on his way home from the ball game in Detroit she remembered that she didn’t cry. A tall policeman in uniform came to the front door and asked to speak to her mother. Her mother cried of course, and so did Aunt Helen. When the policeman left the house Jennifer went into the living room and found them holding each other and sobbing. They were going through Kleenex like there was no tomorrow.

Aunt Helen said that, as she pulled out a handful of tissues from a new box and tried to laugh for Jennifer’s sake, while blowing her nose and sobbing at the same time. “We’re going through Kleenex like there’s no tomorrow.”

Jennifer had already heard a TV announcer say that one afternoon when her father was at home watching a ball game—“There’s no tomorrow folks”—and the words unsettled her. She sat beside her father and asked why there wasn’t going to be a tomorrow. He smiled and explained that it was what people said when you had only one shot at doing something. He tried to explain why there was no tomorrow for the Tigers, but she didn’t really understand baseball. At least she felt better knowing that whatever happened to the Tigers there would be a tomorrow for everyone else.

Now she didn’t understand why her mother and Aunt Helen were crying. Her father would be home soon, and there would be a tomorrow.

Even when she saw him in the open casket she didn’t

think he looked like he'd been in any car accident. He was all dressed up in his dark gray suit, which was a little odd because he was lying in a bed. He looked overdressed lying in the bed. His face was waxy and pale like the big lilies stuck in vases around his bed. She didn't like the lilies because the room was so quiet and the lilies were loud like trumpets. She remembered gazing down at his face. There were traces of talcum powder on his skin, and he had a rosary laced through his fingers. She reached into the casket to touch his hand. It was cold as ice. There was no father there, and no tomorrow.

When she got home after the visitation she dug a hole in the soft earth at the bottom of the garden by the catalpa tree and buried the funny little man with the balloon head that had lost its air and was now just a wrinkled shred of blue rubber. That's when she cried, she told Paul.

Their mother's parents didn't come up from Ingersoll to attend the funeral of the son-in-law they had never met. One day a few months after the funeral, Aunt Helen found a letter they had written to Sarah after Hartman's death. In stiff words they expressed to their daughter their sadness over the loss of "the father to her children" and said that she could come home to visit whenever she wanted to. They wrote that she should see God in all His mysterious workings, and that in her husband's crash she should see a sign and beg forgiveness.

Their mother didn't go downhill right away. She even took Helen's advice and went back to work at the museum where she catalogued artifacts in the Egyptian rooms. Two years later Helen persuaded her to see a dentist because her molar continued to throb through all the painkillers. A friend had recommended Dr. Viktor Crane.

Dr. Crane extracted Sarah's wisdom tooth and then set up further appointments to crown her molars. One day he asked her out to dinner. He was a bit stiff when Sarah eventually introduced him to her, Helen said. But if it came to that, she thought one could do worse than marry a dentist.

Two years after her marriage, when Paul was four, she left her job at the museum. It was all quite sudden; one day she just didn't go back. And then came the day when she didn't go out at all. She stayed up in her room and set up her shrine to the Blessed Virgin. Father Glass, the priest from Christ the Redeemer, came to hear her confession and give her communion.

Dr. Hannah would be interested to hear what she might have confessed to Father Glass, but Paul wasn't able to tell him because he wasn't allowed in the room when Father Glass came to visit.

It wasn't until Sarah's own funeral that Aunt Helen met her parents from Ingersoll for the first time. They introduced themselves with stern and blameless faces and said they had never stopped praying for their daughter's errant soul.

Paul was seven when his mother died. He didn't go to her funeral because he was back in hospital, having collapsed in the heat when he found her.

Helen told him about finally meeting the parents from Ingersoll as she fastened his father's gold links in the stiff double cuffs of his graduation shirt. Later, while he was knotting his tie he ran through the dates in his mind. His parents were married in July, and his sister was born in January the following year. He had always known that. But until Aunt Helen told him about the letter she found, written by his mother's righteous and unforgiving parents, he never thought to count the months between.

Shotgun. No wonder they gave their pregnant daughter's wedding a miss.

A skeleton in the closet back then, and now one in the freezer.

Four

A light breeze came up when the sun dipped behind the trees. The steaks were still marinating inside, so it wasn't yet time to light the grill. He would mark Grant Jeffreys' *Hamlet* essay. He needed a lift and his best student would surely give him that.

The essay didn't begin, thank God, with a reference to the Simpsons spoof that Jason Dowling had earlier cited as witness to the play's *iconic stature*—though the vignette itself was quite clever, the mad Ophelia bouncing across the banquet table, out the window and into the moat with a splash. But hardly relevant in an exam. What the hell was he thinking?

Grant opened with a quote from the final scene where Hamlet is about to enter the throne room to duel with Laertes. He suspects it's a trap and he tells Horatio he might not come out alive.

If it be now,'tis not to come; if it be not to come, it will be now; if it be not now, yet it will come: the readiness is all—Let be.

Jeffreys wrote, "Fate and free will, those eternal opposites, are reconciled in a few simple words." Great start. He knew his stuff. Grant had accepted a scholarship to Ryerson where he would study something called communications. He wasn't interested in law or commerce, though he could have excelled in both. Paul hoped that Grant wouldn't lose his curiosity or his language skills by studying communications.

When Paul was at university there were no courses in things like communications which sounded like something to do with marketing—giving words a positive spin in order to sell something, anything from gas furnaces to government policy. Half the programs offered at universities now didn't exist when he was at school. Even English departments had balkanized into a gaggle of politicized areas of study that seemed to him to have little to do with understanding great writing. But what might he himself have done with a course in communications—Dr. Hannah would have had an easier time with a patient who could communicate.

I could be bounded in a nutshell, and count myself king of infinite space, but that I have bad dreams. Jeffreys wrote, "Like everything else in Hamlet's world, physicality is relative and has less to do with dimension than with perception. Confinement, like its opposite, freedom, is largely a state of mind. And it is Hamlet's mind that provides the arena for the main action of the play. He lives in his own little world."

He should tell Linda. Hamlet had his own little world too.

Anyway, good for Grant. Maybe he'd go on to a brilliant career in communications, something down to earth and practical. Better to have both feet on the ground, like Horatio, and so what if there were more things in heaven and earth than were dreamt of in his philosophy? Wouldn't it be better just to have fantastic days and nights and be released from bad dreams?

His mother didn't have both feet on the ground—neither foot in the end, as it happened. And long before the end, she had lain pale and broken in her bed, in a room with heavy curtains drawn against the daylight, with votive candles that flickered below her statue of the Blessed Virgin and threw dancing shadows on the bedroom wall. In the evenings her tiny voice beckoned

Paul to her grotesque world, where bleached and spent souls stared up at a cold heaven.

Should these things be left alone and not be dreamt about, not be allowed to disturb one's peace? Should they be erased so one can blithely live bounded in a nutshell, oblivious to the primordial murmurings and encroaching thought hordes? And if at all possible, how should one go about erasing them in order to live for the moment and enjoy fantastic days?

He wondered if Dr. Hannah might specialize in removing bad dreams, but then he realized that his mind was wandering again, popping more rivets, unhinging itself. Enough already.

Don't have a cow, Dad.

Linda slid open the patio door and handed him the steaks on a platter. She stared at the grill. "You haven't lit the barbecue. I asked you ten minutes ago. I thought you heard me." She shook her head—"They'll be here soon"—then slid the door shut and went back to the kitchen.

Where had the time gone? He lit the barbecue and finished reading Grant's exam while he kept an eye on the thermostat. When it was at the right level he forked the steaks onto the grill and closed the lid. He graded the exam—95%—and laid it on top of the marked pile. He wondered what books Grant Jeffreys would read while he took courses in communications.

His own university years were happy. Well, happy-ish. He read books he loved and explored them in ways that added little to humankind's collective wisdom but were satisfying anyway. It never mattered to him that reading and talking about great books served no real purpose. It was all rather self-indulgent, he thought now. But they helped him make some sense of his life. Nothing else really interested him, not medicine or architecture, or being an engineer, like his father. Like Dan now. Making money was never a priority, either. How odd to have married an accountant. But he was in love with Linda before he met her, and therefore didn't know she was an accountant. Anyway, Linda wasn't all that interested in money either, which was strange for someone who worked with it every day.

As a boy he'd been earmarked for the priesthood, and so he grew up in the shadow of a vow of poverty, that put paid, as it were, to any thoughts of making money. But it was all a big mistake in the end. A huge accounting error. He left after only a year, so it was a big mistake in the beginning as well as in the end. But it seemed to him now, sitting among exam booklets that were all quite meaningless to the outside world, that even after leaving the seminary he had carried on living a cloistered life.

It was a wonder that Linda had ever taken an interest in him. When she first met him at Chris Turnbull's New Year's party he was immersed in pointless research on *Hamlet* and teaching in an unremarkable private school on England's south coast. Linda hadn't read *Hamlet* but she made an effort to understand his interest in the dithering twerp, as she later referred to him—Hamlet, not Paul—soon after they were married, but when they had to scrap a romantic getaway weekend because chapter four of his thesis was due the next week she could take no more. She had once feigned an interest in his proposal—thesis, not marriage—that Shakespeare might have written into his play a cryptic attack on the Catholic Church in the time of the Reformation. He had found Lutheran parallels in the play. Like Luther, Hamlet and Horatio studied at the university in Wittenberg, along with his two friends Rosencrantz and Guildenstern, whom Linda referred to as Tweedledum and Tweedledee. If the play was read as a political allegory Hamlet was Luther. Professor Little, a Reformation scholar, agreed to supervise Paul's thesis, his own curiosity piqued by Hamlet's line about a dead body being food for worms, suggesting the historic Diet of Worms. It was all quite silly and pointless, really, and eventually came to naught.

He remembered struggling with his thesis late into the night while Linda struggled with her growing indifference to it, which in turn made him feel he was stressing out over something he should have grown out of by then. She was right as it turned out.

The night he emerged from his tiny study in their rented two-up one-down in Chinatown and announced that his project had gone belly up. He was forcing connections where there weren't any. In the end he earned a Masters and a small publication for his efforts—his article, "Lutheran echoes in *Hamlet*", made a largely unnoticed appearance in the spring edition of *The University of Toronto Quarterly*.

A year later Rachel was born. And a year after that Linda was offered a partnership at the new accountancy firm in Burlington, and Paul secured a teaching post at Centennial in Heritage. They weren't sorry to leave their cramped semi in Chinatown and begin a new life.

How quickly it all spun into another life, until now it all seemed to have belonged to someone else. He couldn't remember when Linda stopped updating the photo albums. She used to love cataloguing their life as a family—Rachel's birth and first steps, first bike, first days at school, Halloweens, Christmases, the one birthday party with her little classmates from school. And of course their holidays, some spent with Linda's parents in Winnipeg, a cottage vacation in Muskoka, two weeks of self-imposed exile on the banks of the Miramichi, their England visit when they stayed with Jennifer and Steven and their twin boys—*proper little beefcakes now* his sister called them—and Rachel got flu, and Linda admitted asking Jennifer if she thought Paul needed counseling. Photos of Rachel's piano recitals, until her meltdown at the Kiwanis Festival when she lost her Liszt and walked off the stage muttering "This is horseshit"—an irreversible event that demoted the baby grand to a display unit for the best of all the family photos.

By then Rachel had determined that she was no longer pretty or slim enough to be photographed, and the camera remained in its case. The last time Linda tried to take a picture—the tree one Christmas—the battery had died.

As a family they seemed to have rolled over on their separate beds and faced the wall.

"Bye Daddy. See you later."

"Goodbye sweetheart. Mind how you go. Be careful."

"Bye Mom. I love you."

"Love you too darling. Have a fantastic day."

*

He leapt to his feet and opened the lid of the smoking grill. He'd forgotten the steaks and now they were very well done on one side. And so, not done well at all. He flipped them over and shuffled them around for a few minutes before forking them onto a platter. He hoped they wouldn't be too tough. Holding the platter in one hand he slid open the patio door and stepped into the kitchen just as the doorbell rang.

"Got it," he called up at the ceiling, then dried his hands and removed his apron.

"Hi Dad." Rachel walked into the house like she still lived in it, and then turned to face him. Her blue eyes could harden and glint when she anticipated an unwelcome encounter. She hugged him briefly, not committing to a meaningful embrace with important matters still to be settled. Dan stood behind her in the doorway and mumbled what sounded like a *good evening*.

Linda came down the stairs. "Darling, come in. Dinner's nearly ready. Hello Daniel."

Once they were all seated Linda navigated her way through some safe topics—her way of breaking the surface tension. More like skating across it, free style, like a water strider.

In the middle of the afternoon, would you believe, a gang of youths had swarmed an elderly man in the city centre. During her appointment at the bank the air conditioning died. Water restrictions would be brought in if the dry spell continued—and what a shame about the lawn going dormant so early in the summer. Perhaps they should consider installing an irrigation system. In his assumed role as buffer for the evening, Paul agreed, taking her by surprise. He wasn't sure how it was possible to run an irrigation system with water restrictions imposed, but he let it go, as this wasn't a time for practicalities.

He offered wine but everyone declined. Water was fine, despite the impending restrictions. He filled their tumblers from the pitcher of chilled tap water and remarked, largely to fill the silence that accompanied everyone's sudden fascination with watching him pouring water from the pitcher, that rationed bottled water might one day be everyone's lot if the experts were to be believed. He filled his own glass with red wine to wash down the overcooked steak.

"Paul, dear, use the coaster, would you mind?"

Under the table talk Linda was in a flinty mood. So was Rachel. Dan looked like he wanted to be somewhere else. The evening reminded Paul of a class that wasn't going too well. Might as well bring up the subject of Rachel's decampment.

But she beat him to it. "Why don't you guys just come right out and say it? You think we're making a big mistake. Living together, going off to Africa next year. I know that's what you think, but it doesn't change anything. We've made up our minds." She plunked her knife and fork on the table as though to seal the deal.

Dan looked up from his plate and swallowed. "Can I say something here, if it's okay?" He looked at Rachel, and she nodded. Directing his gaze at the narrow space between Paul and Linda he spoke slowly, finding the words as he went. "I know you think we're a little crazy, and maybe we are. But Rachel and I are together in this. I'm thirty-one, in my final year at McMaster, and one day we're going to be part of that whole nine-to-five thing. But right now we have a chance to travel and work abroad. That whole try-to-make-a difference thing." He looked at Rachel again, then shrugged and went quiet, lowering his head as if aware that he'd skidded off the high road into a cliché.

She reached under the table and took his hand. "So, this is for the record, okay? There's a Toronto company running irrigation projects in Malawi, and they're recruiting engineering grads to go out and work for a couple of years. Dan's contacted them and they're interviewing him next week. I've applied to Youth Without Borders. It's with UNICEF, so it's legit." She looked at her father. "We've done our homework, Dad."

Linda was about to say something but Paul jumped in. He wanted to take the conversation beyond the *too young for all this* stage.

"There's no point in your mother and I objecting. If we tried to stop you you'd do it anyway. Better you go with our blessing, and I'm sorry if that sounds patronizing, but you know what I mean." He glanced at Linda. She poked her fork around her plate and said nothing. "If you need anything from us you know you have it. A loan, or whatever you want to call it. There's money in Rachel's trust fund as well, so you can dip into that." These two wouldn't take a handout, but he wanted to put it out there. He and Linda had spoken about helping their daughter get a start in whatever she wanted to do.

Linda gave a thin smile and her eyes moistened. She took a sip of her water. "I'm not going to feel comfortable with any of this until I know the details—that things are in place and you'll be all right." She looked at Rachel. "It's just so sudden. Last week you were living here, and only a month ago you wanted to be a cosmetician and start your own business one day. Now all this." She shook her head. "Paul, can I have a little wine now please?" She held out her glass and he poured her some red. "Anyway, we need to clear up this other business first."

"Mother, maybe this isn't the time...." She glanced at Dan.

He raised his head again and looked at Linda. "Mrs. Thorne, I know you're upset about Rachel moving in. We wanted to discuss it with you first but...".

Rachel cut in. "But I told Dan it was a conversation we would have *after* I moved in with him. Mom, you know we'd have fought and I'd have left pissed, so it was better I left in a positive frame of mind knowing we could talk about it later." She looked at Dan. "Sorry to interrupt."

"I love Rachel very much." He glanced at Paul and nodded. "We plan to have a family sometime."

Linda cleared her throat. "I'm not sure how I feel about that right now, Dan. Rachel, not discussing your move with us first was hurtful."

She lowered her head. "I'm sorry Mother." She bit her bottom lip. "It's just that we don't discuss things much any more. I mean important things. It's not like I'm giving up on you guys or anything, but it's been tough living in this house, you know. I've watched you two move away from each other for like, I don't know how long. Forever maybe." Her voice was almost pleading. Sad, anyway. She let Dan take her hand. "It's been like a slow death with you two. You don't even talk to each other enough to get into an argument. This house is a morgue sometimes. I had to get out. Dad, I'm sorry but it's even worse when you're at home and not all tied up with school. Summers mostly, when you're not driving up to Toronto to whatever you do at that stupid empty house, and you have no marking or prep, and you and mom step around each other for two months before you go back to school—anyway, I didn't want to get into this whole thing about me and Dan even though I'm the one who brought it up. We want to be together whatever happens, that's all. No fighting any more, it's done."

Paul looked at Linda and remembered the unseasonably warm evening in early April twenty years ago when they sat on a public bench at Queen's Quay and looked out over the lake. He had just asked her to marry him. Only their second time being together. He flew over from England to ask her, knowing she was already with Trevor. But being in love with her long before he met her, and way before she even met Trevor, he thought it right to ask her when he did, especially since it turned out she wasn't sure about Trevor anyway. But that was then, and where did it all go?

Rachel was staring at him. "Let's face it, Dad. That was a pretty random thing you did, asking Mom to marry you when you had just met and she was already nearly engaged to that other guy." She grinned, like she had been reading his mind. Dan's mouth twitched, as he seemed to stifle a smile, maybe at the thought of such wild impulses in this staid middle-aged couple.

"Mom, I'm sorry if you're hurt. I didn't want that. It's not Dan's fault because I told him that we had kind of discussed it here at home. That wasn't true and, Dan, I'm sorry for not being honest with you. We came tonight because we don't want barriers. I'm sorry for hurting you. I mean that." She half rose, leaned across the table and gave her mother a hug.

She didn't have to make peace with her father. He wasn't upset. He reached for the wine because Dan was holding out his glass.

Dan interested him. An engineering student, and

really a very civil, if somewhat awkward one. He too would know his pipes one day out there in Malawi. Rachel always got what she wanted but in a way that had nothing to do with being spoiled. She was determined. They looked at each other now. They would be fine together, he thought. How are these things known?

The rest of the evening passed more easily. So he thought, but after Rachel and Dan left Linda wanted to go straight up to bed. She was tired and had a headache. It had been a stressful day. Paul was happy to clear up. He added the wine glasses to the dishwasher, closed the door, and switched it on. Then he went into his study to enter his marks.

He hung his jacket on the back of the chair, folded his tie and laid it on the desk. He had removed them when he was outside in the heat, marking exams, but he wore the jacket again during dinner because the house was cold. Now he could turn down the A/C a little because Linda was in bed.

He would like to have invited Magnus and Jan to dinner. They would have provided a buffer for the evening and helped to soften the edges between mother and daughter. People behaved civilly, were more considerate with each other, when the Henriksens were in a room.

Linda liked them because they were kind to each other. Magnus was quiet, a little like Paul, she admitted once, though not brooding quiet. Meditative quiet was how she put it. “He relaxes a room, you know?”

She said it in a way that suggested Paul did the opposite to a room.

Before becoming a teacher Magnus was a commercial

diver. He worked from a bell—a bathysphere—laying communication cable at the bottom of Lake Superior. Thirty days was the maximum stretch—saturation they called it. Divers were required to spend all that time beneath the surface because decompressing was a complex procedure. When he wasn't spooling out cable on the lake floor he spent his down time inside the bell reading books. In thirty-day stretches over three years he read a lot of books. There wasn't much Magnus didn't know from all that reading. The bottom of Lake Superior seemed like a good place to read and think.

It was odd, Linda said, that someone so intelligent and well read never wanted *to really make something of himself.* He could have run his own company, she said. He could have been a professor or a doctor. Instead he taught high school history. Okay, so he loved history and he loved teaching, but he could have done more with his life. Like Jan, who was a director in an investment firm. What did Paul think?

Magnus was an alpha male with a mute button, is what Paul thought. He was a friend. And why would he think that Magnus had short-changed himself by becoming a teacher?

Did Linda believe *he* had short-changed himself by becoming a teacher? He never asked her. It wouldn't be a fair question. Anyway, she knew that Magnus and Paul lived in different worlds—Magnus in the real one and Paul in his own little one—for all their being alike in some ways.

But there wasn't time to invite Magnus and Jan for dinner that night. Anyway, dinner hadn't turned out too badly without them. Had he given in too easily though? Should he have at least made a show of resistance to

Rachel moving in with Dan? Did Linda feel he had let her down? Probably. He could never resist his daughter's entreaties.

He remembered the day she was born how she complicated things by pausing half way in order to turn herself around so her head faced down and not up. It was like she had stopped to rethink the whole business of coming into the world. But eventually she resumed her journey and weighed in after subjecting her mother to a twenty-hour labour.

He liked to think of Rachel pausing to reconsider the prospect of being born at all. He had done the same himself, long after being born, more than once. So he thought of her as a kindred spirit, someone who shared his skepticism, and it made him feel close to her, silly as that was.

But he lost her for a time anyway, when she grew into a sadness of her own and left him behind.

There's a point of no return in most lives, unremarked at the time. He had read that somewhere. And so it was with Rachel, who stepped across an invisible line one morning when she was what—eleven maybe or twelve—and never really came back.

On a morning unremarked at the time, she skipped down the street to join up with her friends on their way to school and likely giggled excitedly in the playground before the bell, nursed an innocent crush on some boy in a Blue Jays cap, unrolled her class presentation on songbirds of southern Ontario, ate her peanut butter and jelly sandwiches out of a Hannah Montana lunchbox, and then walked home in the afternoon, suddenly and prematurely aware that life's grind was more of a challenge than she bargained for. With nary a shot being fired, she stared the treadmill in the face—in the manner of a Tessa Barnes mixed metaphor—and felt a new seriousness settle on her life. It all seemed to happen in a day. One day the sadness that she might have contemplated when she paused in the birth canal eventually caught up with her.

Melancholy. n. *A sadness or depression of the spirits. Gloom.*

She'd had her run of therapists, but they weren't required to share what they knew with the parents, and so he at least was never the wiser.

He rarely allowed himself any more to dwell on the early days when she was an untroubled child. He couldn't look at the photo albums that showed her laughing, exploring, musing, and cozily melting into sleep at the end of another rainbow day.

Linda got down to dealing with Rachel's now moody and capricious adolescence in the way she got down to dealing with—everything she dealt with. "It's what girls go through, Paul. It's something fathers don't really get."

He wanted to tell her that boys go through adolescence too—he remembered his own well enough—but he said nothing. His adolescence wasn't important. Not any more. Only Rachel mattered. So at the time he accepted, too easily it seemed to him now, that nothing more was required of him but to stay out of the way.

His parental duties were gradually downsized. He became an extra in Rachel's life, an occasional walk-on, an attendant lord. She seemed to prefer things that way and so he remained in the wings until summoned. Another life-changing decision he never actually made. From a distance, he watched her make her way through troubled adolescent years. Now she had Dan. Together they had Malawi, and he felt happy for her. And hopeful. But fearful still of losing her, even though he had already lost her in a way that was impossible to explain. Or reverse.

"She's a little frightened of you, Paul," Linda said to him once. "She loves you because you're her father, but she doesn't know how to get near you anymore."

"That's silly. I'm right here. She can talk to me any time she wants. How can she be frightened of me?"

"You're *not* here, that's the whole point. Even when you are, you're somewhere else. That's what she feels. It's not your fault, Paul. It's just you sometimes."

It pained him to know how Rachel felt, but sometime later when he tried to speak to her she looked away and didn't say anything. So he knew he had lost her. For the time being, at any rate.

Or—a question that plagued him now, a marauding thought horde kind of question—had he lost his capacity to *feel* for the people who were supposed to matter most to him? Is that what Linda meant by *It's just you sometimes*?

Why did he seem to care more about Tessa Barnes's dreadful essay on *Hamlet* than he did about Rachel's decision to move in with Dan? Why did the riot of adverbs in a student's short story annoy him more than overcooking the family dinner? And why did the missing apostrophes in Bradley Caldwell's semi-literate emails unsettle him more even than a humanitarian crisis on the other side of the world? Why did his students' academic well being matter to him more than his own happiness? Or was it that he had already given up on his own happiness?

He knew in that place it was impossible for him to get to right now that Rachel, so fragile, was precious to him however lost she was to him right now, or however lost he might be to her. He held her life in an infinitesimally fine balance. She was one angel dancing precisely on a pin. Even to imagine her unhappiness was to disturb the precious equipoise. To think of her losing Dan now, for example, or even the Malawi project was—unthinkable. Whatever happened he would help her through it; he just couldn't bring himself to think about it happening. That's how it was. It was easier to think about apostrophes than catastrophes. He had some control over apostrophes even if Bradley Caldwell's emails didn't. Perhaps that was it—what he could still control somehow mattered more.

"Rachel thinks you care more about your students than you do about her." Linda said that to him once, but it wasn't true. Somewhere, he knew, somewhere in that place he just could not get to right now, and hadn't been able to get to for some time, and feared he might never get to again, it just wasn't true.

Would Dr. Hannah understand how he could lose his daughter, and his wife with whom he was in love before they ever met, and still be in thrall to them both in a way that mattered to him more than life itself? Probably not. Maybe it was enough that he himself understood, whether he really did or not.

He admired Rachel and Dan for their zeal and hoped their plans would come to something. Youth Without Borders had their work cut out for them and yes he feared for her safety. Dan's too. He really did care more for them both than he did for apostrophes.

In some African countries the evolution from tribal

society to democratic state had been blown off course by corrupt governments. Not that their predecessors had set a good example. All the colonial oppressors had blood on their hands. But now he struggled to resist thinking that Youth Without Borders, for all their philanthropic intent, might as well empty a bucket of water into the sand.

Compassion fatigue n. *a condition marked by a withdrawal of compassion from a situation that can't be controlled or changed.*

He would never share his misgivings with Rachel. It wouldn't be fair. She believed in change for the better. She would find in Malawi something more fulfilling than ringing up sales in a store that supplied aging women with serums and unguents to stall the wrinkling of skin and sagging of features. Malawi was a step up from all that. A world without cosmetics for menopausal women. And menopausal men. All equal now, even in menopause. She would encounter desperate children who faced the wall in their very first years of life. She too had faced the wall, but she would find a different kind of wall in Malawi. And she would help some of them over it.

Malawi would take her out of herself. Feed an interest, maybe even grow a career. She would meet courageous and passionate people. Deepen her experience. Broaden her horizons.

With all this positivity he was beginning to sound like Rawlings, the annoying career advisor at Centennial.

*

It was nearly midnight when he finished loading his marks into the computer. He poured a scotch and sat down to finish the crossword he had begun while he was proctoring his exam that morning. He didn't check his messages. If Caldwell had sent one it would only keep him awake. A half hour later, the crossword completed, he left his jacket on the back of the chair and his tie folded on the desk, and went up to his bedroom. Linda's door was closed and he could see that her light was out.

Tonight he felt sad for her. Her day had been difficult. Not a fantastic one. He knew she wanted to string the fantastic days together and wear them around her neck, but today the pearls had come loose and bounced all over the floor.

He couldn't remember the last time he had had a fantastic day. Not that it bothered him anymore. He could live with ordinary days. *Thank you for your call, leave a message and just have a day*. It was the nights that troubled him. Now he lay in his bed wishing for a night without dreams.

Could Dr. Hannah help him to live in a nutshell without bad dreams? Just as Hamlet wished. That's what he needed most—in a nutshell.

*

At breakfast the next morning Linda told him she had decided to fly out to her parents and stay for a week. She would book her flights that day. "Rachel's gone. I don't know where you are, Paul. I want to be with someone who needs me." Jim Day, her boss, was okay about her taking the week off; things were always a little slow at work after the tax deadline.

Paul wasn't surprised. This too was inevitable. Another stage in their not being together any more. Way too many stages to count now.

Why did he feel a little relieved at her going even though he never liked being alone in the house? The emptiness was palpable when he was alone in the house. But it was right that she should go home. She worried about her parents, her mother having to care for her dad in his early stages of dementia. There were arrangements to discuss, decisions to be made. Paul would only be in the way. He wasn't very good at planning things. Linda would manage better on her own, and anyway she needed a break from him.

When the time came to move her parents to whatever facility they decided on he would fly out and help. He could help with what had to be done; he just wasn't good at deciding what needed doing. He could do anything so long as someone else, like Linda, decided what it was.

She would know what to do with a frozen corpse if he asked. But he couldn't ask. That one was for him to decide. At least it would be easier with Linda out of his way in Winnipeg. He could concentrate on what he had to do. He had no idea yet how he would do what he had to do, only that it had to be done. But knowing it had to be done was a move in the right direction.

Caldwell had sent another email that morning.

hey neighbour. hope you don't mind ive been clearing out the flyers from your mailbox. dead giveaway these days you know. you want to maybe put up a notice saying no flyers. theyre all in a bag here and ill pass them on to you next time. just so you know im keeping an eye on things here. bradley.

The guy had way too much time on his hands if he could spend his days staring at the house across the street waiting to pounce on the flyers the moment they were delivered.

And the mail. Had he chanced upon a letter addressed to Dr. Crane among all those flyers? When he said *dead giveaway* did he mean he had found something? Viktor Crane continued to receive mail ten years after his death. A request for a donation to the Alzheimer's Society. A questionnaire to assist the market research of a pharmaceutical company. An offer to increase the limit on his credit card. And once a year, even now, a Revenue Canada application form for quarterly income tax payments. Paul had long ago arranged for Crane's pensions to be stopped, and so there was no taxable income now. But how odd that the dead continued to get mail.

It was time. The Canada Day long weekend was coming up and he had no engagements. There would be fireworks to celebrate July First, but he would give those a miss. Fireworks came with everything now: the beginning of a century, the birth of a nation, and the end of a ball game. It ain't over till the fireworks.

Before she left for work Linda came into his study and placed his house keys on the desk in front of him. "Just so you know where they are in case you go out. I'll see you tonight." She spoke softly, like she was hurt and owed an apology. When she left through the side door to the garage she didn't shut it with her usual emphasis. He felt the measured pause before the latch clicked. When she was upset she did everything with exaggerated gentleness—the way Jennifer said their mother did all those years ago when their father was away on business. Nursing the bruise. He heard the ignition catch, and when he stood to look out the window he could see the car backing onto the street. He watched as it pulled away. The heavy garage door rumbled to the familiar thud at the end and then there was silence.

He went to the kitchen to refill his coffee cup and picked up the morning paper from the counter. Time to start on the day's cryptic. It would get his brain going. The news could always wait. It was only news, making its rounds. He set down his cup on the desk, moved his neatly folded tie to one side and laid out the paper in front of him. He picked up a pen and read the first clue.

Pest is seen in shadow (8).

Nuisance, a pest. *Is* inside *nuance*, a word for shadow. *Nuisance*.

Linda would soon be at her desk. She would book her flight to Winnipeg and print up her ticket. She would think all over again of Rachel going to Africa. Her baby. For her it was inconceivable. Malawi. Good God. And how could Paul be so calm about it all? His apparent unresponsiveness to upsets and crises exasperated her he knew.

Don't rush to take a chance after losing opener (5).

Amble. To take a chance was to gamble and without the *g*, the 'opener', the word became *amble* meaning *don't rush*.

Marriages fail, sure, but she never imagined hers would. Why did he think *hers* and not *theirs*? Was it "her" marriage because she had worked so hard to keep it alive long after he had slipped under the surface? And when exactly did he slip under the surface? He wasn't sure. Another point of no return unmarked at the time.

Last evening before dinner when they were out on the back deck and he was marking papers, he knew she wanted him to join forces so they could persuade Rachel to come home. But knowing that Rachel had already made up her mind, he carried on marking *Hamlet* essays. Bloody Hamlet would be her take on it. That dithering twerp again. He'd always been something of a rival. A fifth wheel from the get go.

Had Dr. Hannah ever read *Hamlet*? He would find it slow going of course with not much action until the end when shit finally happens as Tessa Barnes so elegantly put it; but maybe Dr. Hannah would find the Danish prince more interesting than some of his patients. Linda was never sold on *Hamlet.* She found it way too dark. "He needs to get a life," she muttered half way through watching the Olivier film. He thought the more recent Branagh spectacular would engage her, but she was having none of it. "I'm done with Hamlets," she declared, making them sound like a dish she'd gone off. "It's too dark."

She liked light. She grew up in her parents' sprawling bungalow in Winnipeg where she was headed next morning. Their house was built on a rise and overlooked the Red River; its wide windows let sunlight spill into all the rooms and brightened the long snow-filled months of a prairie winter. Paul spent his childhood in a house of dim hallways and rooms with heavy curtains drawn in the early evening, even in summer.

She had waited in the car outside the Crane house just the once when they were in Toronto together and he had stopped by to pick up flyers and *check on things*. She would never go into the house. Not after that whole business they didn't talk about any more—she because it was a can of worms best kept unopened and he because it was now more than his life was worth ever to mention again.

"Why don't you sell the damn house, Paul? It's an albatross. No—a morgue."

He shot a glance at her when she said that, but she was just staring at the house and not looking at him. "Those windows. My God, the place must be dark."

If she owned it she would gut it, she said, re-do it all with open plan rooms and hallways, wide picture windows and skylights to brighten everything inside. But she didn't want to own it. "Just sell it. Sorry, Paul, but it creeps me out."

Except he couldn't sell a house with a body in it. *Historic house for sale. All contents and fittings included.*

His life before Linda unsettled her the more she learned about it. A monastery for heaven's sake, though he had told her about that before they were married. Then a mine where he lived in a bunkhouse with tiny windows way up in the Yukon where the sun didn't rise in the winter. He lived for a time in England where it rained and got dark by four in December—a cramped and damp stone cottage with tiny latticed windows, charming but pokey, with a fireplace that burned smelly coal. When they were first married they moved into a tiny ivy-covered semi in Chinatown. She escaped to her bright office each day and left him at home to work on his doomed thesis about a gloomy no-life prince in a cold dark castle in a place called Elsinore.

Another cloistered life. The secret life of Paul Thorne.

Five

"You're depressing to be around sometimes you know?" she said to him once, after a dinner with friends she had invited over in an attempt to lift his spirits. "Why don't you make an effort and say something when we have people for an evening?"

"I listen. I'm interested in our friends. Their careers, hobbies, vacations. All that."

"Rachel thinks you should go on anti-depressants. I think you need counseling."

In truth, he felt out of his depth when friends came to party. He had little to offer to the conversation. Stock market corrections, the impending Royal visit, reality shows, the new fusion restaurant opening up in Heritage, a charity run for something or other on the weekend, end-of-summer sales and here it was only June—he tried to chip in to that one by saying the day would come when Back to School sales began before school was out for the summer, but someone had already changed the subject, and so his remark was lost.

No one seemed to be reading books any more, and he had stopped going to the movies, so there was a widening gap in shared topics of interest. He found cinemas vast, crowded complexes now, with deafening soundtracks, and he didn't think he'd like the movies anyway. A bride and groom leaping fully clothed into a swimming pool didn't strike him as very funny, and the annihilation of Washington or New York by computer graphics didn't appeal either. The weekend blockbusters now featured superheroes that came out of the comics he read as a boy. But he never voiced his opinions because it would only make his guests uncomfortable. They placed a moratorium on any subject that made anyone uncomfortable while they were enjoying themselves, which was maybe a good thing, because it took politics and religion off the menu.

Not for the first time he wondered if he did have a problem. Why shouldn't people put some fun into their lives? Watch a movie that gave them a laugh and not have to think all the time about the problems of the world? His melancholy wasn't their fault. He cast a long shadow these days. Sometimes he felt he had disappointed life.

From early in their marriage Linda had ridden shotgun for him, explaining and *accounting* for him, so people would excuse a reserve, which she didn't attribute entirely to his hearing loss.

Sometimes there was no *point* in him saying anything because Linda spoke on his behalf, as if he were a child, or not even present.

"Paul doesn't like egg plant, and he's not very keen on asparagus either."

"Paul doesn't know *Survivor* because he doesn't watch television. Really only baseball and documentaries, right Hon?"

"Paul has to go up to his Toronto house this weekend, otherwise we'd love to come to your cottage."

She seemed bent on disarming anyone who might suppose, more from what he didn't have to say for himself than from what he did, that her husband wasn't really in step with the world. In other words—that is to say her words and not his—she wanted to present him as normal, just not in the way the rest of the world was normal.

How much simpler and happier life would have been for her if she had married Trevor, who by all accounts was decent and normal enough. Trevor had both feet on the ground. And one knee on the floor when he offered her that obscenely large diamond.

Why after twenty years did he still consider Trevor as some kind of rival? Why did he feel threatened by a long-ago suitor whom Linda told to keep his ring when she didn't feel sure

about him anymore because she thought—perhaps regrettably now—she might be falling in love with Paul?

He had to admit that all of these concerns—Linda explaining away his peculiar behaviour, her persistence in telling him to visit a therapist, and his own lingering uneasiness about Trevor—fed a growing suspicion that despite all the rationalizing, he was to the world outside and all who knew him, including his wife, unstable.

He felt besieged at times by what he imagined to be their opinions of him. They could think what they liked. He was past caring what they thought. Who were they to judge? Were they all stark raving normal themselves?

What about Linda who spoke for him when he was right there in the room? How is speaking for someone who's sitting right there beside you as if he isn't there at all, different from speaking to yourself? Other couples did it too, especially the ones who'd been together for a few years. Dr. Hannah's notebooks were no doubt full of couples who spoke about each other as if one of them wasn't there, and who discovered, that the longer they lived together, so far from growing more and more alike, they grew more and more unalike. With certain couples, and he and Linda were one such couple, togetherness seemed to diminish in inverse proportion to time spent together.

It was very soon after they returned from their family holiday in England that Linda first tried to persuade him to see a therapist. She told him she had discussed things with his sister while they were in London. Paul and Steven were out playing cricket in the garden with Jeremy and Simon, the *proper little beefcakes*. She said they talked through all the terrible things that had happened, especially in the early days—that awful business of Paul finding his mother and withdrawing *into himself*, as she put it, deciding there and then that the extensive counseling he so inexplicably resisted was absolutely essential.

She didn't elaborate beyond that, but he wondered if Linda and Jennifer had brainstormed a shopping list of symptoms he should share with his therapist, all the things that caused him to be sad and reclusive, and not like normal people who enjoyed restful nights and fantastic days in the uplifting company of their friends.

Things like his father killed in the car crash when Paul was only a year old. So he never knew his dad. That was a shame. A son should be able to do things with his father. Go to a ball game together, something Paul was never able to do, they thought.

But he *did* go to a ball game with his father, that time in the library when he read on microfilm the box score of the game at Wirtz Stadium. He re-lived the event in his head, matching the stats with the unfolding of the game, inning by inning, and imagining his father in the stands on that warm evening, his suit jacket and fedora on his lap and the sleeves of his white shirt neatly rolled up just like in his photographs. He never told anyone about being at the game with his dad because they wouldn't think it normal. Well, that was their problem, not his.

Maybe Jennifer and Linda discussed depression in the family genes. Their poor mother and her rapid decline. Her weird *American Gothic* parents from Ingersoll, Ontario. And the stepfather—psycho or what? Imagine growing up in a house like that. Jennifer escaped early, and it was no surprise that when the time came Paul would bolt to a seminary with all those other reclusive and dysfunctional types. Yes, he should see a professional.

To pacify his wife and daughter, and Jennifer in England, though he would never share the news with her as they didn't communicate much any more, he booked that one session with Dr. Hannah. He had serious misgivings about it doing any good because the shopping list of things his family thought he would bring up in the session contained the very things he would never discuss with anyone.

How had he let the session get out of control? It could have been catastrophic.

After the awkward introduction—Thorne, not Throne, and take a chair if you would—the therapist got right into it.

"Now, Mr. *Thorne*, what do you think you'd like to tell me about yourself?" Dr. Hannah sat back in his chair, opened his folder and smiled, like he'd just planted a second hotel on Boardwalk.

A carriage clock clicked softly on the desk. It was very like his own, in the study at home. Linda had given it to him for his birthday one year.

He examined the carpet at his feet. An awkward question, and the session already becoming like an out of body experience. He imagined his other self getting up from the chair and gliding out the door, all the way down the corridor to the parking lot. But he composed himself and continued to stare at the tan flecks in the navy blue carpet. He counted forty-three tan flecks in a square the size of a record sleeve before he looked up.

Behind his rimless glasses the eyes of *Dr. Sheldon Hannah—Personal and Relationship Counseling and Referral. Appointments Only*—were unblinking. His balding top gleamed under the recessed ceiling lights, and at the back of his head, thick, silver curls gathered like surf.

Paul nodded. “I’ll have to think about that one.”

“Take all the time you want.”

There was nothing about himself he’d like to tell Dr. Hannah. He felt like one of his students being asked to account for a plagiarized assignment. What did he have to say for himself was a lousy prompt. As a teacher he knew something about these things. Leading questions worked better. Did the student buy an online essay because he ran out of time? Did he realize he could ask for an extension? Was something going on in his life right now that made it hard to focus on his work? Were things okay at home? You had to break it down a little.

The way Linda broke it down and left him no option in the end but to surrender to a trial session. Bringing Rachel into her campaign as she did during the latter stages of his resistance was unfair. Two against one he told her.

He *gravitated* to depressing things they said—old films by Bergman and the Coen brothers for starters, novels by Hemingway and Atwood, documentaries about radicalized youths and melted icecaps—and he spent too much time alone.

"You know you're always welcome to join me in my gravitations," he told them, "so I don't have to be alone." But he was missing the point they said.

Gravitated was an apt word he thought. *Gravitas* meant serious, but had nothing to do with depression. Introspection wasn't a mental illness, though they didn't buy that either.

He could understand why they didn't buy that. His was a long list of the things that failed to amuse or enthrall him. The police and doctor serials that his family watched set his teeth on edge, mostly because of pounding music and endless ads. He didn't share their interest in fashion, or cosmetics, or the latest wellness advice for trimming fat or living longer. Weight loss he didn't require, and the idea of lengthening his life seemed less desirable now than it once did.

Linda by contrast was *levitas.* As in a light breeze caressing a still pond and tracing tiny laugh-lines on its surface; as in movies with Sandra Bullock or Gwyneth Paltrow or Jack Lemmon and that actor with the big nose whose name he could never remember. What *was* his name? If he owned a smartphone he could look it up but he found life simpler without a smartphone. Linda said he just liked being out of touch. Aloof she said.

He would manage only a polite smile when someone told a funny story at a dinner party while Linda laughed out loud—split a gut sometimes. But his smile was genuinely polite. He was half deaf, and when the table was noisy, as tables at dinner parties usually were, he didn't always catch what the amusing person said, and so he smiled to contribute in his own impaired way to the mirth. But again, apparently, he was missing the point.

Dr. Hannah smiled, waiting for him to finish thinking about what he might say about himself so he could say it. Only now Paul was trying to remember what point it was that Linda kept telling him he was missing. Then it came to him—they thought he was depressed, and that's why he was sitting now in the office of a shrink.

She had offered to accompany him to the clinic and wait for him in reception until he was done. To be there for him she said. But he suspected she just wanted to make sure he didn't skive off somewhere—gravitate to a *film noir* and kill a couple of hours being morbid and then coming home to announce that the shrink was a complete waste of time. He declined her offer to accompany him.

He remembered that driving to his appointment it came to him. "Walter Matthau. *The Odd Couple.* A movie I actually do find funny, Dr. Hannah, but maybe because Felix and Oscar are depressed too." He spoke aloud, alone in his minivan, at the instant Walter Matthau's name broke the surface because he was rehearsing ways to break the ice with his analyst.

Again he reminded himself that talking to people who weren't there while improvising scenes that hadn't yet happened—and sometimes re-enacting ones that had—were recent developments that he would have to monitor along with his cholesterol count and occasional periods of insomnia.

He would admit to the insomnia if the subject came up during his session. Did Magnus know what it was like to lie awake at night or on occasions when he did drift off, to have dreams that made him wish, when he awoke to his own weight pressing him into the mattress, that he hadn't gone to sleep in the first place?

And now Sheldon Hannah, whose framed doctoral certificate in psychology from Princeton hung on the wall behind him and whose bill would amount to a princely sum, waited for a response to what Paul considered a surprisingly inept question. *What might you like to tell me about yourself?*

Really?

The gold-trimmed, tombstone-shaped carriage clock clicked to accentuate the silence. And to time it Paul supposed. He didn't know how much silence had elapsed since the question was asked but he reckoned it would be logged with everything else.

And after all that lapsed and costly silence, he still could think of nothing to say for himself.

Actually having nothing to say felt good. Linda was always at him to say something when he had nothing to say, but now Dr. Hannah had asked him what he might want to say without making him say anything. He hadn't said anything yet except that he needed time to think about *what* to say, and the good doctor had told him to take all the time he wanted.

Might Dr. Hannah consider scheduling one session a week simply to ask Paul a question that made him *not* think of something to say for sixty minutes? Or how about not even think? Now that would be therapy—a single unanswerable question to send him into an unthinking coma. He could stare at carpet flecks for an hour and then leave the clinic feeling restored to his senses.

"I would like to come here and not think at all," he said without thinking. But the words sounded stupid now they were out, whereas inside his head they sounded like wisdom.

Dr. Hannah tented his fingers, closed his eyes and nodded, as he processed either the wisdom, or the stupidity. Or maybe he was falling asleep.

In the new silence an unguarded thought crawled under the door, tugged at Paul's sleeve and whispered in his ear that he was mad.

Dr. Hannah opened his leather note pad and examined the questionnaire that Paul had filled out in reception—his personal information and answers to some preliminary questions about his "condition".

He hadn't answered all the questions because some were unclear. "How long have you felt this way?" for example. He didn't know what *this way* was, let alone how long he had felt it.

Dr. Hannah turned the page, read a moment longer and then broke the promising silence. "You say that you came on your wife's recommendation." He looked up. "Why do you think she wants you to have counseling?"

"I don't communicate."

Dr. Hannah smiled again. He likely heard little to make him smile in his daily rummage through emotional wreckage in search of a behavioral black box to account for the crash.

"Why do you think she says that?"

Paul supposed now that the questions served to establish his personality type and ultimately determine the appropriate wellness and medication program that would make him normal again. But he didn't feel like a type in the way that, say, blood was a type. Anyway, he could tell Dr. Hannah that Linda had already Googled his symptoms and downloaded a Type D—well grilled on both sides.

Paul, like twenty per cent of the sample group, she said, was prone to worry, anxiety and gloom, and unable to communicate. He avoided company, over-analyzed everything, never admitted to negativity for fear of being rejected, and therefore bottled up a lot of stress that could lead to heart disease and an early death.

When she finished she looked at him like the early death was, or would be when it happened, his own fault. He was Type D in a nutshell—nut*case* the way she presented it—the tag forever strung to his big toe.

Personality labels annoyed him. In the end they had put him off studying psychology himself. But what a session he, as a psychologist himself, could have now with Dr. Hannah. It would be like interrogating himself, answering his own questions about his condition. Except that it wouldn't work, however much he had learned about psychology, because he didn't communicate. Talking to himself didn't count as communicating—it was just another symptom to monitor.

"Has she always found you reluctant to communicate, do you think?"

For a moment he forgot where he was. When he remembered he said, "She would be the one to ask." It was impulsive and sounded sarcastic. "I'm sorry, that just came out. I don't know."

He didn't want to suggest they had issues. He loved her. At least he did once, even before he had met her, though maybe more then, than he supposed he did now. Things had got in the way, as things do. That was normal, was it not? Something all couples deal with? The little irritants that develop over time, like arthritis. Her whole positivity thing, for example. But he thought it best to say nothing to Dr. Hannah about his wife's wish for everyone to be happy. It wasn't a crime to wish for happiness just because it was something he didn't do any more.

"Do you think that maybe you didn't just come here at your wife's request? That somewhere inside, you think I can help you?"

"I don't know that either." He wondered now about Dr. Hannah's annoying qualifier, *do you think,* and thought that the man could reduce his entire clinical catechism to *do you think* and leave it at that. Paul could then answer in truth *Yes, I do think. All the bloody time I think. Therein Dr. Hannah, as a Type D who does nothing BUT think, lies my problem.*

But he said nothing about the annoying qualifier.

He realized that all the nothings that he said were piling up. He seemed able to talk himself out of saying anything.

"When you're inside yourself and not communicating with others, do you like the place where you are?"

"I'm not sure." He thought for a moment. Did he like the place where he was? Where was it anyway? Where did he go when he was inside himself and not communicating? His own little world, Linda called it. But it wasn't any more. It was not a place he could get to any more. Not like he once did.

A tiny snow-covered village, the frosted roofs of its cedar-shingled homes glittering in the afternoon sun. In the middle of the village children skated, round and round, on a frozen pond. They wore woolen hats and mittens and bright scarves that stuck out straight behind them in a make-believe wind. They glided and twirled on the ice and never fell over or bumped into each other. Their laughter was silent but they were happy, and music filled the air. A pretty lady in a blue cloak and thick scarf strolled arm in arm with a handsome man in a long black coat and Russian hat. When the couple reached the lamppost they swiveled on the spot and strolled back the way they had come. Back and forth they walked, with a lifetime ahead of them. A horse-drawn sleigh, trimmed with silent bells and laden with colourfully wrapped parcels, glided over the snow and disappeared through an opening in the hillside, only to emerge again from another opening at the opposite end. A pair of grey horses pulled the sleigh past the busy skating rink, right in front of the faces of holiday shoppers peering spellbound through the glass, oblivious to the icy gusts that swept along Queen Street. Inside the glass there was no icy wind to extinguish the lamplighter's flame; the Christmas trees visible through the windows of the houses were never undecorated; and the driver of the sleigh held a harmless whip that he never used. Mittens clutched snowballs never to be thrown, and the faces of the small children in their bright scarves and woolen hats glowed forever and a day in a snow-blessed world without cavities or dentists, where fathers always came home again.

But he wouldn't tell Dr. Hannah about that place, because he couldn't get to it any more.

"Anywhere I can be alone and comfortable? Though maybe a little anxious too?"

"What makes you anxious do you think?"

"Someone might find me?"

"And what do you think would happen then?"

"I'd have nowhere left to go?"

"Is that what you think I'm doing? Coming to find you?"

"Maybe?"

Answering questions with questions that only sounded like answers was safer than answers themselves, he found.

Dr. Hannah wrote something in his notebook and allowed another silence to grow.

Paul slipped inside the silence to observe him. Answering or not answering his questions seemed to make no difference to Dr. Hannah. He was the same either way. Just like his name—Hannah—the same both ways.

Dr. Palindrome.

He put down his pen and examined Paul's questionnaire again. "You indicate that you have a hearing disability. Was that from birth or an accident?"

His stepfather once struck him hard on the side of his head during an outburst when Paul was ten. But he could never mention his stepfather here. Bringing the unspeakable Viktor Crane into his account would stretch these appointments out to the crack of doom and at a price Paul couldn't afford.

Nor could he trust himself anymore not to let slip during one of his distracted spells that his stepfather's glacial remains lay packed under layer upon layer of ice bags inside his own chest freezer after Paul botched attempt to assist in the ending of his life left him with no choice but to suffocate the bastard and give him the death he had begged for in the first place.

"I worked once in an open-pit mine with heavy machinery—my summer job—and no one wore ear protectors back then. There was an accident. An explosion." He stared at the carpet. The tan flecks began to oscillate inside the deep blue. They danced like the stars in a thousand nights, like the swirling light behind his eyelids. The bright aura before the onset of a migraine.

The room shimmied in a noiseless quiver and the carpet liquefied beneath him. His chair swiveled and then rose like a fairground ride starting up. It floated across the room.

"I was lucky to survive the blast."

His voice rumbled like the boulders now tumbling down the walls of the office. His chair settled into the therapist's spot and he looked across the room at himself in the other chair, the rocks toppling into the space between.

A sharp pain in his head made him open his mouth to shout but no sound came out. Darkness rolled over him, a high breaking wave. He lifted an arm to shield his head. Something sharp pierced his shoulder and he heard bone splintering.

A siren erupted in his head like a sheet of fire. Something popped inside his chest. He couldn't feel his legs, but mercifully his shoulder ached, so he still had that.

When his eyes opened again he peered up through milky light at a clock face with no hands to tell him the time. He reached up to touch his forehead and felt something textured. More texture where the rest of his face was. The siren wailed. Then darkness again.

Someone spoke his name, and his eyes opened now to the moon's white face. "You'll be fine. Just rest," said the moon. But its mouth and the words it spoke didn't happen together.

Sometime later he felt his bed lift into the air and swing away to one side. Above the siren in his head he heard a heavy, sucking, fluttering noise. THUP-THUP-THUP-THUP-THUP-THUP. Like the flapping loose end on a reel of film but much louder. Deafening actually. When his eyes opened, he was flying.

Trees filled the sky outside his glass bubble and then a river washed them away. A familiar mountain floated past, the fresh wound in its side. He slid back into the darkness.

A surgeon told him he had cracked three ribs and broken his left scapula and clavicle. He had multiple scrapes and contusions on his legs, upper body and face, a grade three concussion and very likely, permanent hearing damage. Miraculously he had escaped internal injury. No rib piercing his liver, no rock shard rupturing his spleen. He didn't really understand everything he was told, but tried to feel lucky to be alive.

He learned the details of the accident when he was questioned in the Vancouver hospital as part of the insurance investigation. It turned out not to be an accident at all. The blasting foreman had deliberately piled up enough explosive to take out the entire rock shelf, and himself with it. No one knew why. Paul remembered Frenchie's shadowy figure darting about on the rock ledge, tying up the mouse-tails of fuse cord and teasing out the thin electric wire to connect them to the terminals. All routine preparations. He scuttled amongst the drill holes like a spider crocheting its web. At the appointed time Paul took his usual place inside the shelter along with Johnny Fonseca, his roommate, but there was no Frenchie, and the plunger was missing. Paul had just turned to ask Johnny what was going on, because it was now past five o'clock. He remembered nothing after that.

They found Fonseca's body the next morning. The explosion had pitched him out of the shelter and straight off the ledge; he fell sixty feet onto an outcrop and died instantly.

Paul lay wedged into a gap just below the rock bench. The angle of his trajectory aligned with the slope of the rock face and he had slid to a stop without going over the edge.

The blast sent a hail of rocks down the mountain onto the town site below, the salvo lasting close to a minute. It punctured roofs, smashed windows and punched large holes in company vehicles. One elevated conveyor-belt framed on grasshopper-leg supports collapsed from the shockwave. People ran for cover when the first stones fell out of the night sky. One man never made it. He was running to shelter in a bunkhouse when a single rock the size of a melon smacked him flush on the back of the head and killed him on the spot. His name was Hopewell, and Paul remembered that he was a warehouse assistant.

A month later he was given his final checkup and released. He flew to Toronto and took an airport limo to the house on Maple Street. He had things to pick up before heading down to his residence for the start of the new semester. But his stepfather had been busy while he was away.

He had cleared the house of all of his mother's collectibles. "I was tidying things," he said. "I forgot you wanted me to keep them. I forget things easily now. It's my condition."

"They weren't yours to get rid of."

His stepfather stared at him, his eyes narrowing. "They were rubbish."

"I won't be coming back you know." Why did he think this would matter to the man? But for some reason it did.

"You'll come back. You always do."

*

"What were these *collectibles*? Can you tell me that?"

The voice startled him. Dr. Hannah was in his chair again and Paul was back in his own. The analyst was writing intently. Several pages of his notepad were folded back. He paused and looked up. "You were talking about your stepfather. You said he was clearing house when you came home from the hospital in Vancouver and he had thrown out your mother's *collectibles*. What were these?"

Paul stared at the pages of notes. What else had he said? Had he mentioned the freezer? Somehow let it all slip out as he had sworn never to do?

"They were my real father's records. Jazz mostly. Some opera. My mother listened to them after he died—I was only a year old so I never really knew him—*La Boheme* was her favourite." He stared at the floor.

Mi chiamano Mimì,

ma il mio nome è Lucia.

La storia mia è breve.

As a boy he watched his mother glide around the

room holding an invisible partner. On the record label the revolving white dog angled its head and gazed into the horn. The needle arm moved up and down to the music.

The music stopped that summer morning when he found her. And then he had only her records, until his stepfather took those away too.

When did he mention his stepfather at all and what the hell else had he said? How far did patient confidentiality extend in a case like this? Would Dr. Hannah involve the police if he knew about the freezer?

The silence now was uncomfortable.

"I think we've talked enough for today, Paul. Thank you for telling me."

When did he start calling him Paul? "What did I tell you?"

"That you're unhappy."

"I thought I was telling you about my going deaf."

"That too." He smiled, flipped down the written pages and shut his folder. "I think we've made a good start here. Would you like to do this again?"

"I don't know." What made him think he was unhappy? Or did Dr. Hannah just suppose these things. Thinking as a symptom of depression. Insomnia a subconscious fear of dying? Is that how it worked?

Silence hissed through the recessed ceiling lights and rose up from the tan-flecked carpet. He shifted in his chair.

Dr. Hannah glanced at his clock. "We're past our time here and I do have another appointment. It's good that you talked, Paul. I don't have any answers yet but I can listen. That's what you need I think—someone to listen."

"Is that what you think?" He sounded sarcastic again. "I'll give it some thought, I promise."

"My assistant will send the invoice. You have my number and I hope you'll make another appointment when you've thought more about it. For the time being let's just—put everything on ice shall we?"

Paul shot him a glance, but the smile remained expressionless, like the eyes, nothing to give the ice remark further import. Such an odd comment, though. People put things on hold or on the back burner. They put drinks on ice. And shellfish, or any kind of fish for that matter. Stepfathers too. And further appointments now. Well, there would be no further appointments.

Dr. Hannah had asked him a question about his hearing that caused him somehow to spill his guts answering it. Counseling might work if it didn't include all the *Do you think* questions, and if his answers didn't end up in a notebook that he wasn't allowed to see but which the doctor obviously regarded as evidence of a good therapy session, especially with a patient who didn't communicate.

More than ever now he was bemused by Linda's belief that visiting a shrink would somehow turn bad nights into fantastic days, when all it had done was make him more anxious and even a little fearful. To be fair she said it would take time and he must go through a succession of appointments. But she had no idea that there were things—a whole shopping list of things—he could never tell Dr. Hannah or anyone else, things he hoped he hadn't included in the steaming pile of guts that he had just spilled all over the blue carpet, but if he had, then there would be reason indeed for him to feel anxious and fearful.

Dr. Hannah couldn't reverse Paul's downward spiral into an upward spiral in the way that he could reverse his own name. He had taken lots of notes to determine that Paul was a Type D—for which Paul could give a rat's ass—and recommend medication to make his patient at least *believe* he was having fantastic days when they were still just plain old common-or-garden crappy days because Dr. Hannah and all his recommendations along with all the king's horses and all the king's men couldn't put Humpty together again.

And he wished now he *had* gone to a movie. Something to divert him. *Fargo* maybe. Or *A Serious Man*. But they were all years ago, in a time when he knew his way.

He wished he could go back to when he and Linda first met, so he could feel again what he felt for her then—when they were the only people living at Chris Turnbull's party—and keep it forever in a golden bowl. And later when they visited Oxford, the city of golden cupolas and burnished cobblestone streets, they drank freely from the bowl and believed that everything they did and all they spoke had never been done or spoken before, or since, and would stay with them forever.

But how soon the crack appeared in their golden bowl and the pure love leaked out. How quickly all that once lay ahead was now behind, and how did he not see it trickling away? Was it because all through their marriage he had stood transfixed at the altar, while Linda sailed down the aisle with her arm in the arm of someone who in all the ways that mattered wasn't really with her at all?

If he could go back to that time he would find her

again. Reverse time. Retrace his steps to a time when he knew his way. He couldn't repeat the past, but he could certainly change it.

Six

This may help protect castle in game following stalemate. (10).

The answer was "drawbridge", nothing to do with chess and everything to do with protecting a castle, a stalemate being a *draw* and the game being *bridge*. An easy one, and he felt stupid for not having got it earlier. The puzzle was all but done.

And then what to do with the rest of the day, the first of his long summer? School was done and Linda would leave for Winnipeg next morning. The days stretched in front of him and as yet he had no idea what to do with them. Something would happen soon enough. He knew that much.

Had she phoned Rachel? She would want to say something to her about the discussion last evening. He could see her picking up the phone, and then putting it down again. It's what she did. She and Rachel were once so close. They would still be close if Linda let go a little and allowed Rachel to make her own decisions and her own mistakes. If there were to be mistakes, they should be hers and not her mother's. Everyone made mistakes.

But if Linda were to let Rachel go she would be all alone, a bright moon orbiting a cold, dark planet.

She had suffered him. Married him and then suffered him. Alone until Rachel came and then she bonded with her as he never could.

How she had suffered. In silence. All three of them silent, keeping their thoughts inside. But that would change. He would see to it. Breaking the silence was something he had to do in the days that stretched ahead of him.

His mother made him promise to be silent. It would be their secret she said. He was only six but he promised her because their secret was all they had. It was precious, and dangerous too, because it would cost him his soul if he revealed it. Struck dead on the spot he'd be. That's what she told him. So no one ever knew. Not Jennifer. Not Linda. He had told Linda other things but they only made her sad, so he didn't tell her any more because it was better not to tell her things than to see her look sad in a way he could do nothing about. He found out the hard way that telling things about himself only made people sad and served no earthly purpose. Telling *that* particular secret would also serve no heavenly purpose because it would bar him from heaven for all eternity. It's what she told him, and what he believed then. So he became good at being silent. It was a life skill. His party trick.

Dr. Hannah would no doubt find the whole business about his secret a little melodramatic if Paul were to see him again and tell him, and he'd write it all down in his notebook. But if Paul were ever to tell him the secret he would insist that Dr. Hannah just listen as he was paid to do. Not judge whether a life was melodramatic or exaggerated, but only listen to what Paul never told Linda because he didn't want to make her to look sad in that way again. Things Linda didn't know, and some that even Jennifer didn't know, and so wouldn't be on their shopping list of things to tell his therapist. But he had a shopping list of his own for Dr.—Palindrome.

A case for Dr. Palindrome.

If Dr. P. felt inclined, he could sharpen his pencil right now and start a whole new notepad.

Paul could give him some headings for his notes. Like *The Secret History of Viktor Crane. Cretinous Bastard and Cloven-Hoofed Motherfucker.*

That would do for starters. But where to begin? It was all a muddle.

He had come back from England that one Easter break from the school in Brighton he was teaching at. An interim job while he worked on his languishing thesis, but now there were things to be done at home.

Aunt Helen had fallen and broken her hip—Jennifer told him that.

He had to ask Linda to marry him because she was spending far too much time with Trevor.

His stepfather wanted him to sign some papers, and he said he had something to discuss with Paul when he next came home.

Seeing Aunt Helen would be simple enough. She was in a home now. He would visit her.

He would see Crane and get his business out of the way so he could concentrate on asking Linda to marry him. He would never mention Crane's business, whatever it was, to Linda because Crane was nuclear waste, to be sealed up in a lead container and never allowed to leach into her life.

He would get that part over with—his visit to the house on Maple Street. Dr. Palindrome sat waiting, pen in hand, his notebook open.

•

Crane never left the house now. Sixty-eight, with

Huntington's, he had taken on a live-in caregiver. Sebastian inhabited the newly renovated basement apartment that had once been a cellar. *That* cellar. Back in the day, a large musty storage place with furnace room and laundry room. Now a living area—not a dying area anymore—for Sebastian, with proper ceiling and accent lighting, paneled walls, carpeting and furnishings, an *en suite* bathroom and a small galley kitchen adjacent to the large chest freezer.

Sebastian opened the front door and let him in. The little man tapped on the study door and then disappeared down the hall. Paul watched his stepfather turn slowly in his chair and stand up with some effort. His shoulders were stooped and his grey eyes looked puffy and tired. With his thin face newly shaved down to the white bristle on his chin, he resembled more than ever an aging goat—though this did not yet fully account for the goat in Dr. P.'s heading, which would be revealed in due course—and what hair he had left on his crown was also closely cropped, giving him a yarmulke look. So very ironic for Crane of all people to have a yarmulke look—this irony to be revealed soon enough with all the other ones.

Crane opened the glass door of his study but offered no handshake. Paul hadn't seen him since the day he came to pick up the records. His mother's *collectibles*. And now, only because his stepfather stood at the open door saying nothing for a rather awkward length of time, Paul asked him how he was doing.

The old man's voice was wheezy and strained. The effort of getting up from the chair had left him short of breath. "I am doing as I always do except I move more slowly now and with more pain." He shuffled slowly down the hall to the kitchen, still talking. "My disease is progressive and will one day make life difficult. Impossible really. That's what I have to look forward to." He took a glass from the cupboard and moved to the fridge. "Before that happens I must put my affairs in order." He took out a bottle of water. "Sebastian shops for my organic food at the market. What they put in processed food now can kill you." He filled his glass. "Perhaps that is not a bad thing." He looked at the water and then sipped it as though to test it. "I write and I read. The house is quiet. Sebastian doesn't speak so you won't get a word from him. How old are you?"

"Thirty-one."

"You will outlive me. In the normal course of things. That's all that matters."

What did he mean? Why did it matter to him that Paul should outlive him?

"You are wasting your life. Your students are shaped by Hollywood and television, and there is already now a tidal wave of processed culture that will sweep them away. There is nothing you can teach them. But why do I care? I will be dead soon enough." He turned to go back into the study. "There is something I must discuss with you."

Paul went in behind him and sat on the upholstered leather chair that faced the desk that intrigued him as a child with all its drawers and compartments. He watched him shuffle through his folders, removing papers from envelopes and arranging them on the desk.

Neither spoke while he sorted his papers.

He remembered one evening as a boy watching his stepfather explode like Vesuvius in that same upholstered chair. He heard the roar coming from the study. It was the roar, familiar to them all, that threatened to blow the door glass out of its frames and pour down the hallway like molten lava.

Aunt Helen would roll her eyes, turn up the television and continue to watch her program as if nothing was happening. Jennifer would look at Paul, then go upstairs and shut her door.

So on that one evening when the fresh roar erupted he sidled along the wall from the living room to peer through the glass doors.

His stepfather was heaving in his chair, now pushed well back from the desk and swiveled round so he faced the doors. His eyes bore through the glass and his arms waved in the air. Flecks of spit flew out of his mouth like tooth fragments. His face turned purple and he flailed like someone sealed inside a room without oxygen. His rant shattered the air. Paul didn't understand the words. *Kike. Hymie. Yid.* They meant nothing to him then because he was just a boy and he hadn't yet discovered the magazines from Wisconsin that made his stepfather apoplectic.

Something else that he didn't understand as he watched his stepfather suffocating in a room without air was how the man could look straight back at him, right through the glass doors with his tunnel eyes, and not see him at all.

It wasn't until much later, when he was in his last year of high school, that he entered the study to find paper for a homework assignment and discovered the back issues of the *Neo-Pentagon Press* in Wisconsin. Zion. Nazi. The Protocols. Sons of Israel. The bile leaking out of the pages.

The front page of the Toronto *Telegraph* dated August 17, 1933, was included in the literature he found in the desk.

Dr. Palindrome, when he was *Sheldon Hannah,* would have been especially interested in the newspaper's headline about the riots in Willowvale Park that happened the night before. The grainy photograph showed two young men with shaved heads holding up a white flag with a black swastika. One, his thin face was stretched tight in anger, brandished a metal pipe. The caption identified him as Viktor Crane. Behind these two marched other young men carrying clubs and holding up homemade banners. *Jews Are Vermen. No Dogs Or Jews On The Beeches.*

The paper identified the thugs as members of the Balmy Beach Swastika Club. Crane and his cronies spent their summer evenings prowling the streets in the still, humid air, threatening the newly arrived immigrants who were attired in black linsey-woolsey and brimmed hats, with long strands of their hair curling down behind their ears. These strange-looking people gathered on the weekends by the Lake and cooked their disagreeable, smelly food on portable stoves. They saw the banners that hung from store awnings and along the low windows of apartments on Queen Street, screaming *Hail Hitler (sic)* and *Kikes Not Wellcome (sic) Here,* but they paid no heed.

On the night of August 17 the thugs from the east side gathered at Willowvale Park to disrupt a baseball game played between the Harbord team of mainly Jewish players and the Catholic team of St. Peter's Church. They taunted the immigrant side with their swastika flag and got the desired reaction. Angry red faces burned in the hot dusk, and punches were thrown. Players and supporters on both sides bashed away at each other with bats and metal pipes. Blunt cries of pain mixed with screams of hate and outrage filled the air.

Dr. Palindrome would be surprised to learn that Viktor Crane and his buddies, having spent the night in police cells on Queen Street, walked out of a courtroom the next morning with all charges dismissed. Or maybe he wouldn't be surprised at all. The judge ruled it was a night of high spirits that had got out of hand.

Among the newspaper clippings and the hate pamphlets Paul discovered in one of the drawers was the neatly folded white flag with the black prongs of a swastika—like a Ninja throwing star.

The old man spoke now when he had finished sorting through his papers. "No empty talk of the past. We have no feelings for each other I know but you are the one I depend on. Of your sister I will say nothing. We do not speak."

No empty talk of the past. Of your sister I will say nothing. You and I have had our disagreements but being civilized and intelligent men we can discuss things. Our miserable galaxy is doomed. No one will escape the apocalypse. All will be revealed. *Who spoke like that?*

"I have an adequate collection of assets. The house, some investments, life insurance, my pension. I do not know how long I will live but everything must be completed before I die. I have made my will. I will leave nothing for the jackals. The lawyers, government. Nothing for the bastard sons of Israel." His face tightened. "I leave everything to you. But you will earn it." He smiled without mirth as he set out papers for

Paul to sign.

He glanced through documents that transferred Crane's property and accounts to himself, a paper that made him executor, and signed his name to each.

But all the time, his mind was on Linda. He had flown from England to see her and to tell her he wanted to marry her and he was annoyed at having to listen to the old goat bleat about assets and the bastard sons of Israel while she was at that very moment snuggling up beside Trevor in his parents' living room as he readied himself to pop the question while Paul drowned in talk of investments and jackals. Trevor would soon be making the move and his parents would be hovering just outside the door waiting for him to make it. Once the family get involved it's a whole new ball game, and there's no tomorrow. Trevor would get down on bended knee exactly the way he'd seen people do in some terrible movie. Then he would present the ring. Ten thousand shelled out for a diamond so Linda and the rest of the world would know what a successful man he was. A diamond well beyond Paul's reach but not beyond Linda's because it would soon be on her finger.

He wondered if Trevor's performance on bended knee and his diamond worth its weight in gold were what Linda really wanted. And he asked himself why he was here at all in the house he had vowed never to return to, listening to the goat bleat about jackals and zombies and accounts, but *not* really listening because he was burning time here when he should be with Linda telling her that he loved her and wanted to marry her and would she please let Trevor know that with all his bended knee and king's ransom diamond he was wasting his time.

Still, whatever Trevor and his bended knee and

diamond said or didn't say to her, she had promised to have a drink with Paul before he flew back to England, where he didn't want to live by himself any more because he wanted to live with her, and would happily do so in England, Estonia or the ends of the Earth.

"What you do when the time comes is up to you. It will not matter to me. It is only now that matters. You will be trustee of the estate when I am gone. There is no one else. You will not need me to sign anything when the time comes. By then all will happen as we have agreed."

The goat bleating all this time, like he was addressing the Reichstag, and Paul thinking only of Linda and bloody Trevor.

"When I die there will be no duty or tax. I poked about in the public's stinking mouths for forty years but I invested wisely. I am not rich but I will leave nothing to the Shylocks." A fleck of spittle appeared at the corner of his mouth when he said *Shylocks*. Then he reached across the documents and curled his arthritic fingers around a bottle of pills. He twisted off the cap, shook out one large yellow pill and swallowed it without water. Paul hoped it might lodge in his esophagus and cut off his oxygen supply, so his face would again turn purple as it had done all those years ago when the magazines from Wisconsin made him scream in his chair and flail his arms, and all of this while staring at his little stepson on the other side of the glass and not seeing him. Do it now, large yellow pill, he thought, but of course it didn't.

"This is only business. You will make the pact to see me die in peace. You would like to see me dead I think."

Paul said nothing. He was drowning in sludge. But later that day he would push his way up through the oleaginous liquid and break the surface so he could ask

Linda to marry him.

"When the time comes you must manage things. Do you agree to do this?"

Paul nodded. "I'll do it," he said but only to accompany the nod while he thought about Linda.

"I will die in my own house. Not in a home or a hospital. You will be here."

"Whatever you want."

The words came easily. It wasn't compassion or duty. So why did he say he would do it? Why did he not tell him when the time came—and really the time and the place were right then and there—to go and fuck himself in the way that he had fucked or at least fucked up everyone who had ever come into his life?

So many questions for Dr. Palindrome.

Did he already suspect what his stepfather had in mind? Or did he envision Viktor Crane passing away as they did in Dickens with his family of one gathered round the bed in a candlelit room to watch the poor soul slip away? No. He envisioned nothing. The words came easily because his mind was on Linda, and Trevor on his bended knee holding a diamond as big as the Ritz. He spoke the words easily so he could get out of the house and fast forward the rest of the day to the moment when he could tell Linda he was already in love with her before he even met her. Though he wouldn't actually tell her that because it would give her second thoughts about his mental state right off the bat.

Did he already know somewhere, maybe in that place he could never get to, that his stepfather was actually asking him to help him die? Or did he believe he was only to be present at his bedside when the old man breathed his last as in the natural course of things? He said he would be there when the time came—but surely he meant only that he would be there to watch the cretinous bastard die with all his crimes broad blown as flush as May. But whether he knew that he had actually agreed to trip the bastard himself so that his heels might kick at heaven and his soul be as damned and black as the hell whereto it goes, he was unsure.

I was twelve, Paul. It was a year after Mum died.

He still had his sister's letter. He had considered sharing it with Dr. Palindrome in a later session. But what was wrong with right now? It might as well be right now. Along with the evil talk of kikes and Jew bastards that must be numbered among all his stepfather's crimes broad blown.

You remember he stayed out late some nights, going to his "meetings" and then coming home after everyone was asleep. I woke up whenever I heard him come in the front door. Like I already knew. And sure enough one night he's in my bedroom. I must have drifted off before he came up the stairs. And then he was standing by my bed. I was so scared I couldn't move. I was lying on my side facing the wall. I could hear him breathing and I wanted to turn round and scream at him to leave. It was summer, one of those hot sticky nights. I slept in my underwear with my sheets kicked down to the bottom of the bed. Even over my fan I could hear him breathing. Like he was out of breath from coming up the stairs. He stood by my bed for a long time breathing so I could hear it and then he left. I pulled the sheet up over myself right away. I remember I didn't sleep after that.

A few nights later you had one of your bad dreams. You ran into my room and knocked over all those empty baking tins that I had piled up against the door. Do you remember that? I piled baking tins against the door so he wouldn't come into my room ever again without me knowing. I woke up thinking it was him and I screamed. Aunt Helen came running in from her bedroom and found me sitting up in bed screaming and you sprawled on the floor among all the baking tins. I had told you both that the baking tins were a science project—something to do with trapping nighttime air—and you believed me because you believed everything then.

I knew I had to get out of that house. You know the rest. I haven't told Steven about this and I never will. Writing this to you is as much as I can do.

Love you Paul,

Jennifer

He would have to explain to Dr. P. that all the stuff about crimes broad blown as flush as May and heels kicking at heaven came from *Hamlet*. Hamlet too was on the point of sliding a dagger up through his stepfather's eye into the spongy mass of his temporal lobe while Claudius was at prayer, but Hamlet lost the moment and carried on to his mother's bedroom to tell her she was a whore. Being the dithering twerp he was at times, he thought too much about doing it or not doing it, and decided in the end that to kill a man when he was at prayer might actually *save* the man's soul and not send it kicking its heels at heaven, so in the end he didn't do it. He carried on to his mother's bedroom to make her feel like shit for having sex with her brother-in-law—his uncle, and now stepfather—a mere two months after the death of her first husband, and Paul's father, who was the real King and always would be.

He hadn't said much to Dr. P. about sex so maybe this

would be a good time to get into it. Dr. P. must be wondering when sex would rear its ugly head in this session because every patient he had ever treated during his long and distinguished career got around to it at some point, Freud having laid the foundations.

This would be exactly the time for sex to rear its ugly head, since he had already brought up Jennifer's letter, and mentioned Hamlet popping into his mother's bedroom to tell her she was a whore. This was the time to bring up yet another bedroom visit, one that made him often think of sliding a stiletto of his own up through his stepfather's eyeball into the spongy mass of his temporal lobe, and not just watch him die of natural causes when that time came.

This bedroom visit—the one he would share with Dr. Palindrome—became the wellspring of his own earliest wicked thoughts. The first raiding parties that climbed his unsuspecting battlements and stormed his mind, clearing a path for the thought hordes of later years. By surrendering to these wicked thoughts he feared he had tarred his own soul, so it too would be damned and black as the hell whereto it would go for all eternity, but for all that he was never able to confess them to a priest. Owning up to these wicked thoughts might cause much flecking of spit and gnashing of teeth on the priest's side of the confessional.

But now, if Dr. P. didn't mind improvising as shrink and father confessor at the same time, he would tell all.

Bless him, Dr. P., for he has sinned grievously. He confesses to almighty God and to you. It has been an incalculably long time since his last confession so please forgive him before he even begins, for having no idea when he last confessed. These are his sins.

He had his first experience of sex when he was four. There. That would put the doctor's pencil to work. Though it wasn't what Dr. P. might think, nothing like that, nothing to do with his stepfather being a pedophile and the thing that happened years later when he popped in to see Jennifer when she was twelve and he believed she was sleeping. Like Jennifer, Paul was only an observer and not a participant in his first sexual encounter, but it put him years ahead of his time all the same.

It made him an early developer overnight. And when the time came for his own sexual intimacies, with Laura Swanson up at Great Bear for example, whose hot mouth kissed and caressed him all the way down, it made him an early ejaculator—early in the sense of almost instantaneous—and maybe there was a connection straight up, so to speak, with what he observed that night in his mother's bedroom. That would be for Dr. P. to figure out with all his specialized study of psychology that would certainly include Freud somewhere along the way, if everything Paul had read about psychology was true.

The noise woke him up in the middle of the night. He listened for a while. It came from down the hall and sounded like someone moaning. At first he thought it came from his sister's room but didn't sound like the moans Jennifer sometimes made when she was dreaming. This sounded like someone in pain, and at the same time not in pain. He was curious because he was just four and eventually decided the moans must be coming from his mother's room. He thought she might be ill, so he climbed out of bed and crept down the hall to her door that was open a crack and leaked a sliver of dim light onto the hallway floor.

He peered through the opening into the bedroom. He could see the statue of the Virgin at the foot of the bed. A votive candle was lit and in the dim light he could see Mary's head angled to the side, her eyes cast down. He could also just make out his stepfather's head at the bottom of the bed, cut off by the door at the neck. He was staring up at Mary, his pointed chin beard stuck up in the air, and he was grimacing like maybe his head had really been cut off.

But he wasn't making the moaning sounds.

He pushed the door open a little wider.

Now he could see all of his stepfather stretched out naked on the bed and his mother sitting astride him. With her bare legs bent sharply back at the knees *she* was making the moaning sounds. He lay on his back with his cloven feet thrust into the pillows at the top of the bed. Not that Paul actually thought of cloven feet right then, because being only four he hadn't yet connected his stepfather to the devil.

Anyway, he was fascinated by the sight of his mother rocking back and forth astride his stepfather while she was moaning. She faced the Virgin as she rocked and moaned and she clasped her hands together like she was praying. Her eyes were shut tight like she was praying really hard and meaning it. Her naked breasts jiggled as she rolled back and forth on top of him. His hands gripped her waist and seemed to be moving her back and forth. She moaned all the time that she prayed, rolling back and forth and sometimes up and down and every way at once, but he could see that whatever way she moved it was because his hands gripped her at the waist. Her tangled hair was wet and hung down, the ends plastered to her breasts. Then his stepfather began to moan along with her and turned his head to the side so he was looking at the door where Paul stood, but he didn't see the boy then, just as he didn't see him when he ranted in his study and bared his teeth and made his face go purple like he was suffocating. When he turned his face away from the door again, he arched his back, lifting her up towards the ceiling, and then squeezing his eyes tight shut he shouted "Oh Yes!" His head jerked right back and his eyes opened again, so he was looking straight up at the Virgin behind him, and then he went still.

His mother stopped rocking and slowly came down like a balloon losing air.

"Amen," said his stepfather.

Paul turned and went back to his room.

He lay awake for while after, thinking that what they were doing must have hurt because his mother sounded like she was in pain and so did his stepfather, but however they sounded they didn't seem distressed. And so it was an act of worship. His mother was kneeling and her hands were together, they both faced the Virgin and his stepfather said *Amen* when the prayer finished. *With my body I thee worship*. Father Glass spoke those words in church. *With my body I thee worship* he said.

At first he had wanted to scream and scream and scream when he stood at the door, he wanted to run to the bed and pull her off him, but now he was glad he didn't because they were only praying. Being just four he didn't know that if he had pulled her off him he would see his swollen penis all wet and slippery from being inside her. He didn't know about those things then. He didn't know that his stepfather's penis was capable of being inside her because he didn't know that his mother even had a place for his penis to be. And a penis was just something to pee with, she told him. Pee-nis.

He learned about all these things later of course, and once he discovered what else a penis could do he got what they were doing that night. He couldn't remember how or when he found out. Maybe finding out about sex was like learning you're going to die. Who remembers the moment they learnt they would one day die? Finding out about sex was the same and one day you just realized you knew something you didn't know before. The boys in the schoolyard who sang the rude song about Mrs. Cartwright's name likely told him, maybe at recess, that a penis could do way more than just pee.

So when he thought back to seeing his mother kneeling astride his stepfather he realized they were not actually worshipping the Virgin Mary. Even though his mother's hands were folded in prayer and her eyes were shut tight and she moaned in what only sounded like pain, she was not paying homage to the Blessed Virgin and neither was he, even when he said *Amen*.

What on earth would the Virgin be thinking of it all? *Thy will be done* is what the statue said, Mary answering the angel Gabriel when he told her she was to be the mother of Christ. *Thy will be done.* Maybe his mother was praying to the Virgin for forgiveness as she rocked back and forth on top of his stepfather with his penis inside her. Perhaps that's why there was pain as well as pleasure in her moans. Maybe if she had gone to see Dr. P. herself, had he been around back then, she could have told him what she was thinking while she was having his stepfather's seed spilled into her body, and Dr. P. could now tell Paul what he should understand by it all.

Was it when he watched his stepfather's hands move his mother up and down and round and round while she knelt on top of him, that Paul too felt his power and feared him from that moment? He could see it was all made to happen by his stepfather's will. He lay underneath her with the Virgin at the end of the bed right above his head, and it was his will—and his willy, Paul supposed now—that needed to be done. And when he was older and hated his stepfather and wanted to do something to him that would make him moan with only pain and not pleasure, like insert a stiletto up through his eyeball, he couldn't do it because he was afraid. His stepfather had had powerful hands that made his mother do what she was doing, and he showed his power right there in front of the Virgin, who for her part couldn't watch, but turned her head to one side and cast down her eyes not wishing to see his willy being done.

To go back to his mother for a moment, what might Dr. P. think was going on in her head while she enabled his stepfather to spill his seed into her? Was she afraid of him too, and did she feel helpless with his hands gripping her waist, and so did she carry on worshipping him with her body even as she prayed to the Virgin for forgiveness? And did he make her worship him only that one time, or did he do it every night, and if it was every night or a few other nights than just that one then, why did her moans awaken him only the once? She never had another child so maybe it really was only the once. She would never have used protection because she was Catholic, and so was he along with being a Nazi fucker—like Hitler himself it was rumored, closet Roman Catholic and Nazi fucker all in one—and for all Roman

Catholic fuckers, whether they were Nazis or not, it was a sin to use protection. A sin to put an engorged willy into the forefended place without intending to fertilize an egg with a single sperm out of the millions that come shooting out. He hoped to God his mother hadn't actually *prayed* to the Virgin to make just a single one of those millions of sperm wriggle its way up to a receptive egg and fertilize it, because that would be too ironic for words—Mary being the Immaculate Conception.

Did it all really come down to sex and religion in the end? Being fucked and fucked up at the same time? Hating and fearing, loathing and submitting, screwing and worshipping, all in the same fucked up way? Is that why he himself kept coming back to the house he never wanted to see again? And why he spent an entire morning watching his stepfather sort out his finances and his will and then signing papers? Thy *will* be done now, the willy being long spent.

Did his mother similarly hate the man and give herself to him while hating herself for doing it? Letting him spill his seed and praying to the Virgin for forgiveness all at the same time? And then for insurance, confessing to Father Glass and begging forgiveness all over again when he came to visit her?

He would come back to Father Glass in a moment.

What of his stepfather? Did knowing that his wife prayed with hands folded as she faced the Virgin while he was having his way with her, engorge his penis even more? Was doing it in front of the Virgin some kind of aphrodisiac? Or maybe there was more to it than that and now Paul thought his own soul would for sure be sent to hell with its heels kicking at heaven for thinking that his stepfather maybe fantasized about spilling his seed into the Blessed Virgin herself as she stood above him, with her eyes not watching.

Could anyone apart from the devil incarnate be so depraved as to imagine someone thinking of deflowering the Virgin Mother of Christ who was herself immaculately conceived, as he thrust himself into a moaning and worshipping mother and filled her forefended place with his seed?

The answer was yes. Paul was that depraved person because, five years later, at the tender age of nine, being told about sex by some random dickhead kids behind the bike shed, and being overwhelmed by thoughts of his mother in her bedroom, and trying to work out what such an apparently fucked up act of worship might mean, that's exactly what he imagined. Wicked thoughts to compound his earlier wickedness of watching his mother go at it instead of walking away as he should have done but couldn't, because he had already been turned into a pillar of salt like Lot's wife.

When his stepfather suddenly turned his head to the door just before his *Amen* moment, did he maybe see his little stepson peering through the door and know that he owned him too, and feel even more excited with the boy watching, so that it made him spill his seed all the sooner?

The family that prays together stays together. Father Glass said that too in Sunday school. Maybe Father Glass consoled Paul's mother with the same bumper sticker when he came to her bedroom each day—*every day*—to hear her confession. And yes, Paul's wicked thoughts occasionally strayed to Father Glass coming in a different sense. He too had a serviceable and engorgeable willy under all those consecrated vestments, and he visited Paul's mother every day—in her bedroom, with the door closed, no less.

It was the same when he looked up at the crucifixion in church and tried not to think of Christ's penis. Under the loincloth of the impaled Christ was a loin with an arousable penis that Mary Magdalene—yes it was rumored—was supposed to have *known* in the Biblical sense.

He needed absolution now, but Dr. P. couldn't give him that. Perhaps an ounce of civet, good apothecary, to sweeten his imagination. But the doctor was a shrink, not an apothecary, and while he could listen, he couldn't provide absolution or any other kind of solution.

And so he came back to the original question which was why, during his visit years later when his stepfather asked him to manage things when the time came, he nodded his head without knowing why, saying he would manage things and not understand what that entailed? Was it really because he was thinking about Linda with Trevor on his knee presenting her with a huge motherfucking diamond, and that made him nod his head and say *I'll do it* to anything that would make the old man shut up? Or did some part of him actually understand that when the time came, he would *have* to kill him himself, because more than anything that's what he wanted to do to the man who spilled his seed into his mother as she prayed to Christ's immaculate mother who never had seed of any kind spilled into her except metaphorically God's?

He was asking a lot of questions but he hoped Dr. P. could see how they were not the kind of *do you think* questions that Dr. Hannah had asked in their first session. Paul's questions now came with their own answers, which made them rhetorical, unlike in the earlier session when his answers to Dr. P.'s questions came dressed up as questions themselves, which only made them evasive.

In any case this was turning out to be one hell of a session, and the doctor's hand would be falling off with all that writing, but they were nearly done.

Perhaps he did know, without realizing it, that when the time came of which his stepfather spoke, he was speaking of his time to die, and Paul, again without realizing it, had agreed to be present and do all that was necessary to give him a safe and painless passage into the hereafter.

But somewhere inside himself that he couldn't get to any more, he suspected he agreed to do it all and so remove the sac of bile from his life forever. If that was his hope then he was disappointed because fast-forwarding to the present, as in the right here and now present, he remained tied to the sac of bile in its ice-cold crypt a whole decade after he put it there. It would never be out of his life however much he wanted it to be, and however many bags of ice he piled on top, it would never disappear.

He read the forms and signed them, back in the past present to which he kept returning, all the while thinking of Trevor on his knee with a diamond ring in his hand.

Sebastian came into the study to witness the signatures.

It was early afternoon when Paul left the house. He was tired. There had been a lot of papers to sign. He didn't understand the legal language with its provisional clauses and qualifying statements and bottom lines that were also made up of words that he didn't understand.

He walked up the street and turned back once to look at the house. The upstairs windows stared, impassive under the gables. The verandah gaped. He would sell the house when it became his sometime in the future present and invest the money. It would be a head start for his family, should he and Linda have children. He hadn't asked her to marry him yet and didn't know if she wanted children. If Linda turned him down and married Trevor then the house would help provide for Jennifer and Steven and their little beefcakes. In any event some good to come from their mother's terrible blunder.

But his stepfather was right. He always came back, like a dog to its vomit.

*

And so the memories and time frames linked and locked, intersected and intertwined, inseparable with no beginning and no end like the Olympic rings and Linda's telephone rings—five of them as well— that now, many years on, enjoined each caller to have a fantastic day.

*

Crane was seventy-six when he told Paul he was ready to die. "When the time comes you will manage things. Do what is necessary. Do you remember?"

"I had no idea this is what you meant."

"How could you not know? You signed the papers. Did you not read between the lines? An English teacher?"

His stepfather grinned at his sarcasm. Then his face set again. "You will know exactly what to do. I will dismiss Sebastian and transfer to you my medical records, prescriptions, all that I require. You will tell people when it is over that I have been taken to Victoria to die. I have relatives there. You can say that when people ask."

"I can't do this. I had no idea."

The eyes narrowed and the thin mouth twitched. "I thought you would be happy to see me out."

He was right of course. But Paul needed to be a good deal happier than this before he could bring himself to do it. He still feared the life to come and needed more than loathing to trip the old man so he would kick his heels at heaven.

Crane read his thoughts.

"Are you afraid? Or do you somehow think you are too good? Like your mother perhaps? She was a whore. Maybe you were not aware of that?"

Paul stared back. A whore. The word was a knitting needle pushed into his ear, and forging in his mind the stiletto blade that he imagined piercing his stepfather's eyeball on its way to the temporal lobe.

"Your mother had men. The museum let her go. You didn't know that. Security found her one night in the archives with a student from the university. And so they fired her." His tongue flicked across his lips. "That was your mother. A very good lay, if I say so myself. Others thought so too. Do you even know if you are your father's son?"

His mouth spread into a thin line that narrowed his grey eyes, drawing up the little pouches under them like tiny swag curtains. "And you say you can't do this? You think you are above this? Your mother thought the same." He leaned forward. "She was better off dead."

Of course he was his father's son. Aunt Helen told him he was his father's son and that he was getting to look just like him when she fastened the cufflinks on his shirt.

Helping the bastard to die would be like removing a stone from a shoe. Like snuffing a candle.

*

It's not like putting out a light Mr. Thorne.

He had to tell Dr. P. about his meeting with Gilpin. And what happened earlier that same day. If he dropped a single stitch, the whole story would come apart.

Driving across the Burlington skyway to the lawyer's office on Rachel's ninth birthday, he remembered gazing across the bay at the yellow pall that hung over the steel mills. The smoke was worse on humid days when it had nowhere to go. Smog days they called them now. Suffocating industrial airlessness days. The scene from the bridge quite took his breath away. Like death. Gilpin would tell him all he needed to know about death.

He had never seen someone die. He was there when Frenchie and Johnny Fonseca were killed in the pit explosion at Great Bear, but that didn't count because he was being blown up himself at that moment and didn't see them.

His mother's death was a picture. Her white dress framed in a window. But he didn't actually see her die.

The only death he had ever witnessed, live as it were,

didn't look like a death at all. Lee Harvey Oswald on a black and white TV screen suddenly convulsing, his face creasing up as from a punch line. The man accused of shooting the president of the United States doubling over like he'd just got the joke and died laughing. As a boy, watching the newscast live from the Dallas police station on that Sunday afternoon, Paul thought it wasn't what a death should look like. He didn't know then what a live death should look like, only that it shouldn't look like that.

As he drove, he mused on the phrase, *a fate worse than death*. Scratch at a cliché long enough and it will bleed a little meaning. Could life become a fate worse than death?

Fate and fatality didn't mean the same thing though they came from the same word. A fatalist believed in fate. Whatever happened was intended to happen. Ordained to happen. A priest was ordained. Ordination was one of the seven sacraments. Holy Orders. Paul was fated to be ordained, but it didn't work out. Instead of holy orders he got marching orders. His vocation blew away like dandelion fluff. Like Frenchie and Johnny Fonseca in the mine blast. Maybe they were ordained too.

'Fated. n. *The quality or condition of being predetermined.* Discuss.' An essay he might set for his students one day. Be a spoiler, and give them the dictionary definition up front so they'd have to find another opening sentence.

A fatality on the other hand meant death. Event or person, either could be a fatality.

A traffic fatality was reported on the radio that morning at breakfast. Rachel's ninth birthday. Breaking news gave details live from the scene of a fatal car crash at Highway 401 and Black Creek Drive. The driver of a Taurus family wagon was pronounced dead at the scene. Two people in the second car sustained injuries and were flown by air ambulance to Sunny Brook Health Science Centre. From Black Creek to Sunny Brook. Traffic on the freeway was backed up for a mile. But Paul would be taking the Queen Elizabeth Way not the freeway, and then the Gardiner into Toronto for his eleven o'clock appointment with Gilpin.

Rachel had looked up from her cereal when she heard the radio report.

"What's a fatality?"

Linda gave her considered reply. "It's an accident, darling, where unfortunately someone isn't alive anymore."

"Like when Calypso?"

"Yes dear, just like poor Calypso."

Rachel went back to reading her cereal box.

A month before, she had come home from school to find her pet goldfish on the floor. A bright orange chili pepper lying terminally still on the deep green carpet of her bedroom. Goldfish sometimes leap out of their bowls, Paul told her, though he couldn't explain why. Perhaps Calypso mistook the aquamarine carpet for the open sea and launched herself out of the bowl in a bid for freedom. Or maybe goldfish too can turn suicidal when bound in a glass bowl not much bigger than a nutshell, and the endless circling becomes too much.

Later in the day, Rachel admitted to having a little cry on her own before coming down to ask her father to please come and dispose of the body. Not her exact words, of course. She was only eight, turning nine in a month. All in all, she took the death of her goldfish in stride. No need for grief counselors. No need for Dr. Palindrome.

He duly disposed of the body. Disposing of Calypso's body was comparatively straightforward—plop, into the bowl, and a quick flush. He didn't tell Rachel how easy it was. She never asked for another pet. She got over it and moved on. An enviable trait, moving on. A gift from her mother.

After the accident report that morning he switched off the radio and sipped his coffee, watching Rachel read her cereal box. She was a creature of habit, like her mother, her squinting face now a picture of concentration. Mechanically she tucked a strand of blond hair behind her ear and spooned the cereal into her mouth without taking her eyes off the box.

Cereal boxes had changed. They had got snappier and more colourful with fewer words and more pictures, like a lot of things. Way back in the day they featured monochrome photos of baseball stars like Ted Williams, Joe DiMaggio and Roy Campanella. And Yogi Berra, who hit a double and a home run at Wirtz Stadium in Detroit on the night that Hartman Thorne became a fatality. *It ain't over till it's over.* Now cereal boxes featured pop stars and super models and Ninja Turtles and The Simpsons. It all worked for Rachel though. In a later era they would display tedious statistics about niacin and riboflavin and other serious nutrients that guaranteed unending life measured out in milligrams.

Her face was round like her mother's. And she had blue eyes, though they didn't glint like sapphires because she didn't wear tinted contacts. Her straight blond hair shone in the sun, again like her mother's before the highlights.

Later that morning in the garage, when Paul started up the car for his drive to Toronto, her *Mary Poppins* tape came on in mid-song. *A chimney sweep's lucky as lucky can be.* It was like a note she had left for him. She hung around the edges of his life even when she wasn't there.

Traffic was slow coming off the skyway. He switched to the CBC news at the top of the hour. The last Soviet troops had left Afghanistan. There were problems with the retracting roof of the newly opened baseball stadium in Toronto. Last night's sudden cloudburst had soaked the players and the fans before they got the roof closed. And now there was again *breaking news* of tanks and armed soldiers driving into a crowd of civilian protesters in Beijing. In local news the driver killed in the freeway collision that morning was identified as Barry Chevril, aged thirty-one, from Etobicoke. He left a wife and two small children. Like Hartman Thorne, aged thirty-one a half century ago, and also the father of two.

Crawling in traffic across the skyway over a glassy Burlington Bay shrouded in yellow smog he wondered if Barry Chevril, who had set off that morning for a normal day at work and a short time later lay bleeding and lifeless on Black Creek Drive in the twisted wreckage of his Ford Taurus family wagon, had been pegged from the start to end as a fatality on that lovely June morning.

Father McGrath at Mount St. Michael would have attributed the tragedy to the divinely approved workings of natural law combined with man's freedom to err. For him the immutable physical laws relating to mass and momentum and the accelerated breakdown of molecular adhesion at impact—metal fatigue—contributed to the fatality. Add to that the resulting trauma to brain, vital organs, tissue and nerve endings in their fragile casing of bone and cartilage, and the question would not be, why did it happen, but what did you expect?

As far as Father McGrath, himself a closet agnostic, was concerned, God was in His heaven—maybe—comfortably hibernating as He had done since creation, and so all was as right as it could possibly be in His universe. Everything quietly unfolding as one long, ordained miracle.

Some years ago Paul read of a giant asteroid that had recently missed the earth by a *mere* two hundred thousand miles. A comfortable enough distance he thought, but the tabloids screamed in end-zone-sized headlines: *World Escapes Annihilation by a Hair*. Father McGrath would have smiled at the thought of millions of God-fearing people thanking the Omnipotent for stepping in at the eleventh hour and like Charlton Heston, or maybe now Bruce Willis, diverting the asteroid from its collision course.

We interrupt this bolt from the blue to bring you our regularly scheduled program.

Today was the fortieth anniversary of his mother's death. It was his day to learn about legal fallout from an assisted death, and it was Rachel's ninth birthday. A convergence of fateful moments.

*

It's homicide plain and simple.

Inside his paneled office on the second floor of an old

refurbished building the colour of raw liver, John Gilpin did not mince his words.

Behind the large mahogany desk, his leather-bound legal volumes were shelved in even, scrupulous rows. High on the wall, an oriel window, like a monocle, displayed a circle of hard blue sky. A lidless eye. He wondered if Gilpin was a Mason. Lawyers often were, he had read somewhere.

He was indeed. Paul could see the ring.

He never felt comfortable in the offices of lawyers. Or doctors. Dentists. Even accountants, although he had married one. Real estate people. Insurance brokers. Psychologists. Anyone with a bottom line, usually dotted, to be signed.

Gilpin rose from his desk when Paul was shown in. He put out his hand and offered him a chair. Sunlight from the round window fell on his salt-and-pepper hair, thick and wavy, making it almost glitter. He was tall and thin in his well-made suit, and looked like he might be a marathoner. He had a professional smile.

Paul had written on behalf of a friend who wished to remain anonymous, and whose mother wanted her to assist in her death. He showed Paul a chair and then sat down himself with the letter on the desk in front of him.

"It's homicide plain and simple."

His own statement seemed to unsettle him, his quick eyes sizing Paul up from behind half-moon bifocals, and his brows twitching like antennae. His slender hands darted about, shifting things around on his desk as if he were doing a trick. Or playing a board game. Pen to paper clip two, stapler to letter opener one.

"Strictly in terms of the law we're talking euthanasia

here, Mr. Thorne, and it's still a crime. Your friend would go to jail."

"But this sort of thing happens all the time, doesn't it? People don't go to jail for it, do they? You never hear much about that."

"It all depends on what you mean by *this sort of thing,* Mr. Thorne." He picked up his pen and tapped it end over end on the desk. "Is your friend religious?"

"I don't think she goes to church any more. But we're talking about the law here, aren't we, not religion?"

The lawyer lifted a hand so he could explain. "I'm an Anglican, Mr. Thorne. I go to St Luke's Church on Walmer Road. It would interest your friend to know that our Book of Common Worship now includes a set of prayers to be read on the occasion of life-support systems being removed. And yes, the existence of such a prayer suggests that life-support systems are removed on a regular basis. So, on one hand there is the removal of all obstacles to death taking its natural course as, shall we say, a quasi-religious rite, and on the other there is euthanasia as a criminal act." He rotated the pen along the top of his hand. "That's why it all depends on what you mean by *this sort of thing*. God, we suppose, is merciful and understanding, but the law—which is indeed our concern here—is precise."

Paul shifted in his chair.

Gilpin pulled out a blank sheet of paper from a drawer and unscrewed the top of his fountain pen. Then he drew a horizontal line across the page and pushed the paper forward, so Paul could see.

"The majority of these so-called mercy-killings, like the iceberg, lie under the surface. You don't see them.

The cases that go to court, and even make the headlines, are the politicized ones that provoke discussions about changing the law." He placed the point of the pen in the middle of the page, well below the horizontal line.

"Under the surface—here—are the 'acts of mercy' that we never hear about. Patients in irreversible comas or on life-support systems that are discreetly turned off. Nothing is said. Who's to know?"

"Then there's the terminally ill, comatose patient, from whom nutrition and hydration are gradually withdrawn. The patient dies on their own."

He moved the pen up the page closer to the line. "Here we have a patient who requests that treatment be stopped, so the illness is allowed to take its course. The patient eventually dies, also unassisted, technically speaking."

He pushed the pen nearly to the line. "Now at this point, just below the surface, things become more interesting and a good deal more risky. This is where you don't just withhold treatment, but you actually provide something to hasten the death. Let's say you give pain medication at the patient's request, but you know that a consequence might be death.

You're no longer allowing nature to take its course. Now you're forcing its hand."

He pushed the nib of his pen up through the horizontal line. "Now you're a criminal." He screwed the top back on and put the pen down. "It could be pills or a needle. Even if the woman is able to do it herself, this daughter friend becomes an accomplice by not preventing her. It's not suicide any more, which itself isn't an indictable offence because you can't arrest a corpse. It's homicide—same as actually administering the lethal dose or injection."

He picked up a periodical from his desk and opened it at a page he had earmarked. "Have you ever heard of this man in Michigan they call 'Dr. Death'?"

Paul looked back at him. He had heard of him but wanted to hear what Gilpin had to say.

"His name's Kevorkian and he's on a mission. Dying isn't a crime, he says, and he believes physicians should be allowed to assist people who want to end their lives. He's come up with a push-button device that releases the killer meds into the patient, but here's the thing—it's the patient who pushes the button. So where's the crime in that, he asks. He's already assisted in the death of a woman with Alzheimer's, but he can't be prosecuted because there's no law against it in Michigan. At the moment. You can bet that won't last. The courts are already pursuing the argument that we can never be sure someone with Alzheimer's can actually know they want to die." He held out the journal for Paul to look at, but he declined. He didn't want to read about Dr. Death.

Gilpin laid the magazine on his desk and pushed it slowly to one side. Checkmate. "In Canada the law is clear. Assisted suicide is homicide. For now."

"For now?"

"The good Dr. Kevorkian has started something, no question. Who knows how soon the courts in this country will decide that it's okay for a doctor to assist in the death of a consenting patient whose illness is unbearable and incurable? It will likely happen in our lifetime. But for now the law is clear, if arguably inhumane."

"But if the patient administers the drugs himself—*herself*—isn't that suicide?" He was thinking of the death doctor's push-button device.

"Let me just say our courts would have an easier time convicting someone who used a syringe. Kevorkian's home-made gadget blurs the line." He indicated his sheet of paper. "But gadgetry aside, there's something else your friend should know, Mr. Thorne. An assisted death is almost impossible to conceal. The law requires a coroner to attend a home death by any cause before a certificate can be issued. The police come to a home death as a matter of routine. In suspicious circumstances they do an autopsy."

Game over. The fat lady sings and there's no tomorrow. Paul had heard enough and was ready to leave.

But Gilpin wasn't finished. He removed his glasses, his dark eyes looking pinched above his long thin nose. He seemed to be scrutinizing Paul as he spoke.

"Your friend should not allow herself to be misled by all the medical spin. She may have heard terms like involuntary active euthanasia, voluntary active suicide, passive euthanasia, physician-assisted suicide, and the like. They're all murder, and she has to be clear on that score." He leaned forward. "She should also know that it can all become very messy. Sometimes it doesn't work first time. Sometimes the death force doesn't win. The life force takes over and the will to live conquers the will to die. You'd be surprised to know how much physical strength it takes to end a life. A body can fight death on its own. It's not like putting out a light. More like trying to blow out those trick candles on a birthday cake." His mouth twitched in a half smile, but his eyes remained stern. "Your friend needs to know that."

He stood up and led Paul to the door. "And she needs

to know she will have to make peace with herself when it's all over, whether she's religious or not. The courts don't deal with peace of mind, but that can be the hardest part. You should tell her." He opened the door to the foyer, but stopped Paul in the doorway. "Mr. Thorne, you should do whatever you can to persuade your friend not to go ahead with this. I can tell you stories, believe me. It's just not worth it."

Paul shook his hand and stepped out of the office. His head was spinning, but he remained skeptical. Gilpin had given him the worst-case scenario because he had to. Due diligence and all that. What else would a lawyer advise about such a complicated matter? And he had spoken about Dr. Death in Michigan. Was he maybe hinting that, for all the laws against it, it could still be done? But Paul wouldn't need the doctor's ingenious little dispenser gadget. Crane would do everything himself.

He would swallow the killing pills when the time came, and Paul would watch. Be there with him. The instructions were typed in Times New Roman on cream vellum paper. Crane, for all his cretinous bastardy, was a precise man. Nothing left to chance. A few hours and it would be done. Then he would remove the body to the basement and into the freezer, the reliquary. First things first. No coroner. No death certificate. No police. He would store the body until he figured out what to do with it. When he had a plan he would dispose of it. He would think of something. It wouldn't be difficult. The main thing was to get it done.

On his way home with his head full of murder he stopped at a mall in Burlington and bought Rachel a miniature plastic doll house that swiveled open to reveal a complex of furnished rooms for her tiny doll people. He drove back across the skyway over Burlington Bay watching a dying sun shoot its last salvoes of orange and crimson across the evening sky. It hovered, a dull yolk above the horizon, shrouded by the smoke spewing from the chimneystacks along the shore.

The sky deepened to a bloom of blood-bruise red and Lenten purple with slashes of mustard yellow. He had read somewhere that evening skies over the Great Lakes in summer were especially dramatic because the sun's rays were refracted through layers of factory pollution and engine fumes. *A foul and pestilent congregation of vapours*—smokestacks along the shoreline, and the exhausts of a thousand cars and trucks all around him. Across the sulphurous lake he could see the watery dissolve of Toronto's skyline shimmering in a wash of lake mist and pollutants. An intoxicating aquarelle. Utterly breath-taking. Earlier that year there had been that catastrophe off Alaska where a tanker had sunk, spilling millions of gallons of oil into the sea.

A hundred years ago Siegfried Sassoon described the spectacular beauty of the sunsets over the trenches in France whenever the weather wasn't bleakly, blackly overcast and raining. It was mustard gas with its perfume of lemon blossom that created such gorgeous skies at the end of the day, blinding soldiers by the thousands and melting their faces.

Sassoon had written of officers who shot the severely mangled and maimed on the front lines to put them beyond pain. No homemade pill-dispenser, just a well-aimed bullet to the head.

Accelerating off the skyway he switched on the evening news. More reports coming out of Beijing, dire global events on Rachel's ninth birthday. Certainly one to remember.

Seven

Camus title character seizes large murderer (9).

The final clue. Camus' novel was *L'Etranger. The Stranger.* Insert an L for *large and* you get a murderer—*Strang-L-er.*

He felt on edge, the pulse thudding in his ears. He wouldn't drink any more coffee today. But at least the crossword was finished.

A sudden ping made him start. Another red flag from Caldwell. He stared at the heading... *what's happening pal?*

Pal now for fuck sake. Dr. P. would find Caldwell something of a head case, though Paul hadn't mentioned him—at least he *hoped* he hadn't mentioned him during that one session, just like he hoped he had said nothing about the freezer—because if he had then questions would arise prompting Dr. P. to suspend patient confidentiality and notify the police. And then he remembered that that all happened with Dr. Hannah, whom he would definitely not be seeing again.

In other circumstances, Paul could notify the police himself and have Caldwell done for harassment, what with endless emails and unsolicited encounters whenever Paul pulled up at the curb.

They began back in February when he was raking the dead leaves and winter debris that had collected around the shrubbery and front steps of the Crane house. He had disposed of the flyers that accumulated over the past week until they were spilling out of the mailbox. He made a mental note to put up a sign, *No Flyers.* Not that a sign would ever stop people from shoving their junk mail into his box, but at least they would know he was pissed off enough not to read their stupid advertisements.

The snow had all but disappeared, early for a February. Raking the lawn with his back to the street he felt the eyes on him even before he turned his head. The stocky young man with wispy fair hair, the new owner of the recently built colonial two-storey that had replaced the Harrisons' between-the-wars bungalow, was leaning against a pillar on his front porch, hands in his pockets, staring at him. He waved when he saw Paul peer back at him, so Paul had to turn away and pretend he hadn't looked. But of course he had seen him, and the guy knew he had seen him, and so he was already wrong-footed and at a disadvantage, having lost round one of *Made You Look*. He was on edge anyway whenever he worked around the front yard of his stepfather's house. Someone might suddenly pop up in the old neighbourhood and want to reminisce about days gone by.

He gathered up the leaves and other debris and pushed the wheelbarrow around to the back. When he peered through the curtains on the landing some minutes later, the man had gone.

In March he saw him again. This time the man waved in a quick, hang-on-a-sec manner, then ran down his front steps and crossed the street.

"Hey neighbour. Paul, right?" He held out his hand. "Bradley Caldwell. Saw you a few weeks ago. Thought we should get acquainted this time."

Paul eyed him. Not Brad but the full Monty. The full Montgomery. He took the handshake. "Paul Thorne."

"Oh. Thorne? I thought the name was Crane. Your father's name was Crane, I thought." He cocked his head.

"Only my stepfather. My family name is Thorne."

"There you go. They told me this was the Crane house."

"It was." He wondered who *they* were but didn't ask. He was already further into this conversation than he wanted to be.

Caldwell stared up at the house. His voice was an octave higher than Paul expected from someone of his build. He was Paul's height, but heavier. In his short-sleeved shirt with arms muscled under blond hairs, he looked like he had maybe done weights sometime. Now just weight. A paunch concealed his belt buckle. His wavy pelt of sandy hair looked like it could lift right off his head. The eyebrows were almost white. Hazel eyes heavy-lidded, the rest of his face jowly. He stood blinking in the bright sun, his eyes on the house. A portly lizard on a warm stone.

"Nice old place you've got here. The turret makes it for me. You don't see turrets on many houses these days, no-siree-bob. So this is all yours now?"

Paul looked at him.

"Sorry, I don't mean to be nosey. I just bought the Harrison property and I'm interested in the neighbourhood. History's kind of a hobby of mine. This street's been around a while. I've seen photos of some of the houses that were here long before all these new ones replaced them. I like hearing about the families who lived here." He laughed. "I guess that does make me a bit nosey. Anyway, I know your family lived here the better part of sixty years. Just about everyone else on the street has died or moved away." His cell beeped. "Sorry. Got a message coming through." He stepped to one side and after a moment began texting.

Paul turned away. The man didn't get it. You didn't just pitch up and chat to people you didn't know. It was never that way around here.

In the old days fine neighbourly talk was conducted from a distance, over the hedge or across the verandahs. Actual contact was a quick knock on the door when a garbage can had tipped over or you'd left the garden hose running or someone saw a fox rooting around in your compost. He remembered once in winter there was a knock on the front door and Paul went with Aunt Helen to see who it was—old Jeff Thwaites already backing away from the door almost bowing in apology as he reported a storm window hanging loose at the side of the house.

Neighbourly visits were infrequent and brief, and conversation only touched on local incidents: a child in the west end gone missing, a June hailstorm, a nest of fire ants discovered at the base of George Baker's elm, the death of old Mrs. Gannet *over the next block* at the age of ninety-three. World-changing events like the launch of Sputnik or the invasion of Hungary or Martin Luther King's march on Birmingham weren't much spoken about across the back fences. Paul heard of these events from his teachers or when he watched the news, but for simple folk on Maple Street a neighbor's lost cat carried more clout than a moon shot. Events that changed history drew only the terse disclaimer, *Don't know what the world's coming to,* followed by a friendly nod and a retreat behind closed doors.

"I grew up in this house." He stared up at it now as if for the first time—the deep verandah, the turret and gabled attic, the fish-scale cedar shingles—and then realized he had spoken aloud to no one.

"What was that, Paul?" Caldwell pocketed his cell and came back to the steps.

"I said I grew up here, though a long time ago, of course." *Of course*? Why was he even talking to this man?

"I can't help notice you come up here a lot. Sort of like every week at least, you know?"

"I just maintain the property, Mr. Caldwell, check on things inside, you know, leaks, that sort of thing."

"You should sell. The market's at peak. Now's the time. And this neighbourhood? The Beaches? Are you kidding me? Outa sight. I was lucky to get in when I did."

"I'm in no hurry."

"Fair enough. What was the tree?" He pointed at the polished shield of tree trunk on the bank.

"Chestnut. It was diseased".

"There you go."

The man was annoying him now. The slack face and dead-eyed expression. The endless questions. *There you go.* Time for *him* to go, yes-siree-bob. But he wasn't moving. So, time to change the subject. Talk about him. Make it normal. "Your property belonged to the Harrisons." When Caldwell gave him a curious look he realized that the man had already said he bought the Harrison property.

"Yup. Their old house came down in 'ninety-three. One of the last to go. Old lady Harrison lives in a home up by the City Limits now. The realtor gave me her address, so I called in to introduce myself. We got talking. Boy, she's a talker. She pulled out these photographs of the neighbourhood. The old houses. The families. She took a shitload of photos in her day—excuse my French. She told me about everyone who lived on the street, taking one house at a time. What a memory, and she's got to be pushing ninety."

And getting a telegram from the Queen if she makes it to a hundred. So old Mrs. Harrison was his source. She was the "they". *They told me yours was the Crane house.* Why didn't *they* tell him the family name was Thorne not Crane? Aunt Helen would have told them. Paul remembered her occasionally going across the street for a visit and a chat. Not that he found it odd that she should need a break from life in the Crane house.

Caldwell placed a foot on a step at the end of the path, like he was staking his claim. Like Columbus. "I guess she doesn't get many visitors. She went on and on, let me tell you. Once I got her started there was no stopping her."

That makes two of you.

"Well I guess I should let you get back to your work here. By the way, if you want me to keep an eye on the place when you're not around I'm happy to help. No *problemo.* Got time on my hands. Between jobs, you might say."

He would like to tell him *not* to keep an eye on the place. "Thanks for the offer but I'm okay."

"There you go. Anyway, nice meeting you." He shook his hand again and stepped off the curb, then turned. "One of the photos she showed me is you and your sister with the lemonade stand. Right where you're standing now. On that very spot, just like you never left—how many years is it? Amazing."

He remembered the summer Jennifer decided to have

a lemonade stand, but he didn't know Mrs. Harrison had taken a photograph. What stories had she passed on to Caldwell? *Once I got her started there was no stopping her.* In her declining years with nothing but time on *her* hands, she'd have been quite happy to relate the history of the neighbourhood to such a *charming* young man. Despite the memory lapses, she wouldn't be short of stories compiled while she was stationed at her front window.

At home that same evening he received the first of Caldwell's red flags.

hey there paul got your home address on a search site. good meeting you today. wanted you to know that im happy to help out with anything while youre not here. save you some of those trips you make. Like I said ive got time on my hands and could cut the lawns shovel snow rake leaves anything. good for me to have something to do. time weighs heavy you know. now you have my email let me know.

bradley

Paul studied the message. Did he think he was e.e. cummings? But it was the way now. Everyone in too much of a hurry to punctuate or capitalize, even someone with time on his hands.

Well it was time to send Caldwell a message. Twenty-seven Maple Street was very private property. No flyers, no visitors, no guests, no salesmen and no snoopy drawers as the English would say.

Better to reply right away. Why invite suspicion by delaying, or not responding at all? Caldwell was waiting for a reply. What else did he have to do but wait?

Caldwell. Thanks for your offer. If there's ever an

emergency I know you want to help out. But I like looking after the place. Good memories and all that. Thanks anyway. Paul Thorne.

Too correct maybe? Even an apostrophe. Well, the man could do with a lesson in proper English.

He pressed Send and was about to check his other messages when a loud ping made him start. Caldwell again. Then another ping. *Fuck off.*

He logged off right away. He would read them later or maybe delete them. Just being online right now was like poking his head above the bushes and drawing a volley of red flags.

The guy had way too much time on his hands. He said he watched the street. The way people watch TV. Listening for angry words spoken on an adjacent patio maybe, or looking for a smashed up lamp tossed out with the garbage, a stranger with a briefcase ringing someone's doorbell, a police cruiser pulling up to the curb, a real estate agent pounding a new For Sale sign into a lawn. All duly recorded by private investigator Caldwell, taking over from the old *contessa paparazza* Mrs. Harrison, once concealed behind her hanging baskets with her busy little Brownie Hawkeye.

What had she said to arouse the curiosity of the nice young man who had come all the way out to the home to see her?

Once I got her started there was no stopping her.

*

So Mr. Caldwell—she would never call him Bradley—I'll take you back to the beginning.

Viktor Crane was a dentist and he lived alone in that house when Tom and I moved in across the road. It's a big house for one person, we always thought, so maybe his parents had left it to him. But then again maybe they didn't, because, if memory serves, he grew up in Victoria—the boy told us years later that they took Dr. Crane out to Victoria to die because he had family there. Anyway we first knew him as a young man who lived in the house on his own. He was a clever man—a dentist you know.

And then one day he came home with his new bride. She was young, but already a widow with two kiddies, a girl and a boy. The girl didn't look like her mother but the boy sort of did. The girl was older and her face was rounder than the boy's. He was pale and thin because he was sickly as a baby—the aunt told us that. She moved in with them all soon after. It was a big house, mind you.

The aunt's name was Helen and she was the sister of the widow's first husband. He died in a car accident down Paris way, she told us. With all that she was a cheerful woman, really the only one in the house who spoke much to anyone. She'd come over sometimes for a visit and we'd all sit out on the porch, but she was careful with what she shared. Still, we learned some things over the years.

The house had those large front windows. Well, of course you know that, because you can see them for yourself. But the drapes were drawn, so you never saw inside. And with that big verandah, and the chestnut tree in front, it was like a world hidden away. The tree's gone now. Some kind of beetle infestation made them take it down. I watched them the morning they came. They do it limb by limb, beginning at the top, and they stuff the branches into a chipper. It took most of the morning, and they made a real racket grinding up all those branches.

Here's the boy and his sister selling lemonade long before the tree came down. I took it myself because they looked so sweet together. She became a real tear-away later on, I can tell you.

They all kept pretty much to themselves except for the aunt. We'd wave to Dr. Crane or the two kiddies when we saw them. But we didn't see much of the mother. Maybe once in a while at the beginning, but when the kiddies were a little older, nothing. She never came out on fine evenings to sit. We wondered about that. Maybe she had depression, as they say now. I never understood the whole depression thing. You just get on with life, that's all, the way we all did. But people now—mind you we're not talking about now, are we? It was a long time ago. But still.

There was one afternoon in that horribly hot summer I told you about. It was 'fifty-nine because the Seaway just opened. We saw that on the news. The actual date's in the obituary of course. I'll show you in a minute. But it was such a hot summer we had. 'Fifty-nine. The worst on record they said. We've had a few scorchers since then Mr. Caldwell. They think the planet's melting or something. These experts, what do they know?

Anyway, first we know something's going on is the ambulance pulling into the driveway. Jeff Thwaites from next door found the boy lying face down on the path right there between the two houses when he went to turn on his sprinkler. The ambulance took the poor little soul away right then. He had that heart condition I told you about from when he was a baby. It was the shock, and the heat, we reckon, that did him. We saw Dr. Crane drive up after the ambulance left. Maureen—that's Jeff's wife—was out there by then and they went over to speak to him. The aunt was away in Belleville visiting a friend. She told us afterwards.

Anyway, what a goings-on. A police car pulled up. Then another ambulance. I've never seen so many lights flashing before. They wheeled a stretcher round the back. The sister showed up just as they were loading the mother into the ambulance, and we could see the girl get quite hysterical. Maureen did her best to comfort her after the ambulance pulled away. Tom and I just stayed out of it. Enough going on without us interfering.

There was a lot of coming and going over the next few days. Lots of men in suits, even in that heat. Everyone looking so serious. A terrible tragedy it was.

We didn't see the boy for a couple of weeks. He was in hospital all that time, so the aunt told us after she came back. The mother was already dead of course. Danny Wilkes up the street said she'd fallen down the stairs and broken her neck. We never did find out for sure. Maybe she was a drinker, but I don't think so. Very religious you know. Prayed all the time apparently. So the aunt said one night after she had a sherry or two.

But she never told us what happened. And there was no mention in the obituary. Here, you can read it yourself.

Crane, Sarah Margaret *—née Sanderson—Suddenly on Thursday June 26 in her thirty-sixth year. Wife of Viktor Crane, D.M.D. Mother of Jennifer Ann and Paul Daniel. A service of remembrance was held at Our Lady of Sorrows Roman Catholic Church on June 28 attended* *by family. Interment at Mount Hope Cemetery. In lieu of flowers donations can be made to the Canadian Mental Health Association.*

We knew she wasn't right. It did seem odd that the children's real father, who died in the car crash years earlier, wasn't mentioned in the obituary. The aunt must have been a little upset about that, him being her brother and all. Still, none of my business, and she never said anything.

Jeff Thwaites didn't know what happened to the mother when he found the boy on the path. He was bleeding from where he had put his hand through the cellar window. Jeff told us he made one of those *tanquerines* with his hankie after he called the ambulance. He probably saved the boy's life.

The boy was all right in the end, and he was allowed to come home again. He would come over to stroke our old tomcat, Snowy. He'd talk a bit about school but not much. A couple of times I asked him to come in and have a glass of lemonade but he never did. Always polite though. "No thank you Mrs. Harrison, but I'm not very thirsty at the moment." I laughed. He was always so proper sounding even as a boy. Quite shy though.

The girl was a bright one but hard to handle, I think. Headstrong. Especially later on. She had boys around when she was a teenager, them in their noisy cars and playing the radio loud when they drove up. Like I said, a tear-away. A different boyfriend every week is how it seemed to us. Pretty girl. Too much makeup though. Maybe she wanted to be a movie star or a model. She was never without a fellow. Then we didn't see her anymore. Someone said that they heard she got herself, you know, in trouble and went out West to have the baby. Maybe to Dr. Crane's people in Victoria. But we never saw her again. She was maybe eighteen or nineteen then. The boy told us one time that she'd gone to live downtown and worked in a department store. He never mentioned a baby, so maybe it was just gossip. People talk a lot about things they know nothing about, you know.

Later, he told us she had moved to England to work at a fancy store in London. And that was about the time—1970 I think, I don't know, the years become a blur Mr. Caldwell—that the aunt moved out to Weston to one of those retirement places. Sort of like this one, I suppose.

We didn't hear from the aunt after she moved away.

The boy did high school—Christ the Redeemer over on Tecumseh. Then he went to university. Only it wasn't a normal university. It was a seminary, the aunt told us, where they go to become priests.

Well, we thought that was odd. He seemed a normal boy in spite of everything he'd been through. Mind you he did go to church a lot. He was an altar boy, so he went to Mass most days during the week as well as Sundays. But we hardly saw him after he left to go to the seminary.

Just the one night—it had to be in December because he knocked at our door to wish us a Merry Christmas. He saw our lights were on. I remember it snowed all that night. I'd been on to Tom to get the Christmas lights up before the first snow and he'd just done it that day. The boy had been visiting his stepfather but he didn't stay the night. He was in a hurry because he wanted to catch the last bus he said so he couldn't even come in for a sherry. “Something stronger than lemonade this time,” I said. He laughed at that but he didn’t look at all happy even though it was nearly Christmas. You’d think, eh? He looked a little lost if you want to know the truth Mr. Caldwell. I’m not sure if he was ever very happy at the seminary place. I don’t know much about Catholics to be honest.

*

“So you’re leaving us.”

Father McGrath sat back on the verandah and looked out over the black sodden fields. It was a warm April afternoon, a relief from a winter that had grown tedious. Grey belts of old snow lay in hollows on the shaded side of Mount St. Michael but the air was sweet and the cooing of mourning doves drifted up the lane.

The priest’s face was crevassed like a peach stone and his eyes were a milky blue. White wispy hair lay thin across his head. After a lifetime of cigarettes his breathing rumbled deep inside his chest and his voice sounded gravelly. “You had your reasons for coming here, but I wondered from the beginning if you would stay.”

Paul nodded and stared out over the wet fields at the woods beyond.

“It’s good you’ve decided. And now you mustn’t look back. Time to move on.” The priest looked at him. “What will you do?”

“University I guess. After that I’m not sure. I need to make some money first. Father Mike gave me a contact—he has a cousin who hires for a mining company up in Yellowknife. I'm meeting him in Toronto next week."

"What will you study in university? I don't think you have much interest in mining do you?"

Paul shook his head. "I don't have much interest in anything right now." But then he remembered that people interested him. "Maybe psychology. Behavioural sciences. I'm kind of interested in behaviour." It sounded lame, and he laughed. A career in behaviour.

The priest nodded but didn't look convinced. "You read a lot. I see you. I mean apart from scripture and the saints' lives. You read a lot of novels. So that's an interest I would think."

"I guess I like to escape." Which was true in a way. It got him out of himself. He liked to read about people who weren't always happy, or even at all. Unhappy people seemed more real to him, more interesting. They could be unhappy in different ways, while happy people could only be happy in the same way and so they weren't as interesting. Unhappy people made him feel better about not being happy himself. So maybe reading wasn't about escaping at all. He liked to read about characters who made being unhappy not seem so bad. They made him feel hopeful, whatever happened to them in the end. "Maybe escape isn't the right word."

"But the people you read about don't exist. So isn't that escaping?" The priest lit a cigarette and blew out the first lungful, the smoke continuing to escape through his nose in tiny contrails as he exhaled.

Paul thought he would like to have a cigarette sometime. It would give him something to look forward to during the day. Father McGrath seemed to enjoy his cigarette even though it was shortening his life. Some days Paul thought that shortening a life might not be such a bad thing.

"You read Thomas Hardy. What do you like about Hardy? Most people find his stories depressing."

"I like the people he writes about. I know they're only who they are and they're not like anyone else, but they feel the way I do sometimes."

"What way?"

"It's hard to explain. When I look at Jude or even Tess—they seem like strangers in their own lives. They don't even belong to their own families, and so it's like no one can ever really know them. Except I do. And another thing—I'm not sure how to say this—it's like the only place they belong is being unhappy, thought they haven't exactly given up on not being happy. They've learned to be comfortable with unhappy in case it turns out that's all they'll ever be. It's like a friend they keep coming back to. Someone they can rely on who won't let them down. I don't know. It sounds crazy."

"Aren't you saying they just feel sorry for themselves?"

"But that's what they don't do. They feel sorry for other people. And they feel like other people's unhappiness is their fault, that they've let these people down, or hurt them without even meaning to. Maybe they just want to be forgiven, or something."

"It sounds complicated."

"I'm not explaining it very well." But he hadn't really thought about any of this until now. He watched the old priest take another drag on his cigarette in a way that Paul would remember long after because smoking looked like something he might like to take up one day and not regret.

"Did you ever read Yeats?"

Paul shook his head. "Not much. 'Innisfree' and 'The Second Coming' in high school but I'm not sure I understood them." Though he liked "Innisfree", the poet finding solitude in the bee loud glade. He liked the sound of the words. It seemed enough sometimes with poetry just to like the sound of the words, whatever they meant.

"Yeats wrote about forgiveness. He said that to be forgiven you must have sympathy with all living things—the sinful as well as the righteous. If you have that sympathy then you know what Christ meant by forgiveness. Do you think you can forgive?"

"Who should I forgive?"

"Well—how about Jude, or Tess? You said it's what they want."

"But I have nothing to forgive them for. And they already know that some things they've done are wrong, even while they go on doing them because that's who they are, and they blame themselves more than anyone else possibly could. Their lives are like an atonement for being themselves. So, blaming them's beside the point, and there's nothing to forgive. Not really."

The priest smiled. "I think you understand Yeats." He stubbed out his cigarette. "And what Christ meant by the Redemption." He laughed. "Yeats was an atheist, did you know? So let's even the scales and bring in a believer, a Jesuit no less—Hopkins. If Hopkins were sitting here right now looking out at those fields, he would describe the scene in what he considered words *infused* with the Holy Spirit. Here, right now in our little valley of wet black earth, during this limbo state at the end of an Ontario winter, Hopkins would hear redemption in the bird song, and feel new life pulsing under the soil, thrusting its way up to the surface, to the light. And one day, sure enough, we'll see the tight little hyacinths push up through the earth and breathe the air, the bare branches of maples and oaks and elms will squeeze out their green crayon tips, and the forsythia light its tiny yellow flames. Hopkins believed we can only be close to Christ when we love these simple things as the poet can. And in that state it's possible to forgive."

They sat for a while listening to the trickle of winter melt from a thousand rivulets converging in the ditches along the lane. In the silence Paul imagined he could hear the land breathe, in and out, rising and falling in swells like the ocean. He wished for words that could find beauty everywhere and give it a voice. "What happens after forgiveness?"

The priest thought for a moment. "Love, I would guess. In the end, love. *A bright torch, and a casement ope at night, to let the warm love in.* That's Keats. But you know, it's one thing to forgive others as a way to loving *them*. It's quite another to open yourself up and allow love to enter. The most difficult person to forgive is ourselves. And the hardest to love."

*

Two months later a lurching Land Rover carried him from the small airport in Watson Lake to Great Bear Mine. It pitched and swerved to avoid deep potholes on a winter-crumbled road that threaded forests and wound through muskeg. He watched the changing landscape from the back seat and imagined how he would describe it all to Father McGrath when he wrote to him from the camp.

How the red bursts of bloom and berry flamed in clusters at the base of jack pine and spruce. How the forest opened at intervals like a stage-curtain revealing wetlands of spear grass and wide marshes where sleek ducks troughed the water as they landed. Once, the Land Rover drove past a gawky lanky moose, its own caricature standing knee deep in a marsh on awkward legs. It raised its massive antlers and gazed at the passing jeep. Across the wide valley the mountains rose steeply in the distance, their gleaming snow tops slashed with black crevices. Far below, a dozen round lakes glinted in the sun like old silver coins dropped by some prehistoric hurrying giant in his charge across the broken land.

He imagined what it would be to forgive the hurrying giant, and love the broken land.

It was evening when the Land Rover rounded a final bend in its long descent to the mine site. Below he could see a makeshift arrangement of weatherboard buildings and aluminum sided warehouses. Beyond them, the long wooden bunkhouses painted hospital green and the family homes set on top of the ground. Monopoly buildings. Above the town he could see a huge gouge in the side of the mountain—the pit scooped out of a clean-shaven mountainside.

Bright yellow excavators perched on the flat tiers in the pit and gnawed at the loose rock. Dull green dump trucks crawled up and down the narrow haul road to the pit—in the distance they looked like aphids on a leaf stem.

Slaloming down the narrow road his driver swerved

suddenly to avoid a huge dump truck as it came around a sharp bend. The truck's engine screamed in low gear, its towering half-cab gave it an angry look—a masked gladiator with half its face sliced away. It roared past them and turned up the gravel road on its way to the pit.

Paul's driver threaded his way between high stockpiles of ore and past a large building like a hanger that sprouted long, raised conveyor sheds that crisscrossed like grasshopper legs. Finally, he pulled up outside one of the weatherboard buildings. Ahead, beyond the stretch of bunkhouses and homes the road ended abruptly as a wall of earth pushed up against the rim of trees. It was like the bulldozers had given up and gone home.

*

So yes Mr. Caldwell, he was quite badly injured in an accident up in that mine where he worked. There was an explosion of some kind and he could have died. That's what the aunt told us. He didn't have much luck that's for sure, what with his heart condition and the whole mother business and his arm through the window and then that mine explosion. But you know how they say things always come in threes Mr. Caldwell? Well sure enough they do. Fives or sixes more like with this family.

Eight

Dr. Crane got Huntington's disease, poor man. He gave up his practice and became a shut-in. Just like that we never saw him again. He never went to a hospital or a hospice, but he did have home care—a nurse came some days. And he had a man who lived in and did for him. Foreign by the looks of him, maybe one of them *Dago* fellows. Funny little guy. He never spoke—just smiled and waved when he saw us. We never saw Dr. Crane because he stayed in the house. We only saw the funny little man who didn't speak. Oh, and the boy, but hardly ever, because he moved to England.

But a few years later, he started coming to the house nearly every day. So we knew Dr. Crane must be getting worse. The boy was with him a lot towards the end. The little man who never spoke had left by then because we didn't see him any more. But the boy visited nearly every other day. He was a good son Mr. Caldwell—well, stepson anyway. It's what you hope your children will do for you in your last days. We never had children Tom and me, and Tom's been gone some time now, but it's still what anyone would want from a son. Sorry, *stepson*. It's all the same really. Mind you, we never thought about adopting.

The year before they moved me out here—I got worse after Tom died, you know—the boy came to my door. There I go again, calling him a boy and he was forty by then if he was a day. His hair was even turning grey. Salt and pepper more like. Anyway, he came to tell me that they had taken Dr. Crane out West. He had relations in Victoria, the boy said. He told us very matter-of-fact that's where Dr. Crane had been taken.

Eighty-four he was then. Not bad for someone with Huntingdon's, but I guess life was no picnic. Pretty sure that was in 'ninety-one but I don't keep track of time that well anymore. I'm ninety-one now, did you know that, Mr. Caldwell?

But it was funny that day when he came across the street to tell us that Dr. Crane had been moved out to Victoria. I couldn't make out what he said at first. Like I said, he was agitated.

"Dr. Crane moved out *today*?" I asked.

"No, to die," he said. "Two days ago, not today."

I thought that was funny. At least he came over to tell me. He didn't want me to think the worst had happened there and then, I suppose. Right there in the house, I mean. I didn't know the old man still had people in Victoria, but then I keep myself to myself, if you see what I mean.

You know, it's funny, Mr. Caldwell, but it occurred to me that I never saw Dr. Crane the day the boy said they moved him out. He must have gone very early in the morning. Likely they took him to the airport in an ambulance. But I sat at the front window all that day, like I did most days, and didn't see a thing. I knew nothing until the boy came to tell me the old man had already gone. He was sure agitated.

And you know something else? He never stopped by after that to see me. All the times he came back to the house to do things—I would see him raking leaves, and that—he never came by. I thought of popping my head out the door once to ask him over, but he was so preoccupied I didn't want to bother him. But you'd think he could have just said a quick hello. No accounting for the way folk turn out though, is there?

I did see his family once—his wife and their little girl, it looked like—but they stayed in the car and waited while he went into the house. He came back out after a few minutes and they drove off. I thought it odd that he didn't take his family in to see the house where he grew up. And, you know? It would have been nice if he introduced us to them. We wouldn't have made them stay for tea or anything, but it would have been nice to meet his family. There again, people do change over the years Mr. Caldwell, whatever they say.

So, we never spoke again. Not after that evening he came to tell me Dr. Crane had gone out to Victoria. Never again, with all those times he went back to the house. And then they moved me out here after Tom died.

*

He had just finished painting the window frames and the shutters when Linda broke the silence.

"You don't go and see your stepfather much anymore. Has something happened?"

"Yes something's happened. He's gone."

"You didn't say anything."

"I didn't want to upset anyone."

"Who would be upset? I never met him. Neither did Rachel. Who would be upset?"

"He's gone now so it doesn't matter."

"Where did it happen?"

"I'm sorry?"

"Did it happen at the house or in hospital?"

"At the house. I was there."

"Did the coroner come?"

"What?"

"The coroner. The police call a coroner in when there's a home death. He has to sign the death certificate. You did notify the police, didn't you?"

How did she suddenly know about home deaths and coroners and death certificates? "There was a coroner."

"Did he give you the death certificate after he signed it?"

"Yes, but I gave it to the pathology lab. I donated his organs so the pathology lab had to have the death certificate as well." He could feel the pulse in his temples. "He wanted his body given to science. So they can learn more about his disease."

"Was there an obituary?"

"No. There was no need. I mean it wasn't like he had patients or friends left any more. Like you said, who would be upset? He wasn't a nice man and he was old. Like really old, you know? So there would be no one left to read his obituary."

He knew by the look on her face she was sorry she had started this. Now she wanted him to make it all go away again. Tell her anything as long as it made sense, so she didn't have to think the unthinkable. She knew enough to know she didn't want the unthinkable. Just something acceptable or a facsimile of it. She waited.

"He died in the night. I was asleep in another room. When I found him in the morning I called the home care people and they called the police who notified the coroner. Once the coroner had signed the death certificate the constable left with my statement. I had already made arrangements with Pathology and they came for him later that morning. I signed the death certificate over to the lab. There was no burial or cremation, no funeral or obituary. Just a body gone to science."

It was good enough. She nodded and walked out of the room to get on with her life and think no more about what might have happened. Better to fold up his explanation like a sales receipt and place it in a drawer, let it work its way to the bottom where receipts and statements and guarantees of purchase eventually end up forgotten.

But then one day, a few months later, she asked him why he kept driving up to Toronto. If there was no one at the house any more, why did he keep driving up there? Was there another woman? She asked in a way that made him think she would be okay with another woman in his life if the alternative was the unthinkable. They could talk through something like an affair. But she needed another sales receipt. Another guarantee.

He stared at her. "The house has to look lived in. Otherwise you get break-ins. Squatters. All the furniture's antique. It's all valuable stuff."

And that was enough. No affair. Just a house full of antiques that she would be sure not to mention again.

Ten years on and he had been spared any official inquiries about the disappearance of Dr. Viktor Crane. Not a one. It wasn't all that surprising really. Crane had vanished years before he died. No one cared, so no one knew. In a way his death had already happened long before it did.

But now he had interrupted Mrs. Harrison's reminiscences. She was sharing her memories with Mr. Caldwell. Of course, they were only his own imagined version of what she might have shared with Caldwell, but at least he wasn't speaking it out loud to himself. And he had stopped short of providing Caldwell's responses to her questions. That would have amounted to inventing an entire dialogue in his head, which would surely signify another popped rivet. A monologue in one's head is one thing, but doing the whole dialogue would be a real cause for concern.

If Dr. P. were to have written it all down, would he be able to make any sense of it? Did he know enough about the stepfather to identify his condition, or might he suspect now that *the boy* was the real issue? Maybe he would suspect that the boy didn't actually *want* to find a way to dispose of the body or sell the house, in which case Dr. P. could safely conclude that *the boy* was a bigger head case than anyone in the family, including the stepfather, and maybe anyone he had ever encountered in a lifetime of shrinkery.

How would Dr. P. identify the boy's dysfunction? Post Traumatic Stepfather Disorder, perhaps? And what of the mother? Captive complex? Stockholm Syndrome? Would Dr. P. research his previous cases of partners who bond with abusive significant others, and children who remain attached to pernicious stepfathers even after dispatching them to their next port of call? What was the correct term for killing a stepfather? Neo-parricide? Pseudo-parricide? Maybe quasi-parricide? Or how about just plain murder in any language? *It's homicide pure and simple,* said Gilpin the lawyer. Anyway Dr. P. would no doubt recall textbook cases spouses who stay loyal to their abusers—even abusers who get their rocks off while the good wife is at prayer to the Virgin at the bottom of the bed.

The Virgin saw nothing because she bowed her head and looked away, and dear old Mrs. Harrison saw nothing either because her view was obscured by the night and the old chestnut tree that grew in front of the window and the heavy drapes that were always closed except for that one bright day in summer when they were opened at last, and so she didn't have a clue what went on inside the tenebrous house on Maple Street.

Why the boy hangs onto it is beyond me, Mr. Caldwell. He could get a lot of money for a house like that in this neighbourhood, what with people buying a tear-down now for the price of three houses not so long ago. That house you wouldn't have to tear down and start again. Fine old bricks and mortar as they say, that house.

You can see he keeps the electricity going because the lights come on every evening. The porch light and a lamp in each of the two front rooms. He must have put in a timer you know, so no one would think the place empty and burgle it. They have these modern alarms now, but I don't know if he had one of those put in. And you can tell he keeps the furnace going in winter. I see those big icicles hanging all around the house from the roof melt. Bad insulation you see, like a lot of the old houses. Maybe the new ones too for all I know. But you have to keep the furnace going in winter or the pipes will freeze. You don't want frozen pipes Mr. Caldwell.

Not on your nellie, Mr. Caldwell. With him around there could never be enough insulation.

*

He shivered now, sitting at his desk. Linda had set the A/C at a frigid level. "You're doing your bit to bring on another ice age," he said to her on an afternoon when the temperature outside the house had dipped below the temperature inside. He didn't understand the global warming thing—hydro fluorocarbons being released into the atmosphere and punching large holes in the ozone layer, something like that—but he thought he would mention it anyway. The polar ice caps would melt and flood the continents, which would bring on a second ice age, he told her. When she asked him how that worked, he said he had no idea, but technicalities notwithstanding, it made sense to switch off the A/C and open the windows when the air outside dropped to a degree lower than the air inside and charged nothing for its services.

But he might as well have been talking to himself.

He turned up the manual override until he heard a click inside the thermostat.

And at that very moment the phone rang—call display showing Linda's office number. Like she was ringing to tell him to turn the A/C back on. But it was only to say she and Rachel had arranged to meet up after work. They would go out for dinner and then a movie. There were salad things in the fridge for him, and he could finish the slices of very well done steak from last night. She'd be home by ten.

The house was silent. His desk clock ticked as the second hand twitched its way around the dial. A carriage clock, a birthday gift from Linda—he had chuckled when he opened his present, then looked at her and said, "My clock's ticking, that's what you're telling me?"

The clock in Dr. Hannah's office was a near replica.

He remembered it on the desk, clicking through the silences.

And now, remembering Dr. Hannah had stirred the thought hordes. He could feel them gathering for another assault. Imagining Mrs. Harrison's history of the house on Maple Street had helped to trigger them, he supposed, even though he had stopped short of imagining Caldwell's replies, because to imagine what Caldwell might have to say would ramp up his anxiety levels even further. That's how the thought hordes worked, how they multiplied and swarmed like black flies inside his head.

The house somehow felt bigger around him now than it did before Linda called. He felt reduced, knowing she was going out for the evening with Rachel who didn't live with them anymore. And Caldwell hovering at the back of his mind like one humongous cloud of black flies himself.

He went out onto the patio for a cigarette.

He was one of a self-conscious minority who still smoked, if only occasionally.

Linda and Rachel did not like him smoking but Rachel lived with Dan now and they occasionally shared a joint themselves. She told him. He remembered Linda smoking a cigarette at Chris Turnbull's New Year's party when they met. Just the one. Half of one really, before she tossed it into the snow. He never knew her to smoke another.

He had started the practice—it had never really become a habit, he liked to believe—the summer he worked at Great Bear. Everyone smoked at the mine. Frenchie would light a fresh one off the cigarette he just finished, but he blew himself up before he suffered any ill effects from smoking. Father McGrath got him thinking he'd like a cigarette sometime when they talked about Hardy and Yeats and Hopkins, and McGrath was long gone too, but it was Laura Swanson who really got him started. She had come out from Vancouver to visit her sister Lisa who was married to Tom the mill foreman, and Paul had been invited to make up a four at dinner. After the meal they all sat out on the porch finishing off a second bottle of wine and watching the northern lights dance high above them in the Arctic night. Laura offered him a cigarette. His first.

She offered him another "first" a couple of nights later when they were alone. She had taken his hand and guided it, whispering to him and touching him. Outside her bedroom window the fluorescent green lights slithered and leapt in the purple sky.

He missed her when she left to return home—her sparkling eyes and the crescents that formed at each end of her smile like tiny parentheses. She was thirty and recently divorced, and she left him breathless. They talked about him going out to see her after the winter and they wrote for a time. He would fly out to Vancouver for a week when spring came. But the winter seemed endless and the snow fell for a month and filled the valley. No mail got through for until early March and when the long overdue delivery arrived there was nothing from Laura. He wrote her another letter and sent it off. But when spring came he still hadn't heard from her. He asked Lisa if she knew anything and she looked at him sadly. "Laura's Laura, I'm afraid…she gets ideas in her head and then something else happens. She said she's with some guy now. I'm sorry, Paul."

He thought for a time that he might have fallen for

her, but that wasn't possible because he was already in love with Linda whom he hadn't yet met. So it was just infatuation. And sex, of course. She was his first time. He didn't know what he was to her.

He still thought of her sometimes when he smoked a cigarette. Like they still shared something beyond a memory. Same with Father McGrath, only different of course.

The most difficult person to forgive is ourselves. And we are the hardest to love.

He stubbed out his cigarette and flipped it into the compost bin. All biodegradable. He slid open the glass door and entered the house. The cigarette had made him feel light-headed. He wouldn't check his mail right now. There would only be red flags from the importunate Caldwell, and again the thought of Caldwell and his red flags disturbed the hordes once more—he sensed them gathering, preparing to swarm. And only a moment ago he had enjoyed such peace, with his cigarette and memories of Laura Swanson.

Back in his study he sat in his armchair and looked across at this desk, the carriage clock ticking, his tie neatly folded beside it, and his jacket hanging on the back of the chair. Dr. P. would be in his shirtsleeves, tieless, and the top button of his shirt undone. He would look tired, like he had had himself a day, not a fantastic day, just a day.

Paul would control himself this time. He had lost control last time, when he told Dr. P. about the sac of bile and cloven-hoofed goat-faced motherfucker, even though he was aware of everything he said. Not like that time with Dr. Hannah. Now he would tell Dr. P. about the casement, not the one with the toxic waste frozen inside, but the one that had to be opened to *let the warm love in.* Forgiveness first. Then love. Dr. P. would understand because he knew all about Father McGrath and Yeats and Hopkins. Dr. P. would help him open the casement.

How would he begin this particular session? Not with *what might you like to tell me about yourself do you think*? But he knew Paul was comfortable with silence, and so he would say nothing, give him time to settle and stare at the carpet. A different one this time, plain oatmeal carpet, with no flecks like black flies to agitate him and make him hallucinate.

After a reasonable interlude, Dr. P. would begin. *Is there something specific you might like me to ask you?*

"No."

So I can ask you anything I want?

"Yes."

How did you and your wife meet?

"I thought you'd never ask." That was to lighten the mood, and he thought the good doctor smiled like he was actually amused this time.

Take all the time you want. Tell me everything.

It was important to tell Dr. P. everything about meeting Linda because when he met her he was in that place he wanted to get back to. There would be no going forward until he went back to where he was before the beady-eyed serpent with the sac of bile crawled under the gate and poisoned the garden. He wondered if he should include a mention of Gerry Gold's amateur production of *Paradise Lost* in the Trinity College gardens. Gerry required the leads to perform naked, and on opening night Adam and Eve committed two sins in one go when Adam's personal serpent experienced an unrehearsed arousal and went where such serpents go when aroused, with or without rehearsal, all of which shocked the audience and resulted in the Dean canceling the play and suspending Gerry Gold along with Adam and Eve who got double jeopardy for the very *un*original sin that they tacked on to the original one.

But he wouldn't tell Dr. P. about that *Paradise Lost*—his own mattered more right now.

"We met at a friend's party one New Year's. I was in love with her already. I was in love with her before I met her. I know that doesn't make sense. But it's true."

And she loved you?

"No. She didn't know I existed until we met at the party. And then she started to see someone else right after, so I can't say I swept her off her feet."

How would Dr. P. proceed from here? *Tell me about the New Year's party and what made you think you were in love with her even before you met her?*

He thought for a moment. It did sound stupid to say that he was already in love with her before they met. Then again it would only sound stupid to someone who didn't understand that Linda made him feel he had known her all his life, and so he had to make Dr. P. realize what it was to live in the night knowing there actually was a sun somewhere else. Living on his own in England he didn't see a lot of sun, because the skies were mostly overcast like pewter, and low enough to put a fist through, but that's not the kind of sun he meant when he talked about the Linda he thought about when he was alone.

He should have been happy in England. He enjoyed

teaching his classes and in his spare time he worked on his thesis in the little stone cottage that the school rented to him in a nearby village called East Dean. Some weekends he drove up to London to do research at the Reading Room in what was then called the British Museum, and he would stay with Jennifer and Steven sometime before they had the twins. His sister managed a high-end clothing store on Oxford Street. Steven played first cello with the BBC Radio Orchestra and did wedding gigs with his own chamber group.

The playing fields at Brighton Academy overlooked the English Channel, and when he coached the junior harrier team he could look out and see France on a clear day. Sometimes if the weather was fine he would run alone along the chalk cliffs and feel the soft turf under his feet. He would run for miles feeling the breeze from the Channel on his face. He had every reason to be happy, but he wasn't. He carried his own pewter skies around with him and he needed to find the sun to melt away the feeling, deeper than the loneliness he had learned to live with, that life was passing him by, like all of his birthdays in a row, all unmarked at the time. Like all the ferries he could see out in the Channel heading for somewhere else where the sun was, where someone named Linda was—and had always been—waiting for him.

It was complicated, and maybe Dr. P. wouldn't understand this was a place he had to get back to. Dr. P. would understand only if Paul took him there and then he could see for himself. And Paul could see again what it was about Linda—her head held at an angle when she listened to him, her hand reaching to touch his arm but not quite making contact, a word she spoke, or maybe the way she said any word, the quizzical glance from her impossibly blue eyes—something anyway that made the sun melt away the pewter skies and stopped his life from sliding past like a succession of unmarked birthdays.

He had lost her, and now he had to go back to where she was because she wasn't here anymore, and neither was he. She was locked away in that place he kept thinking about and now must get back to. If she was there, then no doctor, even one with a Princeton degree and years of clinical experience could find it on his own. But if Paul was able to take him there, there was a chance he could retrieve her, even if she was locked away in a cold grey castle with the drawbridge raised. He would need ladders and a battering ram, archers and siege engines and catapults on wheels, so he could storm the ramparts and vanquish whatever had shut her away. He needed now his arrows of desire and his chariots of fire so he could destroy the dark satanic mills and build Jerusalem once more on England's green and pleasant land, metaphorically speaking of course, because he didn't live in the real England anymore but in Heritage, Ontario.

Do you think maybe you yourself are the thing you seek to destroy?

Dr. P. was absolutely right, of course, and finally earning his exorbitant fee. It took a Princeton degree to understand that Paul was indeed the one keeping Linda hostage in the place he couldn't get to, and so he would have to storm the fortress from the inside, and release her, so they could ride away together on his dashing white charger.

No need for ladders or battering ram after all, no archers or siege engines and catapults on wheels, to set her free. He needed only *a bright torch.* Before he could love her again he must love himself. So Father McGrath had told him. But forgiveness before love. And atonement before forgiveness. Things would all work out now that he had them straight in his head.

*

It was well after nine when he rang the bell and waited under the porch light at Chris Turnbull's front door. He wasn't looking forward to the party, with its large rooms full of noise and people he didn't know.

He never felt comfortable in a large room full of people he didn't know. He would feel the same in a large room full of people he did know, except that all the people he knew would fit comfortably in a small room. Chris Turnbull was his roommate at university for a year, but that was some time ago. Chris had done well for himself—the house was imposing, and there were expensive cars parked in the long driveway and on the street.

Chris opened the door. "Paul! Great seeing you again. Give me your coat. Let me get you some wine and then I'll introduce you to Denise. We have to catch up. I'm afraid it's already crazy in here."

The noise level was beyond tolerable despite the high-ceilinged rooms, and he decided not to stay long. He would never make it to midnight in this crowd. Chris returned with his wife and introduced her. Denise told Paul that Chris had spoken a lot about him. He was going to compliment her on her beautiful house, but she was already introducing him, as an English professor from England, to Gerald, who owned a heating company, and Darlene in real estate. Denise said they all must be sure to have some of the lovely baked salmon before it disappeared, then she did, after waving at a couple coming in the front door and going off to greet them. Gerald and Darlene smiled at him and nodded, having no idea what to say to an English professor from England, but before Paul could explain that he was a high school teacher not a professor and he *lived* in England but wasn't *from* there, Gerald suggested they raise a glass to the old year. Then he and Darlene resumed discussing the hidden costs of gentrification. Gerald specialized in high efficiency furnaces and state of the art fireplace inserts and therefore, as he put it, knew whereof he spoke. For a time Paul listened to them talk about paneled doors and thermal windows, or it might have been enamel floors and infernal inflows—he wasn't sure, because the room had become even louder—and then decided to move off in the direction of the baked salmon.

He excused himself, and turned to see Chris Turnbull coming towards him with a young woman in a blue dress. The woman smiled at him as she approached. Her eyes were bright and so very, very blue—impossibly blue, he thought. And then she was standing in front of him.

"Paul, this is Linda Franklin. She's from Winnipeg and has just joined the firm. Linda, this is my very good friend, Paul Thorne. We were roommates. Now he's an English professor who actually lives in England. Uh, oh, doorbell." He turned and started to move away. "So glad you could come, Paul. And we'll catch up, okay?"

Paul nodded. He hadn't heard a doorbell, but that wasn't surprising. Then he looked at Linda Franklin and realized she was saying something to him. “I’m sorry. I’m having trouble with all this noise.”

She smiled and took him by the elbow, as though he were a little blind as well as deaf, then guided him through the crowd and into the hall. Maybe it was when she took him by the elbow that he became crazy for her. There were fewer people in the hall, and conversation was more subdued. Still smiling, she turned to him. “I was just asking how long you’ve lived in England.” She took a sip of her wine.

Her eyes were blue like her dress. Sapphire blue. More blue than that. He didn’t know then that contact lenses could be tinted. How could he possibly know that when he didn’t know she was even wearing them?

*

Would things have been any different if he had known? For that matter, were tinted contacts dishonest? Or a harmless enhancement? Who doesn’t enhance whatever can use a little help?

Even Dr. P. had those rimless glasses that made him look intelligent and vaguely Ivy League, so clients would trust him with their personal histories and hope he could straighten them out. And what about the precisely groomed silver hair that curled like surf at the back of his head?

Paul would have tried to enhance his own appearance if he had any accessories. But he had none then, and even now he had only the hearing aid that he infrequently wore, and the wedding ring that he never removed. He sometimes chose not to wear the hearing aid, not because it did nothing to enhance his appearance but because it didn't really aid his hearing. In fact, it screwed up his hearing by making him hear more than he wanted to. It enabled him to hear, among all the things he didn't want to hear, atmosphere. Unencoded, or unencrypted, or whatever the word was, it enabled him to hear unnecessary things that drowned out what he wanted to hear. So he didn't wear it. That left his wedding ring, maybe a dishonest accessory in recent years, but he was on a mission to fix that.

Atonement. Forgiveness. Love. In that order.

*

"How. Long. In. England." She asked him in an exaggeratedly patient voice that suggested she was doing it for maybe the second or third time.

"Sorry. About a year and a half."

"What made you go there in the first place? You're Canadian, right? I mean you don't sound English."

"My sister lives in London. I was visiting her, and ran into an old friend of Chris and mine from university—Gerry Gold—who had a bad experience here and went off to teach in a school in Brighton. I spent a few days with him and met his headmaster. Things just happened after that, and they gave me a job. I'm just a teacher, not a professor. Chris misunderstood." He took a slurp of his wine. What a convoluted reply. "Have you been to England? Or, you know, traveled much?"

"I've always wanted to go to England. One day maybe. I'm just a prairie girl. Quite a step for me even to move here."

She missed her parents in Winnipeg, she said. Dr. P. had to understand how important they were to her. She was their only child and it was very hard for her to leave them. And she missed Winnipeg. She found Toronto intimidating after life in a small prairie city, but she was making progress, she thought. Chris Turnbull was a nice person to work for, and she had made some new acquaintances. "It's such an exciting city. Toronto, I mean, not Winnipeg."

But he could tell she wasn't excited by Toronto. Dr. P. would know she wasn't really lying when she said Toronto excited her. She was trying, in the way people do, to overcompensate for the disappointment of the city and its unwelcoming residents. Maybe for all her positivity, she too felt she was a stranger in her own life, and so she was overcompensating for that. Maybe he would suggest she read Thomas Hardy, so she would understand that she wasn't alone in feeling isolated. But he wouldn't suggest that right now. He would do it later, after they were married.

Other guests stepped past them, moving through the hall to the bar and the baked salmon laid out on the buffet table in another room. As people shuffled past, they moved closer together, two stones in the middle of a stream.

She was flying home the next day to be with her parents for the New Year. They had just returned from their timeshare in Florida.

"When do you come back?"

She put out her hand to pick a loose thread off his sleeve. "Sorry, I'm a bit of a neat freak. Next Saturday."

Dr. P. might decide that was the moment—when she reached to pick a loose thread off his sleeve. She had already taken him by the elbow and led him into the hall, away from the noise, and that was bad enough, not the noise, although it was also bad enough, but her taking him by the elbow, because it made him a little crazy as soon as he met her.

He wasn't sure what to say next. It was way too early to ask her to marry him. "Can I get you another glass of wine?"

She handed him her glass. "Sure, why not. After all it's goodbye to the 'seventies, thank God."

He forgot tonight was the end of the decade as well as the year. He was too busy wanting to marry the woman in the blue dress with the impossibly blue eyes and the warm smile, who would be flying off to the ends of the earth in the morning and not returning until the very day he had to fly back to England, the woman with whom he had been in love all his life and whose wine glass he was about to replenish.

Making his way back to her with the glasses he saw that someone had taken his place. The man speaking to her now stood exactly where Paul had stood a moment ago and was running his eyes all over her like he was looking for somewhere to take a bite out of her.

She glanced at Paul as he approached and excused herself, leaving the young man in mid-bite. She came up and took what she thought was her glass. It was Paul's glass but he didn't say anything. Instead he sipped from the glass that had been hers. Sipping from her glass was like kissing her. He could have drained the glass and then eaten it. Crunched it into little shards and swallowed them, like a circus act. But at the time he felt it was normal to feel like that, though Dr. P. might have something to say about it all sounding a little weird to him.

"Do you mind if we step out for a cigarette?" she asked. "I'm sorry, do you smoke?"

"I'll come with you."

Outside on the deck it was chilly but clear, a relief from the congestion of the party. The night was still. No moon and just a powdering of new snow below the deck. She offered him a cigarette. He took it and they smoked in silence for a moment.

"Thanks for coming out here with me," she said. "I had to get away from that guy. His name's Derek, he works in our office and he's been coming on to me since I started the job. I really don't like him. He thinks he's God's gift. He took me out to dinner once and then gave me the cold shoulder for a week after that because I didn't invite him in when he drove me home." She smiled, took a short puff of her cigarette and tossed it over the railing into the snow. She shivered. "I don't really smoke. Just at parties. I hate the taste. Do you want to go back inside?"

The heat and noise of the party had escalated during their brief spell outside.

"When do you go back to England?"

"I leave next Saturday. That's the day you—.

"—get back from Winnipeg. So we'll just miss each other." She seemed not to know what to say next.

He would go so far as to say she seemed perplexed. Was that the word? Or was it all wishful thinking on his part? Not that he wanted her to be uncomfortable, but if she was perplexed it might mean she hoped they could see each other again after she got back and before he left, but she couldn't tell him that because they had just met and so she was at a loss for words.

"Would you mind if I asked you for your address? I'll send you a post card from England. Maybe your phone number? I come back to Toronto every once in a while and maybe we could meet up for a drink sometime? Could I give you a call? I mean, if you're busy, well don't worry. But if you want to have a drink sometime when I'm over—even lunch maybe—we can talk, you know, about anything you want. If you want to." If that wasn't exactly the way he put it, it was close enough, and so it wouldn't take rocket science or even much in the way of behavioral science for Dr. P. to know that he didn't have a lot of experience in *making a move*, if that was the expression back then. Not that *making a move* would ever be the right expression for his inept overtures—it was more like fumbling for something to say to prevent him from asking her to marry him on the spot.

She smiled. "I'd like that." She gave him her glass to hold. "I can give you a number though it's only temporary right now. I have a tiny apartment, a closet really, but I plan to move into something bigger." She fumbled in her purse, pushing things aside, looking for something to write with.

Was she also feeling a little crazy by then or was that again wishful thinking on his part as he stood transfixed by her looking for something to write with, like maybe a pen?

She took out a small gold-edged address book that had its own tiny gold pen slotted into the spine. She wrote in it and then tore out the page. "I wrote down my name as well, otherwise you might not remember whose number it is. Can you give me yours?" She held out her book.

"Of course." He took the book and gave her the wine glasses to hold. "Except I don't have a phone. I live in an old cottage belonging to the school that's never been hooked up. It's England remember. There's a pay phone outside the pub but that's no use." Even calling his sister in London required him to stuff coaster-sized coins into a pay phone every time the beeps threatened to cut him off. He'd need a bucket of loose change for a trans-Atlantic call. It would be cheaper to have a phone installed, and he would certainly discuss the matter with the school bursar when he got back. "I plan to have a phone installed but I can give you my address right now." He wrote down the details of his unconnected stone cottage in East Dean, a village that was on the wrong side of the world all of a sudden. She smiled at him with her head at an angle the whole time that he spoke.

At midnight everyone raised their glasses to toast the new year and the new decade, and with the chorus of cheers filling the room she gave him a kiss on the cheek and wished him—how did she put it—a year to remember. He was on the point of asking if she wanted to share a cab when she was ready to go home, when she was suddenly pulled away. A conga line had started up and was making its way down the hall when someone—not the biter—grabbed her hand, spilling her champagne, and pulled her into the shuffling line of revelers. She turned to look back at him, her free hand outstretched for him to grab hold of, like Catherine reaching for Heathcliff in the movie. And then she was gone.

He didn't feel like joining the conga line. He didn't want to grab hold of the woman he had just met and take her by the hips and kick his legs out for no other reason than a new decade had just kicked in and everyone was pissed. He wasn't pissed, but a little pissed off because the woman he wanted to marry got swallowed up in a conga line that would weave its way many times over through Chris Turnbull's sprawling home before it collapsed in hysterics on sofas and chairs and the floor, and he didn't want to see her having to do that. Anyway he had her address.

He found his coat in an upstairs bedroom and managed to slip unnoticed out the front door when the conga had taken a timeout to refresh itself at the bar at the other end of the house.

*

Dr. P. might want to follow up on that moment and ask him why he left the woman he wanted to marry without even saying goodbye? Someone had pulled her into the conga line and she turned to look back at him, thinking he would join in. It was a party for heaven's sake. Everyone was having fun so why wouldn't he kick up his heels and dance even if it was just a stupid conga line. But there were so many reasons why he didn't do it and it was all too complicated to get into. It was easier for him to leave the party and so he left. Slipped away into the night like a thief. He would write a thank you note to Chris and Denise and mail it before he returned to England. He would say he got very tired suddenly and didn't want to be a downer. He would thank them for the party and for introducing him to their nice friends. Denise and Chris had an amazing life and they deserved everything they had, he would say.

But it wasn't his life and they weren't his people, however nice, though he wouldn't say that. They weren't Linda's people either but she would find that out for herself. In time. None of this would help Dr. P. understand why he left the party just when it was ramping up, though no one used that expression back then. *Ramping up.* One day when he'd gone through all his notes, Dr. P. would discover that whenever things ramped up, his patient had a tendency to ramp down and slip away into the shadows. Dr. P. would see a pattern and confirm his original assessment of a Type D personality.

*

There were no cabs around so he caught a streetcar at the St. Clair and Mount Pleasant loop and then took the subway downtown. The trains ran late into the night on New Year's and they were free. Seated in the near empty car he took out the slip of paper she had given him and examined the writing. Linda Franklin. She wrote her *a*'s like they came off a typewriter; they weren't at all like cursive *a*'s. All her letters were perfectly formed and simple. No flourishes or pirouettes. *Linda Franklin.* The circle in the *d* was complete, the *f* and the *k* were exact and assertive. Her telephone figures—*432-7373*—were economical: the corners precise, the curves firm and the lines unerring. All quite remarkable for someone trying to write in a tiny notebook while standing in the midst of drunken revelers at a crowded party.

The following Saturday at the airport, after his departure was announced and he lined up for the passport check, he scanned the Arrivals board for the

Ward Air flight from Winnipeg.

Landing at 21:30. He would be in the air before her plane touched down.

He'd be somewhere over Labrador heading across the Atlantic to a grey English dawn by the time she got out of the airport taxi and fumbled for her keys at the door. No. She would have her keys ready in her hand before she got out of the taxi. And when she got in the door she would phone her parents to tell them she'd arrived safely. They wouldn't think about dinner until they heard from her. Then she would unpack her suitcase and boil the kettle for a cup of tea. Or maybe she'd have a glass of wine and watch the late night news before going to bed. She drank wine at Chris Turnbull's. And had at least one refill before the champagne at midnight. But perhaps she was just a social drinker who had gone a little overboard that night and kicked her heels out in the conga line and possibly regretted it the next morning. She would drink tea before going to bed. Or maybe cocoa. Probably cocoa.

The man in uniform at the departure booth smiled and asked to see his ticket and passport, looking at him in a way that indicated he was repeating the request.

Nine

Back in Sussex he wrote her a letter to explain why he had left the party without trying to find her. He gave her the same reason he would give to Chris Turnbull when he wrote to him—that he became suddenly tired—and so Dr. P. would immediately twig that this was first time he lied to her.

Telling her he became suddenly tired was indeed a lie. Whereas *not* explaining to her that he left the party—just when it was starting to ramp up—because he didn't know how to have fun and didn't want her to know that, wasn't a lie but an omission. Telling her he hoped she had a good visit with her parents was the truth, but it was followed by another omission—this wasn't his real reason for writing to her.

The real reason was to remind her they had met. He couldn't stop thinking about her. He didn't tell her any of that. That wasn't lying, either, though when he finished writing his letter he realized that it was all in one way or another a complete fabrication: telling her a lie, half-telling her a truth or two, and omitting everything he didn't want her to know. He resolved to tell her only the truth from now on. Then he unpacked his bags.

Term was well under way by the time he received her reply. He kept all of her letters. When he was stuck in England without her and without a phone, the letters were all he had. He had read them so many times he could recite them from memory if he ever had to. But he kept her letters—they were in his desk now and he could read them to Dr. P. to prove that everything he said was true.

February 20, 1980

Dear Paul,

What a surprise to get your letter last month. It did me good to hear from you. Red ink in the office all day and even Chris was in a bad mood. February blahs. So when I came home and saw your letter I was happy. I love getting mail anyway but I don't think I've ever had an aerogramme before. I'm afraid I didn't follow the instructions properly and so I mangled it—sliced it open in all the wrong places and had to scotch tape the pieces together so I could read it. Next time I'll be more careful.

(He liked *next time.*)

I enjoyed meeting you too. I felt guilty when I went home after the party because I was supposed to be helping Chris and Denise, making sure people mixed, that sort of thing. But I'm kind of shy with people I don't know so I was really the wrong person to ask! I hardly spoke to anyone else all evening. Apart from Derek the jerk. Then all the nonsense began at midnight and by the time the conga line finished you were gone. I was hoping to say goodnight but I do understand if you were tired. Jet lag too, right? I hope you had fun all the same.

I'd have written back sooner but I've been kind of busy since I got back from Winnipeg. I had a good time with my parents and thanks for asking. Since then I've been preparing our clients for tax deadline, but a lot of our clients are pretty slow with their returns. I thought people would be a lot more on the ball down here in T.O., but they can be prairie-slow like people back in Man.

Derek doesn't bother me anymore by the way. I let him think I'm interested in this other guy Trevor who's a lawyer in a firm we partner with and comes into our office a lot. Trevor's a nice guy and he always says hi. Derek seems to be getting the message.

Chris mentioned you the other day—that's what got me going on this letter—and he said you were going to be a priest before you guys met up in residence. That's kind of interesting. Funny you never mentioned that. What else in your dark and mysterious past are you keeping from me? You're different Paul, I'll say that. And that's a compliment by the way.

I'd like you to call when you're back here again. And good luck with your teaching and your doctorate—that whole Hamlet thing. Shakespeare was never easy for me, sceptered isles and bare bodkins and all that, so I think you must be very clever!

Well I'd better finish this and get ready for the week. Write back and tell me all that you're doing. Maybe one day you can tell me why you wanted to teach. Most of the teachers I had in school were kind of nerdy (sorry) but you don't seem that way at all.

Okay, time for Motor mouth (my nickname in high school!) to shut down for the night. Thanks for being my escort (sort of) at the party. I really enjoyed talking to you. Take care. Write back okay?

Fondly,

Linda.

P.S. Note the change of address. I've moved from my closet apartment! I've come out of the closet. Ha! L.

He wrote back that night. He told her he was coming to Toronto in April at the start of his Easter break. He had to make the trip he said. His aunt had fallen and broken her hip. His supervisor wanted to go through the latest draft of his thesis. *Resuscitate it* was the phrase he used. Both reasons were real enough though not as urgent as he let on. Aunt Helen had fallen a couple of weeks ago and she was getting good care. He had less time for the thesis now that he had started teaching. But the half-truths served a greater truth: he had to see her. He didn't like the sound of Trevor.

He committed one major omission in his letter this time but it was an essential one. He said nothing about going to see his stepfather while he was there, because he would never mention his stepfather to Linda and poison the well.

Not mentioning Trevor was another forgivable omission.

He heard nothing for a couple of weeks and then her second letter arrived.

It was addressed to *Paul Thorn* without the *e*. Not an auspicious start.

Toronto, 15 March, 1980

Dear Paul,

Your letter came yesterday. Thanks for keeping in touch. I laughed out loud at your hilarious comments about the English weather and having no central heating. And that poor kid who broke wind in class and his teacher made him go outside to spin round and jump up and down and flap his arms in the air to get it out of his clothes. I had to look up "whirling dervish". I laughed myself silly. You are very funny! Ironic? Is that the right word? Funny ironic, that's what you are.

Anyway, to bring you up to date. I feel I can talk to you about anything at all. Like you're kind of the brother I never had. I hope it's okay to say that.

I told you when I first wrote last month about this guy Trevor? The lawyer? Well it seems that all along he really has been interested in me and he asked me out a couple of times. He doesn't pressure me at all but I kind of know he likes me. And he's considerate. You know, thoughtful? So we've been out a few times, mostly double dating, that kind of thing. But we've moved on a bit since then and now he's asked me to go to Nassau with him for a week. He wants to make this a relationship, and though I like him a lot I'm not sure yet about a long-term commitment. So I figured we could go on holiday together and see how we get on. You'd like him. Being a lawyer isn't his whole life. He's into skiing and diving and he plays a lot of tennis. He has a ton of trophies. Plus he likes movies and jazz. You said you liked jazz.

We're away the last week of March but I'll send you a postcard from Nassau. If you're in Toronto this summer give me a call and we can "do" lunch as everyone says now. You have my office number.

Have a good semester and take care.

Always yours,

Linda.

He didn't especially like jazz. That would come later when he drifted into melancholy. And it would be the throaty saxophone and unbridled piano jazz of cigarette smoke and bourbon and never the plinkety-plink-after-dinner-black-tie jazz that Trevor no doubt listened to. He had no idea if that's what Trevor listened to, but he felt better imagining it was.

His reply to her second letter contained an abundance of omissions. Not liking jazz for one. Her forgetting or maybe ignoring that he was planning to fly over at

Easter and not in the summer. The impossibility of his marrying her if she was with someone named Trevor with whom she planned to holiday in the sunny Bahamas while Paul was marooned on his sceptered isle with a pewter sky above his head that he could punch a hole through.

So he asked if she might have lunch with him when he came to Toronto in April—*not* the summer any more—to manage all the things he had to do.

It was an English spring, colourful and brutally deceptive. Daffodils nodded in bright clusters along the roadsides and then lay flattened after a sudden squall of horizontal sleet. Magnolia blossoms emerged hopefully, only to shiver on their branches when the temperature plunged under darkening skies. But an English spring was not important right now.

At the end of classes the next day he drove into Brighton and booked his flight. He tried not to look at all the posters in the travel agent's advertising sunny holidays in the Canaries and Seychelles and the Caribbean. In the last week of March he tried not to think of her and Trevor in the Bahamas, but of course that was impossible. He imagined Trevor dressed in whites giving her tennis lessons at some club, standing behind her, looking like a glass of milk, with one hand on her waist and the other adjusting her grip. Then the two of them in bathing suits sitting at the pool bar half-submerged on a stool and sipping large colourful drinks with little umbrellas in the glasses, before enjoying lunch and an indolent afternoon, with maybe a siesta in their hotel room.

He flew out the day after term finished and called her as soon as he had settled into his rooms on campus.

"Hi Linda. It's Paul Thorne. I'm here."

"Paul? Hi! My God! What a surprise. Are you calling from England?"

"No. I'm here. In Toronto."

"You're here now? I hadn't realized. I mean wow. This is a surprise. Is everything okay?"

"Everything's fine. Did you get my letter? I wrote that I was planning to come in April. I sent it maybe three weeks ago?"

"Oh God yes I did get it. I'm so sorry Paul. I completely forgot. I mean I had it in my head that you were coming in the summer and the letter arrived at a crazy time here. Me trying to get ahead with all my clients before I went on holiday. I'm just—sorry Paul. It didn't register I'm afraid. But you're here now, that's the main thing."

He wondered what she meant by *that's the main thing*. Probably nothing at all, from the sound of it. "So how *was* Nassau?"

"Well it was interesting. Thanks for asking. Yes. The islands are beautiful. Such gorgeous sand. My God, I can't believe you're here. Anyway yes. We loved it. The ocean there is like an emerald. What can I say? We had a good time. We both needed the rest." She paused, and he thought about the two of them resting. "So you're in Toronto. How was your flight? Where are you staying?"

"The flight was fine. I'm staying in residence. They let out rooms for grad students during the holidays. Listen Linda, is there a time this weekend when you might be free? You know, to have a drink and catch up? Or maybe we can do that lunch?"

Another pause. "Okay, so this is going to be a little

awkward. I'm sorry Paul, I don't know when I'll be free. You know with Easter weekend and all that. We just got back and I have a backlog of work on my desk so I've been staying late at the office. I'm meeting Trev's parents. We're spending the weekend at their home in Richmond Hill. And then Sunday, well, we thought about dinner somewhere, just the two of us, you know, after the stress of the weekend. But maybe later in the week, if I can get to leave work at a decent hour. How long are you in town?"

"I'm here till next Saturday. So there are a lot of days. But there's something you should know." He went in blind. Her weekend with Trevor—*Trev* now—and meeting his parents had thrown him off. "I came to see you. That's why I came now. It was to see you. I mean my aunt broke her hip and I'll see her too while I'm here of course. And my supervisor wants to look at my thesis, which is in pretty bad shape, and I'm okay with that, really. But I wanted to see you."

A long silence and he thought the line had gone dead.

"Why?"

"I'm sorry?"

"Why did you come just to see me?"

"I don't know. I did that's all. I felt at the time I had to. I still do now I'm here. It's hard to explain. Anyway just a drink Linda. Nothing else. Not even lunch if you'd rather not. Would you be available for a drink next week? Coffee?"

"Paul can I get something straight here? You flew all the way here from England and all you want is for us to have a drink with me before you fly back?"

"Yes. Well I mean my aunt isn't well, as well—so I

can kill two birds with one stone—not literally of course—three birds if you include my thesis. Okay, forget the birds and the stone. I know what you must think. Well, I don't know what you must think but—what day might you be free to have a drink?"

Another pause. He wanted to hang up, call back and start the conversation all over again.

"Okay Paul I'll have a drink with you. It can't be this weekend though because Trev and I—"

"Yes I know, you're with his family this weekend. I get it." He hoped he hadn't sounded impatient. He didn't want her to think he was impatient. He wanted her to know that she was wasting her time with Trevor who struck him as the calculating type for all his being nice and pretending to ride shotgun for her when Derek was being a jerk at the office, but he couldn't say that now.

"Call me on Monday, okay? I'll have a better idea of what my week will be like. Call me at my office." She gave him the number and her extension.

"Okay. And thanks." He wasn't sure what he thanked her for. For putting up with his absurd behaviour perhaps?

"Paul—just a small thing. You don't have to answer if you don't want to because maybe I shouldn't even be asking, but—"

"Yes, I think I'm in love with you. Or at least I think I could be in love with you very easily if I'm not already. Pretty sure, actually."

"Oh."

Oh meant he should have let her finish her sentence. Dr. P. would be surprised at how his *un*communicative patient actually required a gag order back then.

"Okay. I just wanted to know if something was wrong. Like if something's going on in your life right now because you don't sound the way I remember you. But I guess you've kind of answered my question."

"No, no. Everything's fine, Linda. I'm sorry. I didn't mean to make things awkward. Really."

She laughed but it sounded like someone else's laugh, or maybe now in the present time he just forgot exactly how she laughed.

Then she spoke. "Oh don't worry about that. Listen, I hope your aunt is okay. And Hamlet too. We'll talk on Monday okay?"

"Ok. Thanks. Monday. Bye. Bye Linda."

He stared at the phone after the line went dead. Christ. Out of the blue. What was he thinking? But now it was done. The cat out of the bag, and stone the bloody crows. All three of them. Still, he had come over to tell her and now he had, though not quite as planned. How would Trevor have done it? He of the tennis trophies and lean athletic figure in whites. Serve and volley all the way through to game, set and *match,* what else?

The home was depressing. Aunt Helen did her best to be upbeat and talkative, but she was too aware of her morose and silent companions. She was in a wheelchair but seemed comfortable enough after her surgery. He didn't stay long because she was tired, but he arranged for a disabled transport vehicle to bring her to the restaurant he'd invited her to for a brunch on Easter Sunday.

She was in better spirits on Easter morning when the attendant wheeled her into the restaurant. She said she didn't like the home though she was comfortable enough there and the staff was wonderful. "It's the women. They're catty and they gossip all the time. Some of them think they're above the rest of us. I don't like them at all."

"What about the men?"

"They go quickly. You don't really get time to know them."

They didn't speak about the past. Nothing of Sarah, or Jennifer. It was like she had wiped the slate clean, or maybe it was being done for her. Except she looked at him one time, focusing her gaze and finding the words. "Your father was a wonderful man and you look just like him now."

He smiled. "Thank you Aunt Helen."

Her face had got puffy, probably from the steroids she was taking for her thyroid condition. She seemed to have withdrawn inside her ballooning figure. And he remembered even when she looked after him and Jennifer, all living together in the house on Maple Street, she seemed already to have begun to pull away from the world. Now she looked like she could just float up out of her seat and disappear into the clouds.

After lunch he wheeled her around the block in the sweet spring air so she could see the magnolia buds and the first daffodil shoots. It was too early for blossoms, but it was warm, and they had an hour before her ride came to collect her.

For a time as he pushed her slowly around the block they didn't speak, and Paul tried not to think of Trevor perhaps at this very moment going down on a knee and presenting Linda with the ring. If he had asked her to marry him while they were in the Bahamas she would have mentioned it on the phone. *I'm so excited I can't think right now Paul; I'm going to get married.* Something like that. So Trevor would be asking her this weekend for sure. Have the parents size her up, get the nod, then pop the question. But he tried not to think about any of that while he wheeled Aunt Helen around the block, knowing she was just enjoying the lovely spring day.

He took her back to the restaurant and they waited for the transit vehicle. She wanted to go back on her own and he understood. She would sleep in the afternoon. When the van arrived he rolled her chair onto the mobile platform and the attendant raised it, then wheeled the chair inside. She waved at him after she was in, as she might to a hired chaperon when she was safely home.

He waved back. "Thank you Aunt Helen. Just, thank you—for everything."

"Goodbye. Goodbye."

The door slid shut and the vehicle moved out into the thin downtown traffic of a Sunday afternoon. He felt completely alone in the world, watching the van drive her away. Sadness filled the spring air around him, like pollen.

Early Monday morning his phone woke him.

"Paul, it's Linda. I'm sorry this is so early but I won't be in the office this morning. I have to drive to Kitchener for a meeting. So you wouldn't get me when you called."

"That's okay. So today's no good?"

"No, today will work. I get back late afternoon and then I have to clear up some things in the office before I can get away for good. Trevor is working late. I can be free by five-thirty. Are you okay for a drink then? Or if you want we can grab dinner somewhere."

"Great. Where is it convenient for us to meet?" She had called him Trevor, not Trev. *Trevor is working late.*

"Corner of Richmond and Bay. Six o'clock?"

"I'll be there."

•

The breeze caught her blond hair when she stepped out of the cab. She wore a lemon-coloured spring coat. She saw him and waved then turned to pay the driver. She was wearing gloves when she waved to him. She kept them on while she picked out some bills to pay her fare, so they had to be very fine leather. She was smiling when she came forward to give him a hug. But she looked tired. "So great to see you again Paul."

"It's great to see you too. How was your drive?" He didn't ask how her meeting went because she would only say that it went fine but would spare him the details, knowing that a meeting between accountants and clients would be meaningless to someone buried in *Hamlet*. By the time he realized that he should have asked her anyway it was too late.

"Hectic. Traffic both ways like you wouldn't believe. I feel like I spent the day in a parking lot. Anyway I made it. Let's go round the corner and grab a table at this new place I know before it gets crazy busy. Even on a Monday it's popular."

D'Accord! was already filling up when they entered, but they were shown to a table towards the back. The walls of exposed and tastefully crumbling brick were hung with framed prints of Degas and Van Gogh and

Toulouse-Lautrec, interspersed with grainy black and white photos of the Eiffel Tower, the Champs-Elysees and Montmartre. Each table was laid with a checkered cloth and lit by a candle stuck in a wax-encrusted wine bottle. The menu was in English only. He wasn't hungry but he began to relax when they were seated and the wine came. Concertina music played through mounted speakers, and when he said the restaurant should be named *D'Accordion!* she laughed like she actually found it funny. It pleased him because he didn't make people laugh as a rule.

*

Dr. P. would understand that this was casual supper and not elegant dinner because Linda was going with Trevor now and only doing Paul a favour by meeting up with him at all.

*

But when she removed her thin leather gloves and laid them with her lemon coat on the chair beside her, he saw she wasn't wearing a ring. So Trevor had not gone down on bended knee over the weekend. Or maybe he had but she didn't wear the ring tonight because knowing that Paul might be in love with her as well she would have to break things gently to him rather than shove Trevor's very large and expensive diamond in his face when she removed her gloves.

They got through dinner and the loud concertina music without much talk of Trevor or Nassau or diamonds or Paul telling her he might be in love with her. She said nothing about his remark on the phone because she didn't want to embarrass him. She didn't say that of course but he knew. They talked about England and Hamlet and teaching, and then she spoke about how she still missed her life at home, how difficult it was to make even casual friends in Toronto with everyone so busy, and how she had always been good with figures, so it was kind of obvious that she would be either an accountant or an architect. He had to keep asking her to repeat what she said because the music and the talk in the restaurant were quite loud. He lost some of what she said because he didn't want to keep asking her to repeat what she just said in case she might think twice about spending the rest of her life with someone whose impairment could become really annoying. And then he reminded himself all over again that she would be spending the rest of her life not with him but with Trevor, who heard everything, had no impairments of any kind, and whose shelves groaned with tennis trophies.

But the dinner went well he thought, all things considered.

They split the bill and he suggested they take a cab down to the lakeshore and enjoy the mild April evening at the water if she had time to spare. He had no idea what they would talk about when they got there but at least it would be quieter. He didn't expect her to agree to it because she had already had a long day and maybe figured they had run out of things to talk about, but she said yes and without even checking her watch, which meant that Trevor was working very late that night.

By Queen's Quay they sat on a bench under the lights

of the pier. The city had had little snow that winter she said, so unlike the prairies, and she was relieved at the mild winter temperatures. She could never wear such a light coat this early when she lived in Winnipeg. He remarked that it was milder in Toronto than in England when he left. People there said that the blossoms always came out too early. He began to rethink their visit to the Quay. It seemed like they had run out of things to talk about after all.

They sat without speaking for a moment or two, and he sensed that they both felt the mild panic of not knowing what to say while a million things remained unspoken. A breeze came up across the lake but the evening air was still soft. They gazed out over the thickening water towards the islands and watched the early lights of the houses flicker behind the stirring branches. The ferry was just leaving Hanlan's Point to return to the city docks. Its air-horn sounded a deep grunt. Above the end of the pier, illuminated by the lamps, a sea gull hovered and squawked, its spread wings twitching against the breeze as it eyed the white belly of a dead fish floating on the surface.

He had asked her to come with him to the Quay, and so now it was up to him to make a start with one of the things that weren't to be mentioned. "How was your weekend with Trevor?"

She didn't answer right away. When she did, she measured her words. "It was fine. Thank you for asking. His parents were very nice. They have a lovely place in Richmond Hill."

He could feel her looking at him as he gazed out over the darkening water. The seagull splashed down onto the surface and then flew up again with the dead fish in its beak. He nodded. "Well, I'm glad of that." Knowing exactly what she was going to say next he waited, following the gull's low flight until it flopped onto the boardwalk and set down its catch.

"He asked me to marry him."

He kept his eyes on the gull. Was Trevor on bended knee at the time, he wanted to ask her because he was dying to know, having played out the scene so often in his head, but he resisted. Obviously, she had removed the ring before meeting him for dinner. His chest was about to explode.

The seagull was tearing the fish to shreds, standing on its body as it ripped off bits of flesh with its beak.

He looked at her and forced a smile. "Congratulations. I really mean that." He tried very hard to mean it. "I'm happy for you. For both of you." His heart was beating fast and he knew that he shouldn't look away now, not if he wanted to convince her that he meant his words.

She gazed back at him, her eyes a little sad. "I told him I wasn't sure. I don't know yet."

"Oh." What else to say? He had so say something. "How did he take it?"

"He was surprised. Kind of shocked really. We talked a bit, but that's pretty well where I left it. I said I needed time to think." She breathed out like she had been holding it for time. "The rest of Sunday was awkward, as you can imagine. It's not like I could go anywhere. I tried to be kind to him, but of course he was upset." She shook her head. "What surprised me was the way he seemed more angry than hurt, like it wasn't the answer I was supposed to give. I mean I know it wasn't what he wanted to hear, but the way he reacted, I felt like I hadn't followed the script. Do you know what I mean?"

He nodded, feeling sorry for her distress. She didn't deserve to be distressed. And he hoped that she felt comfortable telling him all this and wasn't adding to her distress by thinking maybe she shouldn't be sharing it.

"Don't get me wrong. Trevor's a wonderful guy, and he's considerate. From the start he never came onto me the way guys sometimes do."

"You mean like your friend at the party."

She laughed. "Exactly. Nothing like him. With Trevor, I didn't feel like I was supposed to sleep with him, and it wasn't until we went away—okay, I'm sorry, forget that part. *Motor mouth*, see?"

The seagull shrieked as it rose over the water into the purple sky and flapped away into the night, leaving fish remains on the boardwalk. His chest was on fire, like indigestion suddenly. He thought of the two of them together in their hotel during a whole week of indolent Nassau afternoons.

But now she wasn't sure, she said. And she wasn't wearing the ring because she hadn't accepted it.

"Trevor's one of these guys who always wins, you know? Nice guys aren't supposed to win as a rule but he's a nice guy who wins, and I was attracted to that—his being a winner and being nice at the same time—but he was cross when I said I had to think about it. Like I'd failed him. He just stared at me and said nothing for the longest time. It scared me a little." She looked at him. "So now I'm really not sure."

"I'm sorry. It's all I can say. I'm just sorry."

She took his hand. He felt the soft leather. "Listen

Paul, I had a really great time with you this evening and I'm glad we did this. I like you. You're smart and you're thoughtful. I feel I can be me when I'm around you. I remember feeling that way at the party, not really wanting to talk to anyone else. Do you mind that I told you everything just now?"

He shook his head. It filled up with a dozen cartoon thought-balloons and all of them were bursting at once. "I'm glad you felt you could trust me enough."

She looked down at the water lapping against the pier. "I'm not sure about anything right now."

"I want to marry you as well, Linda." The words were out before he realized he was saying them. But they kept coming. "I mean as well as Trevor."

She laughed suddenly, and then tried to stifle it. "Oh God, I'm sorry Paul, but it sounded like you want to marry Trevor too." Then she shook her head. "I'm sorry. I think you were being serious."

"That's okay. I didn't mean to just say it like that. But it's why I came over. To tell you I want to marry you." He waited to see if more words would come out, but they didn't. He wondered if he should get up and dive into the freezing lake, then swim across to Hanlan's Point and beyond, all the way back to the sceptered isle with its pewter skies.

She squeezed his hand. "Can I tell you something?" She was smiling now as she looked at him. "I remember feeling a little disappointed when I realized you had left Chris's party before I could say goodbye. And also the next day flying out to visit my parents, knowing you'd be gone when I got back. So I've been a little confused all this time. When you called the other night and said what you said—you know, how you felt—I was happy to hear you say it. I shouldn't have been, I suppose, but I was. So I'm confused. About everything right now." She squeezed his hand again. "I don't know if I want to marry you, Paul. I know I feel good when I'm around you, but I don't know if that's enough. It's only our second time seeing each other. That's a bit crazy, don't you think? We don't really know each other do we?"

"You don't have to say anything right now. I can't promise you much on a teacher's salary, but we can be happy together maybe. Do you think that's possible?"

*

It occurred to him as he recalled the scene now, that he was using the phrase *do you think* in exactly the way that Dr. Hannah used it. So now he couldn't be sure if he was imagining exactly what he said to Linda at the time, or if Dr. Hannah's *do you thinks* all those years later had worked their way into the remembered conversation. Heaven forbid that he should start talking like his own shrink.

*

She leaned across and kissed him on the cheek. "I like you Paul. Maybe I could love you. Maybe I've already started to. But yes, I need time to think."

They sat and looked out into the darkness descending on the lake. The silence felt comfortable. He remembered it now, how he felt completely at peace. He and Linda together, at the still point of the turning world. Just that one time. Then she shivered and pulled her coat around her. "I have an early start tomorrow. Can we get a cab?"

He nodded. "I go back on Saturday. If you want to talk, I mean just talk, you have my number at the residence. I won't be a nuisance I promise. I'll give you your space."

"Thank you Paul. I know I'm going to be busy at work and"—she shook her head again—"trying to sort myself out." They stood up together. "What are you doing this week? Oh, stupid me. How could I forget? *Hamlet.* You're seeing your supervisor."

"Right. And if my aunt's up for it I'll see her again." But he didn't think she'd be up for it. "I'll see how things go."

He said nothing to her about his stepfather or signing papers that morning.

*

Signing his life away, he thought now, sitting in his study, on the wrong side of all the ironies of another time.

Dr. P. understood why he said nothing about his stepfather. He understood why even mentioning his stepfather when he and Linda had just been to the still point of the turning world would permit the worm to burrow its way into their new bud and blight it before it ever bloomed.

*

The evening before his flight she phoned him. "Paul, it's

Linda. Please don't speak. I need to say something." He could hear her breathing. "I'm calling to wish you a safe trip back. I'll write you a letter tonight and mail it tomorrow morning straightaway. But just to say, please save me a little bit of your long teacher's summer holiday if you feel you want to. Maybe you can show me around England."

"What's going on, Linda? Is everything okay?"

"I can't get into it all now. Just wait for my letter. And get a phone over there, okay? Have a safe flight." She was silent for a moment. "I've done some thinking like I promised and I think maybe I could love you too."

He could have floated all the way back to England, he felt. The sun was rising when he flew over Dublin, a gold medallion exactly poised on the horizon at the moment he looked. By the time he walked out of the airport at Gatwick, it burned bright in a clear morning sky.

*

With Linda and Rachel still at the movies and Dr. P. naturally wanting to know what Linda said in the letter she was sending, he would have to read it to him, so he would know that his patient had his feet planted on *terra firma* and wasn't tilting at windmills.

*

29 April 1980

Dear Paul,

I hope you got back safely with no delays. Okay, I'm

going to get straight to it.

Life's a mess. I've been trying to sort things out but not doing very well.

I broke up with Trevor after you left. We went out for a drink so there would be people around because I didn't want to be alone with him when I told him. Before I could say anything he tried to give me a gold bracelet but I told him I couldn't accept it. So I had to tell him why right there. He didn't take it well. I won't go into details—let's just leave it at I'm grateful there were people around.

I've had to change my phone number because he kept calling me and I've changed the lock on my apartment. I'll be okay, I'm sure. I've always been a little paranoid about security to be honest.

You should understand something here. I was already having doubts about Trevor before you came over. After Nassau I felt there was nothing more to know and nothing to do except get married. Marriage should be the beginning of something not the end. And obviously there was a lot about him I didn't realize. Like he can't deal with setbacks. I told you, he's scary when things don't go as planned. Maybe not such a nice guy after all.

This whole thing has deflated me. He said things that didn't make me feel good about myself. Maybe he was right to do that, I don't know. I'm not perfect. Who is, right?

Which brings me to us. The 'us' we hardly know yet. Am I who you think I am? Do I even know who I am any more? Are you really who I think you are? I hope so. I'm all bright and breezy—usually—so you can be the ballast, I'll be the sails and let's see where we go with this.

Here's what I suggest—my turn to take a blind leap here, frying pan into the fire sort of thing—I'd like to come to England this summer, if you still think you want me. We can travel around and you can show me places. I've always wanted to visit England, I think I mentioned that at New Year's.

Do you have a phone yet? Let me have your number and I'll call you. It's cheaper from here. I checked already.

I think I'm glad I've written this. I don't feel scared anymore, just excited.

Love,

Linda.

•

He met her at Heathrow, and they drove up to the Cotswolds. He had bought tickets for Stratford one night—*The Comedy of Errors*. They explored Warwick Castle with its deep dungeons and an oubliette underneath the stone floor that made them both shudder—she said she could *never* forget the oubliette, and didn't realize what she'd said until he raised an eyebrow at her, and then they both laughed. They drove to Oxford and stayed in a small hotel on Boar's Hill that gave them a grand view of the city below. From their bedroom window they could see the colleges, the ornate obelisks and gold spires that gleamed in the sun like tines on a crown.

The next day they walked hand in hand along the cobbled streets. The high crenelated walls of the colleges burned bronze in the sun, and gowned scholars fluttered like large bats in and out of the arched entrances. Dons clutching books and satchels disappeared like Alice through low wooden doorways that offered glimpses of green velvet lawns and gigantic blooms.

"They look like monasteries."

"Exactly what they once were."

"Well, you'd know, wouldn't you?" She laughed and squeezed his hand.

"I guess. But can you imagine how dreary this would all look in the rain?"

"Well, it's not raining now, and it looks like a city in Heaven, and yes, I'll marry you, Paul." She stopped, looked into his eyes and nodded. "I want to stay here, right on this spot where we are now, and love you." They kissed where they stood, on a busy pavement in the middle of a golden city.

That evening, after an intimate dinner, they strolled along St. Aldate's, and she asked him about the seminary.

"What made you think you wanted to be a priest in the first place? I've always wanted to ask you, and now I can."

Dr. P. would want to ask the same question. He couldn't remember if he'd ever told Dr. P. that he once thought he would be a priest. But he remembered what he said to Linda.

"I was taught by priests at my high school, Christ the Redeemer. It wasn't unusual for them to single out a few boys and suggest to them they might have a vocation. Maybe because I was always a bit of a loner they figured I could handle seminary life. But it didn't work out, and I left after only a year."

It was a gigantic lie. A real whopper. Not the part about him lasting only a year, and not the part about him being a loner, but telling her that the priests at

Christ the Redeemer led him to believe he had a vocation—that was the whopper.

But he couldn't tell her the truth. He had promised his mother on his life to keep his secret.

It was stupid to have made a promise that required him to lie to Linda, but he was only six when he made it, and had no idea how stupid such a promise would turn out to be. A promise made on his life. And on his mother's too, though she must have known even then, with what wits she had left, that she'd be checking out anytime soon.

It still bothered him that on the very day Linda said she would marry him, he lied to her. But he couldn't tell her then, and there was no point in telling her now, as in when she came home from seeing a movie with Rachel. What could he achieve by telling her now? She wanted him to see a shrink so he could *deal* with his issues, not tell her how he got stuck with them in the first place.

He remembered something she said to him that evening in Oxford as kind of funny now. *Once we're married you'll never feel like going back.* At the time she said that, they were standing by the high wall outside Christ Church, Tom Tower a shadow against an aubergine sky, the two of them under a streetlamp that showered them with gold. It was just after she raised her bright face up to him, and they kissed.

He should maybe have asked her then what she meant by *going back*. Did she mean going back to the seminary or just going back? If she meant the seminary then it would be funny amusing because he would never go back there. If she meant just going back, as in time, then it would be funny ironic because going back was pretty well all he had done since he had started.

Dr. P. would accompany him on this last leg of the journey.

Even with Caldwell's red flags pinging away somewhere inside his computer this was turning out to be a damned good session. It was all working out now, and he would be sure to thank Dr. P. for his time when they were finished.

He had found Linda again. It wasn't a glance or a gesture that made him fall in love with her. He was already in love with her before any glances or gestures. In love with the very thought of her. A thought made incarnate under the streetlamp's golden light at Christ Church.

A bright torch, and the casement ope at night, to let the warm love in. The warmth surged through him now. He would tell her when she came home from being at the movies with Rachel.

But not the secret. No one could know the boy's secret. Except Dr. P. because he was the boy's confessor now. And he should know who the boy's real mother was. He might get confused about that because when Paul and Linda drove back from Oxford to the cottage in East Dean he found a telegram inside the door.

Aunt Helen passed away in her sleep. Am flying out to arrange funeral. Please come soonest. She was our mother. Jennifer.

But Helen was never the boy's mother whatever she was to his sister. An aunt, and a guardian for a time but not the boy's real mother, whatever the sister said in her telegram.

Sarah was the boy's mother, pure and simple. Or maybe not so pure, and far from simple. Beautiful, haunted, broken Sarah who sucked the soul right out of the boy's body. Was there a technical name for a child whose soul got slurped up like placenta by the mother who gave it birth? Not a foundling, or a changeling. A foundling was abandoned at birth; a changeling was substituted by fairies when they stole a child.

Lostling, perhaps. A child without a soul. A Lostling. There. Dr. P. could add that to his list of neurotic conditions.

Paul would take him back to the very beginning now. They had begun at the end with *do you think* and now they would end at the beginning. Dr. P. was good at this. He made a name for himself by starting at the end and going back to the beginning.

And when they got to the beginning of this, they would be at an end.

Dr. P. could cancel any further appointments he might have this evening, and send his receptionist home. He should turn off his phone, so there would be no interruptions.

When Paul finished telling the boy's story he would settle his own account and be on his way.

But first, the boy's account. Dr. P. should think of a piano falling out of a window. Not much happening at first but then it becomes interesting. He already had his pages of notes from Paul's account of the mother's *Terrible Blunder* and *Long Decline*, but now he could record the *Final Rapid Descent*. And he wouldn't need notes to remember this one.

Ten

The boy was in the backyard with his sister when his Aunt Helen came down the back steps to tell him that his mother wanted to see him.

He looked at his sister. He couldn't remember ever being asked to go to his mother's bedroom. He didn't like the idea of going to her bedroom because that's where she worshipped at Mary's shrine with his new father. His sister glanced up at him from where she sat on the ground, then shrugged and returned to her alfalfa trays. For her science project she had planted alfalfa seeds in little irrigation trays and she was showing him the first tiny green shoots splitting their kernels. She wrote down her observations in a notebook, just like Dr. P. did much later in the boy's life. For now, the boy planned to leave school when he finished grade eight because that was his sister's grade, and he thought there could not be much of importance to learn after that.

He followed his aunt out of the sun and into the house. She remained in the kitchen while he walked on into the hall and began to climb the dark stairs. He took each stair slowly, eyeing the corners of the high ceiling, looking for the bat that had got into the house. His aunt spotted it one morning, hanging upside down in a corner above the landing, its wings folded around it like it was pretending not to be there. He watched her poke at it with a broom handle until it took off and swooped and looped all over, driving them both into the kitchen where she shut the door. They never saw it again, but now in the gloom he scanned the high ceiling on his way up the stairs. When he got to the landing he switched on the light. Nothing. He walked slowly down the hall to his mother's bedroom.

When he got to the door he knocked, then waited until he heard her say his name. He put his head around the door and saw her propped up against the pillows, her shoulders wrapped in a white woolen shawl. She smiled at him but he could see deep shadows around her eyes. "Come and sit here by me, love. There's an angel."

Standing in the doorway he turned to see the angel, but there wasn't one. There was only his sister at the other end of the hall peering at him from the top of the stairs.

"Close the door love."

With the heavy curtains closed the flames from the votive lights flickered brightly around Mary's statue. They illuminated her face and threw dancing shadows around the room. The shrine was decked out with tiny plastic sprays of roses, violets and lily-of-the-valley.

"Come over to my bed, there's a love."

When he went to her she put out a cold hand and held his. "Don't be afraid my darling boy. Are you a little afraid?"

He shook his head. Then she leaned over and hugged him hard so that he did feel a little afraid. When he pulled back so he could look at her in the dancing light from the candle flame, he saw her wedding face. He looked up at the framed photo on the mantel above her bed where she stood beside her brand new husband. His new father. She held a small bouquet of white lilies but her smile in the photo, as now, was hard, like she was clenching her teeth behind it. That's what he called her wedding face.

"Are you feeling stronger now my dear one? Do you

feel better? I pray to Mary every day to make you strong."

"I can run to the park and all the way back. It's two whole blocks and when I come back I'm not even breathing hard."

"That means your heart is stronger and Mary is answering my prayers. If we believe in Mary she will always answer our prayers."

"Why does Mary answer your prayers but she doesn't answer mine? I pray to her every day and I ask her to make it so you can come downstairs and be with us like before."

"Mary doesn't do everything all at once," she said. "Neither does God. Their time isn't our time, and so we must be patient." She stared at him, and even though he couldn't always see her hooded eyes in the flickering light he knew they were on him. He felt uncomfortable again. After a long silence she spoke.

"God wants you to be with Him. Mary said I was to tell you."

Her words alarmed him. "I'm going to die?" How could that be? She had just told him his heart was stronger, that Mary had answered his mother's prayers. She just told him that.

"No, my love, you're not going to die. It means God wants you to be His priest." She smiled when she said *priest*, and her face seemed to brighten on its own, without the candles. She smiled a proper smile and not the wedding smile any more. It was a smile like she was happy. God wanted him to be a priest, like Father Glass, and it made his mother happy to tell him.

But he didn't know how to be a priest like that.

Father Glass said Mass at Christ the Redeemer. When he spoke the prayers, his voice boomed down the aisles, and he glided around the great marble altar in his gold and crimson robes like a giant kite.

"Is God sure?"

"Yes, God's sure. Mary told me. She was here last night and she spoke to me. But you must never tell anyone. Promise me that you will never tell anyone."

Her face was so soft now. She seemed to glow. Father Glass had spoken to the Sunday school class about beatification. His mother's face beamed like she was beatified. The Blessed Virgin had come to her bedroom and spoken to her. Did she stand by her own shrine at the foot of the bed? Maybe she was still here in the room and that was another reason why his mother's face glowed. He glanced around the room. He couldn't see anyone, but that didn't mean she wasn't still here. It was, regardless, a miracle that the Virgin had appeared to his mother.

Father Glass had also spoken about divine visitations. Jesus appeared in front of special people even today. His sacred heart bled real blood in a church in Italy. People saw Him drip blood from his statue and it was because He was sad for all the sinners. That was a miracle, Father Glass said. The Virgin Mary visited the three children at Fatima, and she appeared to Bernadette at Lourdes, and then to the peasant girl in a place called Guadeloupe. Those were miracles too and the children were either beatified or canonized. His mother wouldn't make up a story about the Virgin coming to see her. She had a Special Devotion to Mary and that meant his mother was special.

If his sister told him that the Blessed Virgin had

spoken to *her* he wouldn't believe her. Jennifer sometimes played tricks on her brother because she knew he believed everything she said. But she had stopped going to Mass, so Mary would never speak to her now. He worried about the state of her soul.

Now in the bedroom he looked at the Virgin who had visited his mother and told her that God wanted him to be a priest. He tried not to think of the Virgin averting her eyes that time when his mother was worshipping her and his stepfather was saying *Oh yes*—the veiled head lowered and the hands spread out at its sides, the palms open. Thy will be done. And now it was his turn. To have thy will be done.

"Paul?"

"I promise."

"Good boy. I'm going to teach you a special prayer. I know you remember things and I want you to remember the words of this prayer. Will you do it for me?"

He nodded. At school he memorized poems. He was able to recite them at home that same night. Mrs. Cartwright told him in first grade that he was a fast learner. He had a wonderful memory she said, and now he would show his mother how quickly he could learn her new prayer. "Tell me the prayer."

She said the prayer right through and he listened. It wasn't a long prayer, not like the Apostles Creed.

Dear God in heaven.

Thank You for my life and for making me special.

Keep me pure in thought and word and deed.

Make me worthy of You.

Strike me dead if I should be impure.

Strike me dead if I should disobey You.

Strike me dead if I should ever tell my secret.

My love and my life to You and to dear Mother Mary. Amen.

Then she spoke the words line by line and he repeated them. Then they did two lines at a time, and then more at a time until he had them all by heart.

The *strike me deads* frightened him at first, and he hesitated when his mother asked him to say them.

But he said them because he felt safe in the presence of Mary. When he had memorized the whole prayer, and recited it over and over until his knees ached from the hard floor, she squeezed him again. She was tired now, she said, and wanted to sleep.

He moved towards the door. When he turned to look back she was on her knees at the end of the bed and leaning forward to light a fresh candle in front of Our Lady. Their two faces flickered together in the light. His mother's face had got hard again and her smile was clenched like in her wedding photo. Her face and the face of the statue looked the same. He closed the door and moved down the hall to the stairs, checking for the bat. Maybe the Blessed Virgin came as a bat when she visited his mother, and that would explain why he and his aunt had seen one in the house, and then not seen it again. But why would someone as beautiful as Mary appear as such an ugly creature? Then he remembered his mother saying that the Virgin came to her last night, and it was more than a week ago that they had seen the bat. But whatever form the Virgin appeared to her in it was to tell her that he was to be a priest. He would let his sister know right away. At last he had something important to tell her. He hoped she wouldn't be mad that God wanted him and not her, but that wasn't God's fault because she was the one who stopped going to Mass.

And then on the stairs he remembered the *strike me deads*. He had promised to keep the secret, so he could never tell his sister that the Blessed Virgin visited their house or that he was going to be a priest. It saddened him then to know there was this wonderful and important secret that he couldn't share with his sister whom he loved dearly, and it saddened Paul now as was telling Dr. P. the boy's story that it was probably at that very moment, when the boy left the room with the secret he could never share with his sister, that he began to separate himself from her.

Maybe, at that moment, the boy began to separate himself from everyone.

Dr. P. should make a mental note of something here. The glow on the mother's face when she spoke to the boy about Mary. The sudden flush of beatification. It looked like fever, but really it was love, and he had warmed himself by it as by a stove in winter. So Dr. P. would understand that the boy did know love as a child. His mother loved him, and he would do anything so her all-consuming love would never go out.

Every night through the months that followed he went to her room to pray.

His sister said to him one morning on their way to school "Boy, you must have said about a hundred rosaries up there. I got so bored."

She had listened at the door while he was in the room. Anyway, they said three rosaries not a hundred. Still, a lot of Hail Mary's with fifty in each rosary, but at least they didn't mention the secret while his sister was listening outside the door. She would have said something if she'd heard anything about that.

"I'm just glad it's not me having to do all that praying." After that she never mentioned his visits again.

He began to dream of Father Glass. In his dream the boy sat in a pew alone in the back of the church and Father Glass was up at the altar. His voice cracked like black thunder and hurt his ears. The priest turned and fixed his huge crater eyes on him at the back of the church. Then he moved down the altar steps, his deep purple chasuble filling with air until his feet left the floor. He rose into the air and floated down the aisle towards the back, lifting his arms so the chasuble spread out across the church and blocked the light from the high windows. Then the giant head swung down straight at him until he was staring into two large holes where the eyes had been. He would wake up shouting, and then Aunt Helen would be at his bedside.

At breakfast one morning she told his sister that she must stop reading to him from her fairy tale book, because it was full of bears and sorcerers and that poor little girl whose red shoes cut her feet and made them bleed.

So his sister stopped reading to him at night before bed. She had already stopped saying her nursery rhyme prayer with him and he wasn't unhappy about that. It was supposed to be a simple prayer but he never really understood it.

Now I lay me down to sleep,

I pray the Lord my soul to keep,

If I should die before I wake,

I pray the Lord my soul to take.

Some of the words made no sense. If the Lord already had his soul to keep then how could he come and take his soul if he died in the night? And the rhyming prayer was very like the *strike me dead* prayer. Two prayers to make him think about dying in the dead of night, last thing before he went to sleep. It seemed so final. At least the rhyming prayer sounded like music and was gentler than the thought of being struck dead just like that, like stepping on a June bug and hearing it crackle.

Anyway, she didn't read to him anymore because she had moved on herself. When it was his bedtime now she was still on the phone talking and giggling with her friends. That meant he could say his mother's secret prayer out loud instead of just in his head so his sister didn't hear it.

She told him that she sometimes heard him talking in his sleep and he worried that he might say something about his secret. He thought it wouldn't be fair if God struck him dead for speaking his secret in his sleep, but then he supposed that God wouldn't trick him like that, letting him talk about the secret in his sleep and then striking him dead for it. In any case the problem was solved later that summer when she moved into her own bedroom across the hall and he didn't have to worry any more about God not being fair.

She was different now. Even with a room all to herself she took longer to get ready for school. She dressed and undressed several times most mornings. Skirts and blouses in different combinations, her hair going up and then down, into a ponytail and out again, this colour lipstick and that colour lipstick. Across the hall in his own room he could hear drawers being opened and closed and she would come out and go back in again five minutes later, shut her door and do it all over again.

One night when he was drifting off to sleep after his prayers he was shocked to hear her shouting at their stepfather downstairs and using words he didn't know but which sounded ugly. She was in the hall at the front of the house where the study was so he heard everything.

"I'm not going to any school with a name like a fucking concentration camp, run by a bunch of know-nothing dyke nuns! So you can fuck yourself." He heard her run up the stairs and slam her bedroom door. Then he heard his stepfather go out the front door. Moments later his car pulled out of the driveway. He would be going to one of his meetings.

He lay awake for a long time after that, thinking he would have to move his sister to the top of his list of people to pray for. It wasn't a long list, but he thought she should be at the top of it.

Every night and first thing each morning he prayed for his mother who looked as pale as the Virgin and hadn't come out of her bedroom yet, though he knew she would one day if he kept praying for her because God and Mary liked to take their time about things.

He prayed for his father who was already in heaven. A good man and much loved by everyone who knew him, so his aunt had said. He prayed for him anyway, because he was his real father and he wasn't coming back.

He said a short prayer for his aunt. She was okay. There must be times he thought when she would prefer to live with the troll under the three little billy goats' bridge, but her heart was a sunflower, and she sang to herself in the kitchen when she prepared supper and cleared up afterwards. She crocheted doilies as she watched TV and spread them around on all the furniture in the house. They made the boy think of frosted cobwebs in the hedges on winter mornings.

He wondered now if frosted cobwebs were what the boy actually thought the doilies looked like then or if they were just how he himself imagined them now. It really didn't matter. Dr. Palindrome wouldn't care one way or the other. They were just doilies and not all that important, but they made the rooms they were in look less dismal.

He didn't pray for his stepfather's soul because he didn't know where to begin and he didn't understand his stepfather's way of praying, because all he said that one time was *Oh yes,* and then *Amen.* And he was afraid *of* his stepfather and not afraid *for* him, so he didn't feel like praying last thing at night for someone that he was afraid *of.* There were too many things going on in his head already last thing at night without having even to *think* of his stepfather's soul, and it would be many years before the boy would read *Hamlet* and think of a soul kicking its heels at heaven, being as damned and black as the hell whereto it goes.

But at the top of his prayer list was his sister, who had taken to going out the front door on summer evenings to talk to boys who wore their ball caps back to front. They sometimes smoked cigarettes and rode their bikes up and down the street with no hands on the turned-around handlebars. She spent a long time in the mornings looking sideways at herself in the mirror. He could see her from his own room when she didn't close her door properly. Of course she had stopped going to Mass *cold turkey* by then. She once told him she was going to stop smoking *cold turkey.* But she still smoked.

She quit going to Mass cold turkey instead. And now she used ugly words like *fuck* and *dyke* that sounded like they could send her straight to hell even though he had no idea what they meant. And she refused to go to school at Our Lady of Sorrows. So he had lots of reasons to move her to the top of his prayer list.

At lunchtime he would gobble his sandwich in the boys' locker room so he could nip across the road to Christ the Redeemer and squeeze in a quick rosary or light a votive candle if he had a spare nickel. Every Friday, at the risk of being late for afternoon school, he would run a circuit of the Stations of the Cross and always avert his eyes from Christ's loins when he came to the crucifixion at Station Twelve.

Life went on and everything became just a different kind of normal. That's how it seemed to the boy.

It was normal for his mother to make him tell her all that he had done during the day, so Mary and God could hear. Had he been worthy of his calling? Had he told his secret to anyone? Had he given in to the desires of the flesh? Of course he had no idea what it meant to give in to the desires of the flesh. He thought it had something to do with eating too much meat.

It was normal for him to tell her about his day and then read to her from his book of bible stories. In the beginning he read to her from a bible that had more pictures than words. He loved the pictures. Moses in the bulrushes. The Gadarine swine stampeding off the cliff. Jesus in the deep blue Garden of Gethsemane being led away by the soldiers with burning torches that lit up their angry red faces. When she moved him on to a real bible she started at the beginning again, at Genesis. And so it went on.

And then one day, during the hottest summer in living memory, just when they were about to start reading the Song of Solomon in his real bible, she left him.

Looking back now, staring at Dr. P.'s jacket on the back of the chair and his tie folded neatly on the desk, he wondered why no one saw it coming. Someone should have seen the signs.

But life on the boy's street was a broken barometer—the daily forecast stuck on NORMAL whatever the weather.

Neighbours were just decent, simple souls who minded their own business. They put out their garbage bins the night before, paid their bills ahead of time, trimmed their lawns, weeded their borders and exchanged polite hellos when they passed on the street.

They would observe the very respectable Dr. Crane pull into his driveway each day, walk up the front steps, pick up the evening paper, check the mailbox, deadhead a geranium in the window box as easily as he might pinch a jugular and open his front door to enter. But they wouldn't see him after he closed his door inside a wax museum of virgins and satyrs, saints and devils, sanctity and sex. Who would know? Who would care to know, apart from old Mrs. Harrison sitting at her front window across the street?

No one saw it coming. And when it came they attributed it to the heat.

Old Mrs. Thwaites who lived next door declared to the boy's aunt that *in all her born days* she had never known the likes of it.

From the shade of the back porch he watched his aunt

hang out the washing while she chatted with her neighbour over the privet hedge.

"Not a drop of rain for weeks," Mrs. Thwaites muttered, "and not a sign of it anywhere. It's not natural, you mark my words. It's all to do with that *nucular bomb* testing in the desert." Her dentures clicked as she spoke. Dipping the brim of her wide sun hat to shield her eyes she squinted up through the still haze at a hot sky bleached to the colour of moonstone, as if willing a cloud into view. "The spuds'll do well enough in this, but likely as not it'll be a poorly bunch of radish." *Click click.*

Mercifully, June twenty-six was the last day of school. In the airless classroom, Sister Enid informed the children that the St. Lawrence Seaway would open that very afternoon. The boy stared out at the playground, watching the heat shimmers rise off the tarry surface. When the final bell released them for the summer he stepped across the playground, avoiding the spots where the baking asphalt leaked out in inky pools. Some of the boys wanted to play work-ups on the diamond where the large elm shaded home plate, but he didn't join them. He had brought his bat and mitt to school, but the day was too hot, even in the shade, and he wasn't supposed to exert himself in the heat. With his schoolbag strapped to his back, and carrying his bat and mitt, he headed home.

He took his usual short cut through the dirt lane that ran behind the homes on Tecumseh. Heat waves shimmered on the corrugated tin roofs of the garages. One garage had its door up and with the heat rising off the roof it seemed to gasp for air.

His bare arms tingled, like a fine sprinkling of rain on his skin, but there wasn't a cloud in the sky. He didn't have far to go now.

A tiny dust storm in the lane up ahead caught his eye. It wasn't a breeze because the air was dead still. Drawing near he made out an injured sparrow with one wing held horizontally to the side. The bird spun round and round in the dust like a wind-up toy missing a wheel.

He stood over it for a moment watching it spin and then stop, as though to catch its breath. There was nothing else he could do. Looking around he saw an oil-stained rag lying at the side of a garage. He picked it up and draped it over the stricken bird. It stopped moving. He laid his mitt on top of the lump, then raised his bat and pounded at the glove until he was panting with the effort. Sweating now and with his pulse hammering in his ears he lifted the mitt. He tucked the edges of the cloth under the flattened mush and dropped the wad into a garbage can at the side of the lane. He said a prayer to St. Francis of Assisi, the patron saint of all living creatures, and dead ones too he hoped, and then proceeded to where the dirt lane ended on Maple Street.

He turned left at the corner and headed down the street towards his house. No one was out and about. Only the Harrisons' white tomcat Snowy. He lay stretched out in the shade on the top step of the verandah watching the boy approach. The boy would have gone up the path to stroke him but he wanted to get home and cool off.

He crossed the street and walked up his own front path in the shade of the chestnut, and then turned down the walkway at the side of the house. Entering the backyard he saw Mr. Thwaites at the bottom of his garden next door pruning the shrubbery. Wearing a wide-brimmed hat against the sun he looked like a Chinese peasant from a picture book, bent to his task in a rice paddy. The boy didn't call out. He was thirsty and went straight inside to the fridge. He drank from the water pitcher first and then filled a glass. The house was quiet—his aunt was away for a few days visiting friends, his sister would be at the malt shop, and their stepfather wouldn't be home until later. The kitchen, at the back of the house away from the afternoon sun, was almost cool.

After some minutes he went upstairs to dump his schoolbag in his room and wash his hands—he had handled the oily rag with the mashed up sparrow inside.

At the top of the stairs he stopped in his tracks.

Ahead of him he could see bright sunlight spilling out of his mother's bedroom into the hall. She always kept her door closed in the hot afternoons while she slept in a room made dark by heavy curtains drawn against the day.

Maybe she was having another visitation from Mary, and it wasn't sunlight at all.

He dropped his bag inside his bedroom door and crept down the corridor, his heart racing again. When he reached her doorway he looked in.

The room was empty, the bed made up and his mother gone.

Daylight everywhere. The curtains were pulled well back, and outside the surprising glass the broad leaves of the chestnut tree drooped in the heat. He had forgotten that the bedroom looked out on the chestnut tree. At the foot of the bed stood the plaster statue of the Virgin. Pale blue and white, her head inclined towards the floor, her arms held out, beckoning. Though now, in the light of day, she looked like she was shrugging. Giving up. Not thy will be done, but what's to be done?

Where had she gone?

He checked the upstairs rooms one at a time. "Mother?"

He went back down to the main floor. The tick of the hall clock sounded like pebbles dropping down a dry well, one at a time. "Mother, where are you?" She wasn't outside or he would have seen her when he walked up the path. In the kitchen again he sat at the table to finish his glass of water and think.

He looked at the door to the basement but it was closed. He never liked the basement, its musty smell—all mothballs and damp—and it was creepy, dark with only a bare bulb on the ceiling at either end. Aunt Helen would sometimes send him down to get something from the freezer. But on a hot day like this, it was the coolest place in the house. He went to the door and worked the knob several times, but it wouldn't release. There was a latch on the kitchen side, but there was no way to lock the door from the inside. He banged on it. "Mother, are you down there?"

The clock ticked in the hall.

He went out the back door into the sudden wall of heat. Mr. Thwaites in his Chinese hat was still pruning shrubs at the bottom of his garden.

His stomach felt cold in the heat, and he could hear the pulse thump in his ears. His mouth had gone dry again. Maybe a burglar had jammed the door shut from inside when he heard someone enter the house. But it couldn't be a burglar. Not with his mother upstairs. Except she wasn't now.

He went down the back steps and round to the side of the house with the small basement window. He knelt on the concrete path, cupped his hands against the glass and peered through.

As he got used to the dimness inside, he could make out a chair upended on the bare stone floor. Above the chair, between the floor and the high ceiling, he could see something white and still. A white dress and a blue veil, and so definitely not a burglar. Adjusting further to the half-light, he could see a life-sized doll—a mannequin thing—floating in the space between the floor and the ceiling. It wore the white dress and blue veil. Its arms were at its sides and now he could see its bare feet in the air. Was it Mary? Her face was white and her eyes wide open and she was floating above the floor. It was the Virgin, staring at him through the window.

Then he saw the scarf. Around Mary's neck and stretched up to the ceiling. And no, it wasn't Mary.

The tingling in his arms erupted into a thousand needle jabs and despite the heat of the alleyway he felt himself shaking. He punched his hand through the glass so he could reach for her, but the pavement rushed up and struck him hard in the face.

Eleven

So Dr. P. had it all now, the whole enchilada: *Terrible Blunder* to *Slow Decline* to *Very Rapid Descent*. It was time to thank him and bid farewell.

The very thought of him.

He stepped out onto the deck and lit another cigarette. Linda would soon be back from the movies. He hoped that she and Rachel had enjoyed the evening together. Once he had envied their togetherness, but not any more. And a very long time ago he had gone to the movies with her himself. They would do it again, he was sure. Whatever she wanted to see.

It was cooler now and growing dark, as already the longest day of the year had passed. The Canada Day weekend was coming up, and then the summer would race away as it always did, shortening by the day until autumn, and another school year.

It might have to start without him this time. He couldn't know for certain. Not yet.

He finished his cigarette and went inside. The phone light was flashing, but he hadn't heard it ring while he was out on the deck. Lost in thought, again.

A message from Magnus inviting him and Linda to a barbecue on Canada Day. Just family. Bring Rachel too, of course. He would have to decline. Linda would be out west and Rachel was with Dan now. Paul might not be around either. But it was kind of Magnus and Jan to invite them.

A half hour or so later he heard the rumble of the garage door and Linda's car pull in. The engine died, and then he heard the car door. Then the garage door.

Moments later, she came in the front. He went out to the hall to greet her. He wanted to give her a hug but refrained, thinking it might make her uncomfortable. He understood that. No matter. Everything would work out in time. “How was the movie?”

She responded as she put away her things. “Oh, you wouldn’t have liked it, but it was fine. You know, another rom-com, not your favourite. Anyway, just a movie. Rachel liked it. And dinner was good. We had a nice time. How was your evening?”

“I had a quiet time. You know. Just sorting out some things.” Then he remembered the phone message. “Magnus and Jan invited us to dinner this weekend. But I told them you’d be away.”

“Too bad. I’d love to have dinner with them. Maybe we can have them here after I get back.”

“Sure, some weekend when they’re not at the cottage. Why not?” There was nothing else to tell her. There was everything else to tell her, but this wasn’t the time. So he said nothing and just looked at her. He smiled then because just looking at her and not saying anything made him suddenly feel awkward. But she didn’t see him looking at her right then.

She checked the thermostat. “You’ve turned down the A/C. I’m finding it kind of warm in here—can we turn it on again for the night?”

“Of course. I opened the windows in both bedrooms but we can have the A/C.” These things weren’t important any more. Why had he ever allowed them to be?

“Thank you.” Now she looked at him. “Are you okay, Paul?”

"Everything's good. You all packed?"

"I just have some last things to put in." She continued to look at him. "What will you do while I'm gone? You have a whole two weeks without me to annoy you."

"I'll be fine. I'm going to clear things up in Toronto. I'll be starting on that while you're away."

"You're not selling the house?"

"There are things I have to do first, but yes, I'll be selling the house."

"Oh, thank God. Rachel will be so relieved. You must tell her. What made you decide?"

He shook his head. "Long overdue, that's all."

She nodded. "Better late than never."

He hoped she wouldn't get into it, and she didn't. It wasn't her favourite subject.

"She wants to have lunch with you."

"Great. I'll let her know about the house once I've sorted things out. It's all quite complicated—all the paperwork and the clearing out—but I'll tell her for sure when I'm straight on what's to be done."

"You don't have to share the details. I'm just glad you're getting rid of it. But let her know when you can have lunch."

She went into the kitchen and he heard her open the fridge. She was speaking to him again, but he couldn't make out what she said.

"Sorry Hon?" He headed down the passage, but she was already standing in the doorway, with the plate of cold steak in her hand.

"You didn't eat. I told you I prepared a salad and there was this."

“I’m sorry, Hon. I just didn’t feel hungry. Thanks for getting it ready. I’ll have it tomorrow.”

“It would have been better today. And it’s not good to go without dinner.” She put the plate back in the fridge and closed the door. Then she turned to face him again. “Are you sure you’re okay, Paul? You don’t eat much these days, and I can smell cigarettes. Did you smoke on the deck? You told me you had quit. Now you’re selling the house, and you never call me Hon, so what’s going on?”

He had sucked a mint but the tobacco smell was on his clothes. “I used to call you Hon.”

“That was a long time ago.”

“I know. I just felt like saying it now.” He smiled and felt awkward again. *Hon* had come out by itself, after he said, “I’m sorry.” *I’m sorry, Hon*. And so he guessed that maybe the last time he had called her *Hon* was the last time he had said he was sorry. That would explain it. But to tell her that now would only complicate a situation best left as it was.

She reached a hand out to fix his collar. “Take care of yourself while I’m gone, and call Rachel. You will have lunch with her, won’t you?”

He took her hand without feeling awkward. “Don’t worry about anything, okay? I’ll call Rachel. She’ll be okay. Everything will be okay.”

She nodded. “Rachel and I sorted things out. We had a long talk over dinner. I think Dan’s okay too. I know he cares about her.” Now she was looking into his eyes, first one side then the other, frisking him. “When you say everything will be okay—not just Rachel but everything—what do you mean?”

"I don't know, exactly. I want us to be what we were. We both want that, right? We've talked about that. Isn't that what we both want?"

She looked straight at him now, the way she always did when *she* was about to say exactly what she meant. "We haven't talked for a long time, Paul. Too much has happened. No one can ever be again what they were in the beginning. You said that."

He looked at the tiny crow's feet at the corners of her eyes and felt the tug of something else lost. After they were married, she changed the sapphire blue contacts to neutral ones. So her eyes were normal blue—just blue. "I've been wrong before."

She frowned and shook her head. "What do you want?"

"I want us. We've gone too long without us. Listen. There are things I have to do. I can't be more clear right now. Clearer, I mean. I don't know any more than what I'm telling you."

"You're not telling me anything. I just want you to tell me you'll see Dr. Hannah again. Tell me that. Rachel and I are still worried. We talked about it again tonight."

He nodded. "I've been thinking about Dr. Hannah. I really have. And it's helped. I mean I actually feel better just thinking about him." He smiled, for real this time. "You were right. That one appointment was never enough. So I've thought about him a lot."

"You need to *see* him, not just think about him Paul. Therapy doesn't work that way."

Her gaze switched to far away again like she was looking at something just behind him—years behind him maybe. She seemed unaware that he was still holding her hand.

"What time is the limo picking you up in the morning?" He had offered to drive her to the airport, but she was anxious about not getting there in time if she went with him. Traffic on the expressway was unpredictable. The limo company guaranteed a punctual arrival at the correct terminal.

"Six. My flight's at ten. I asked for the early pickup. I'll leave a note for you with my flight info and contact numbers. I'll have my cell with me." She let go of his hand and went into the hall to get her purse from the table. She took out her car keys and hung them on the key holder by the door and then returned to the kitchen. He took his house keys from his pocket and hung them on an empty hook next to hers. This time he would remember the spare one in the empty paint tin if he ever needed it.

She called from the kitchen. "Do you have their address?"

"I do. Somewhere."

She came back into the hall. "Okay, I'll write it down with everything else." She smiled briefly. Her tolerant smile. "Do you remember they live in Winnipeg?"

When she said Winnipeg the word came off her lips like a blown kiss. He remembered her lips making the tiny O when she told him at Chris Turnbull's party that she grew up in Winnipeg. The syllables lodged in his mind now as a phonetic absurdity. Winnipeg. Lake Winnipegosis. Winny Peg. Winnie the Pooh was apparently named after something to do with Winnipeg. That too was absurd. Something ever so English and stuffed cozy bear and tea and honey and a tree-house in the Hundred Acre Wood all named after a freeze-your-blood, windswept prairie city beneath the Manitoba hinterland where towns were named Moose Lake, Flin Flon and Caribou. But it was where she had grown up under the care of loving parents who needed her now. In Winnipeg.

Her preparations were under way: car keys in their proper place, so she would know exactly where to find them on her return. Suitcase already packed except for some last things. Limo ordered for early pickup. A salad in the fridge all ready for him for when he would next eat. *When* being the unknown with him. He the variable, and she the constant. For now.

When she went to the stairs he spoke. "I'll make coffee and toast in the morning. You just focus on getting ready. Print your boarding pass, all that."

"I already have my boarding pass." She kissed him lightly on the cheek. "Goodnight, Paul, sleep well. I'll see you in the morning." He watched her go up the stairs to her bedroom.

Their bedroom once. One day maybe it would be again. He would set his alarm for five, so he could prepare her toast and coffee before she left.

He lay awake for a time staring at his closed bedroom door and thinking that when he opened that door in the morning it would trip a wire to set off a whole new chain of events. It comforted him to think that. Whatever tomorrow brought it would mean change. Not knowing what that meant was strangely comforting. In the hands of the ordained now. *If it be not now, yet it will come.* He was ready.

•

In the morning he remembered not having had a single dream.

The limo arrived a few minutes late, and she was already anxious. He took her suitcase to the car. She kissed him quickly on the lips and slid into the back seat. As the car pulled away he raised his hand in a wave, but she was already leaning forward and talking to the driver, no doubt telling him her flight time. Not Wardair to Winnipeg this time. WestJet now. Changed like everything else. Crow's feet stamped at the eyes, caring parents now needing care, Malawi not Nyasaland, the end of one school year the beginning of another. Change was always the end of one thing and the start of another. A blinding flash of the obvious, that, but he had missed the obvious for a whole decade now. Maybe longer even than that.

On his desk he found an envelope propped up against the lamp. *Paul.* Inside was a note with her travel details and a message.

I need time to think about us. And Rachel. This year has been especially difficult. You're depressed and you're in a rut. You tell me there are things you have to do but you don't know what they are. And you want things to be as they were with us but that's gone now. You have my number if there's an emergency but I'd rather you didn't call just to talk. I need a break from us. I'll be busy with Mom and Dad anyway. Maybe by the time I get back you'll know what you want to do.

I love you Paul. It might surprise you to know I've never stopped. But I'm not sure where you are anymore and that's kind of like not knowing who you are anymore. No matter what, I still love you Paul. Maybe this sounds stupid but you need to start thinking better of yourself again.

So call Dr. Hannah. One appointment was never enough. Promise me you'll see him before I get back.

Linda.

No. That was something he couldn't promise. He had an appointment coming up, but it wasn't with Dr. Hannah.

He switched on his computer and opened his email. Five red flags. The first was from Rachel.

Hey Dad what's going on? I thought you guys were heading out to Grammy and Grampy's together? Mom just told me she's going alone because you have stuff to do. Aren't you done with marking and meetings? She said everything was fine but I'm worried. Call me and we'll have lunch. Dan and I are okay. *We have an interview next week with the people from YWB. Things should start moving. And thanks for the support. Meant a lot. Mom will take longer I know. But I'm kind of worried about you two. You seemed okay the other night when we came for dinner but now I'm not sure. Call me. Love you. Rachel xxoo.*

Btw we need to talk about my fund. I want to pay my way.

The other messages were from Caldwell. He deleted all but the first because the rest would just be variations on a theme.

Hey neighbor—letting you know Im in town if youre up this weekend so you can show me the house. I have a friend whos interested even tho i told him you werent selling. if you change your mind youve got a buyer. private sale, no agent but maybe we could agree on a small commission? real estates gone up 12% in the last year. and I deal in old furniture and stuff. so if you have any pieces you want valued I could do that. just letting you know. being a neighbor. bradley.

He would drive up on Saturday morning. The long weekend. Friday would be impossible with the highway a parking lot right across the peninsula. It would be the same thing from Toronto all the way to Muskoka, people riding the brakes for two hundred miles to suffer a weekend of mosquitos and jet skis and motorboats buzz-sawing their way through the heat. The lake waters were laced with engine oil and e-coli. Good luck to them all, he thought, and then reproached himself for being negative when he had resolved not to anymore.

He would drive up on Saturday morning and let happen whatever was to be. Click on any key to start. It was past time.

Caldwell. I'll be there by noon tomorrow. Doing some clearing out so I'll be busy.

He pressed Send and then rang Rachel's cell.

"Hi Dad."

"Hi darling. It's me."

"Yes Dad, I have call display. What's going on?"

Nothing was going on quite yet. "Just calling to take you for lunch."

"Mom told you. Are you and her okay?"

"We're fine. She got off okay this morning. Why?"

"I know, she texted me. That's not what I meant. She wasn't herself at dinner. We talked about Dan and me and, yeah, she's better about that now. And the movie cheered her up too, but I can tell she's not happy. You guys have had your issues, but there's something different going on. How come you're not going out there with her? She'll need help you know."

"Sweetheart, everything's fine. She wants to be with gram and gramps right now. They have a lot to talk through and I'd just be in the way. Really. We discussed it. So, lunch today or tomorrow? Just us. I mean would Dan be okay with that?" There was silence. "Rachel, she was fine when she left."

"Are you guys going to split?"

"No, we're not going to split. We're never going to split. We just thought she'd be better going by herself this time. I'll go next time to help with any moving."

Her voice became quiet, resigned. "What are you doing this weekend? Are you getting together with anyone?"

"Well, I'm going up to the house."

"Oh Jesus, Dad, why don't you just get rid of that place and be done with it?"

"Funny you should ask. It's what I'm thinking of doing."

"Thinking's what you're good at, Dad." She sighed. "Okay. I'm working today, so let's have lunch tomorrow. I'm done at two. Does that work?"

"I'll pick you up at two. Usual place?"

"Yup, thanks. Bye Dad. I love you."

"I love you too."

He looked again at Linda's note. *No matter what Paul, I love you.* He had felt all over again what it was to love her, and so it was still inside him. More than just a memory. Not long ago he couldn't distinguish between loving her and not loving her. He didn't know the difference. He even wondered then if Rachel had slipped out of his love without him being aware. Like a body slipping away under the surface. Imagine not knowing if you loved your own child. He couldn't bear to think of that, and yet he was thinking of it. That was the way with the thought hordes—this time a single horde, but still.

Not so long ago, love was a dying sun touching the blood-red water at the edge of the world and emitting a long steaming hiss. Now he felt its warm glow under the night, returning to him from the other side of the world.

What would it be to love someone so much you would die for that person? Greater love hath no man than to lay down his life for his friends? Did the man in the water, the hero among the ice floes in the Potomac River, and blinded by fuel from the submerged jetliner, love the people he brought to the rescue cable as the helicopter shimmied in the wintry gusts overhead? He didn't know the people, so how could he have loved them? He only saved them, as many as he could, until the current swept him under the ice. Arland D. Williams was his name, and he saved people he never even knew, before disappearing himself. They named the bridge after him, the bridge in Washington that clipped a wing of the jetliner and caused it to plunge into the river.

He could give up his own life for Linda and Rachel. But could he ever be sure that wasn't a wish for his own death? Keats wrote of being half in love with easeful death. Maybe it's what Arland D. Williams felt as the current took him under the ice.

Like putting out a light.

•

He didn't expect lunch with Rachel to be easy, and it wasn't.

She picked at her Greek salad, poking her fork at the black olives and the small white cubes of feta. Without looking up she said, "Do you think maybe you and Mom would be happier if you lived apart?"

The question surprised him. He had never considered it. "I don't know. Maybe she would be happier in the long run. But we're not enemies you know. We don't dislike each other." He hadn't thought about living apart because they were already doing it, sleeping in separate bedrooms, living in separate worlds. They'd been doing it for years. The day he started painting the apple white window frames and the forest green shutters and she asked him that night if he would mind sleeping in the guest room because he smelled of paint. But he knew it wasn't just the paint.

"You're supposed to love each other. It's that simple."

"In a way we do. I mean you can love someone and care about what happens to them and always think about them, and at the same time you can be happier if you aren't on top of each other." Not the most appropriate way of putting it, he thought, even as he was saying it. When was the last time he and Linda were on top of each other? He couldn't remember that either. It was even some time before the night he came to bed smelling of house paint.

She looked at him, waiting for more.

But he was floundering again. Waist deep. "Your mother's away right now and that gives us both time to think about things. Like what we still love about each other. Or why we *can't* live without each other. But whatever happens, we love *you*. That means something, I hope."

She stared at him across the table. "I guess. It's funny how you refer to her as *my mother*. Is that all she is to you now?"

"No." He didn't know what else to say. He wasn't ready for this one either. "What should I call her?"

"How about just Linda? It's not difficult Dad."

It shouldn't be difficult, but right now it was. What's in a name? Everything, it seemed to Rachel. *Call them as you see them, Dad.* He didn't really feel like calling her Linda in front of his daughter. "Okay. Linda. But I have some things to work out. Will that do?" He smiled to take the edge off his words.

She stared. The icy blue fix. "Is there someone else?"

"Good God, no."

"What about Mom?"

"No. I mean I don't think so." He had never considered it. Could he blame her if she found someone else? She once thought she loved Trevor. But she wasn't sure, and she had been honest with him about that. "She would have told me."

"Well, that's something. You can work from there, can't you? Being honest? Are you always honest with Mom? Because you can't love her if you're not."

"I know. We'll make it work again. By being honest. We can pick up where we left off—you know—wherever that was. We can find out what got lost and get it back." He wished that he sounded more convincing. He felt convinced, but he knew he didn't sound it.

She continued to stare at him. "What is it, Dad?"

He turned away and gazed out the window by their table. On the street a traffic warden was writing out a parking ticket, leaning over to one side to read the license number. She slapped down the wiper and clamped the ticket onto the windshield. Then she moved on down the row of parked cars, leaving the ticket to flutter in the breeze. "There isn't more I can say right now. When the time comes you'll know everything."

"Sounds ominous, Dad. What's that all about?"

"I'm selling the house in Toronto. It's become an issue with your mother and me, and it's time for it to go."

"*Become* an issue? Have you told her?"

"Yes. The other night."

"Wow, Dad. All these years. Why didn't you just sell it when the old guy died? Not like it had sentimental value."

"No. But the market wasn't good then. It's better now. The property has appreciated, so I was right to wait." He hoped she wouldn't hate him when she knew the truth. He was taking things one step at a time, all he could do now. Saying he wanted to sell the house was only part of the truth but it was at least true. "I'm getting started this weekend. It's why I'm going up there." He wanted to ask her now. "Are you and Dan always honest with each other?"

"I'm honest with Dan. Why would I not be? I love him. It's like I said."

"Is he always honest with you?"

"Dad, we're honest with each other, all the time. It's the only way." She stirred her coffee and looked thoughtful for a moment. "Mom doesn't know this yet, but Dan and I have decided to go on living together but not get married. We talked about it."

He nodded. Her announcement didn't surprise him somehow. "Any particular reason?"

She shrugged. "It's sort of like not needing a church to believe in God. I mean, if you're a believer at all. Sometimes being in a church makes it harder. And neither of us has seen the whole marriage thing really work. Sorry to say, Dad, but it's true. It's even worse with Dan's family. We think we've a better chance of staying together this way. And if we have kids and we're not married, that's okay too. It's no one's business any more. But I won't tell Mom yet. It's not like she needs to know everything right now."

That was true. She was only now coming around to the idea of Dan. "You'll let her know when you think it's time?"

"Of course."

He liked that she didn't ask him not to tell what he knew. But that made him an accomplice in his daughter's—what—strategizing? He didn't want to think that she learned strategizing from him. Her honesty was always her defining trait and there were times when it scared him. Like when she slammed down the piano lid in the Kiwanis final. She wasn't throwing in the towel; she'd just come to the end of pretending. She hated the hours of practice and the pride that everyone else took in her command performances, and she was having no more of it. Now dissembling had become part of her growing up—a rite of passage. Discovering you can't tell the truth all the time is part of being adult about things.

"Hello? Dad? You still here? Are you disappointed?"

"Yes, I'm here. No, I'm not disappointed. I was actually thinking I'm proud of you." He smiled. "And maybe envious."

"Why would you be envious?" She said it like an accusation. Like she didn't buy it.

"You have everything in front of you. Who wouldn't wish for that again?"

She laughed. "You're not pegging out yet, Dad. And in case you're wondering, I love you. One day you'll be proud."

He shook his head. "I'm proud of you now."

She changed the subject and talked about Malawi. "I'm ready for this. I need to get away. I haven't been anywhere yet. Winnipeg. Camp. New Brunswick. And one time to England which doesn't really count because I was just twelve and I got sick."

He spoke about her fund. She just needed to go to the bank with proof of age and sign some forms. He knew she had money saved from all her jobs as well. He told her that when he sold the Crane house there would be security for her and Linda. He said Linda this time. It just came out and it wasn't that big a deal.

She wasn't ruling out university after Malawi. Anthropology interested her she said.

His mother once worked in the museum in Toronto. What goes 'round as they say.

Again he felt a twinge of envy for the simplicity of her belief—and Dan's—that they could make life turn out as they wanted. He envied her being on the right side of mistakes she might never make. Dan was a good young man—cut from a different cloth and a little off the wall, but earnest. An engineer. Good with his pipes, as Aunt

Helen had said of his own father all those years ago.

What goes 'round.

Dan was honest and he cared for Rachel. They would love each other and love their children if they had them. It all seemed so simple. So unlike how he had complicated everything.

You're supposed to love each other. It's that simple. He needed simplicity now. What happens, happens. Move on and don't look back. Jennifer to England. Now Rachel to Malawi. His mother had moved on to simplify things.

"I have to go Dad. I'm meeting Dan." She reached for her cell. "We're getting our passport photos and we have to make appointments for our vaccines and a million other things in case all this comes through. Crazy busy right now. Let me check where he is." She tucked her hair back behind her ear and started texting him.

Later, he pulled up outside Dan's apartment building and told her he'd call in a day or two when he had settled a few things. "Say hi to Dan."

She opened the car door and then looked over her shoulder at him. "It's Mom you have to settle with Dad. She needs you, and you need her more than you think. I love you, Dad. It's not your fault, you know. It's just you sometimes. Good luck with the house." She leaned across and kissed him on the cheek. "Thanks for lunch. Talk soon." She got out of the car, shut the door with the usual emphasis and walked up the pathway to Dan's apartment. Then she was gone.

It's not your fault.

What wasn't his fault? Or maybe, what *wasn't* his fault? The marriage going stale? His ability to make people unhappy? He didn't *try* to make people unhappy but he was good at it anyway. A talent, like Johnny Appleseed, only Paul seemed to sow despondency wherever he went. It was a penchant. It was just him. Linda had said the same thing. *It's just you, sometimes, Paul.*

Well, not any more.

Twelve

It was late the next morning when he turned the minivan down Maple Street. Branches heavy with leaves hung over the sidewalks. Once, they laced their branches and braided a canopy over the street, but now the City cut them back when they grew too close to the hydro wires. As he drove down the street he could see the Crane house set back among the newer homes—a dead tooth in a row of gleaming implants.

And he could see Caldwell on his front porch looking up at a sky the colour of skim milk. The man waved when the van pulled in to the curb and he was already crossing the road when Paul killed the engine.

Even before he could get out of the vehicle Caldwell was at the passenger door, peering inside and smiling.

Paul lowered the window.

"Hey neighbour. How was traffic coming in?" He stretched out his arms across the top of the van, and spread his feet so his head was level with the window. Anyone looking might think he was trying to push the vehicle onto its side.

"Hello Caldwell."

"So, yeah, looks like another hot one. Anyway, I've been hanging around, you know, minding my business. Everything okay for a look-see? Like a quick perusal if you've got a moment?" He backed away from the van and shoved his hands deep into his pockets in an irritating *aw shucks* manner, grinning like a boy.

A quick perusal. Did he do 'Word Power' in *Reader's Digest* to help him kill time when he wasn't nosey-parkering outside the Crane house, or maybe even inside it? Had he found a way to get inside? There was still no alarm system. Paul had planned to install one this summer. But now that he was managing things there was no need for it. If Caldwell had found a way in, then Paul would just have to deal with whatever came up. He was here to deal with whatever came up.

"Give me time to get settled. Open a couple of windows, put on some coffee." He regretted saying that because now he would have to offer him coffee and prolong the stay. But he'd said it, and it didn't matter. Things would take their course. If there was providence in the fall of a sparrow, then so too in the making of coffee. Or not. It didn't matter. *Let be.*

Caldwell was looking at him. "Sounds good. I'll be on my porch, so give me a shout when you're ready."

"Say half an hour."

"See you then." Still grinning, he turned and marched across the street.

Once inside the house Paul began to perspire. He opened some windows to let in any drafts that would stir the musty air. Then he went down to the basement. In the far corner the freezer hummed, and the beady-eyed light glowed on the lid by the padlock.

He asked himself again what was the point of keeping the freezer locked. Caldwell's *perusal* would include the basement, and so Paul would have to remove the lock to put him off thinking there was something like a body inside. He turned the dial. But when he removed the lock he felt anxious. Anyone could lift the lid now and see the ice bags. Layer upon layer of them. *Whatcha got in there Paul?* Or maybe *who ya got in there?* All the same it would be prudent to remove the lock.

He didn't open the lid. He hadn't opened the lid for years. Not since the electric storm caused the brownout and required him to pile more ice bags on top. Otherwise he had never disturbed the undearly departed. Crane's resting place. Resting house. An old Elmer Fudd joke—*Hey wabbit what are you doing sweeping in my fwidge?* Punch line—*It's a Westinghouse doc.*

He wondered if a body left long enough in a freezer might sublimate. Crystalize and disappear over time. Probably not, and was sublimate even the right word? If he owned a cellphone he could Google it. But none of that mattered any more—neither the word nor the chemistry involved.

The doorbell rang. Curse the man. It wasn't even fifteen minutes. He looked at his watch—half an hour exactly. Where had the time gone? He hadn't made coffee. But why should he? He owed the man nothing. Fuck Caldwell and the horse he rode in on.

He was at the door sporting the vacant grin. He held out a book. "Brought this along in case you wanted to check out your antiques. You know, for pricing. It's a reference catalogue." He moved past Paul into the corridor. "Wow, look at this one for starters."

He made for the escritoire at the end of the passage. It had a dropdown writing surface and slots for envelopes, invitation cards and the like. "Early re-pro Chippendale, walnut, *circa* 1900," he announced. "They made a bunch of these up in Fergus, Ontario. Limited edition. I forget the maker's name but it should be right under here." He lifted the desk surface. "Yup. Knudsen. A Mennonite. Worth something these days I can tell you." He looked pleased with himself, grinning all over again like it was his.

In the living room he commented on the upholstered footstool with its embroidered butterflies—Third Reich eagles maybe—the carved nest of side-tables and the brass standard lamp. From there to the dining room and the draw-leaf mahogany table with eight chairs and matching Welsh dresser. "Everything so well preserved." He winked at Paul.

Through the paneled glass doors of the study he saw the desk and his face lit up. "Can we go in?"

Paul shrugged. Open house, why not? He turned the solid brass engraved door lever— *circa haven't a fucking clue Caldwell*—and they entered the study.

Caldwell went up to the desk. Its honeyed surface glowed in the noon sun flooding through the window. "This is something else. Awesome Paul. I've never actually seen one of these but I'm pretty sure it's a Wycherley, from Chatham." He tugged at the handle, rolled back the concertina panel cover and jabbed a finger at the brass plate. "There you go." He examined the desk and rattled off a description like he was some kind of auctioneer. "Mahogany three-drawer cylinder desk with fitted interior. Eight internal drawers plus dummies, pigeonholes, tooled leather adjustable writing slope, finely figured veneers and boxwood string lines. The cylinder opens by pulling out the top drawer"—he pulled out the top drawer—"providing access to the interior when you slide back the writing surface." He slid back the writing surface. "Do you have any idea what you've got here Paul?"

Awesome *Paul. Hey there Paul. Fuck off Caldwell.*

"I guess not. You grow up with stuff you know, you take it for granted." He looked at the man. How did he know all this stuff? And then he realized.

"Worth a small fortune I can tell you. There were only twenty made in all, did you know that?"

"No I didn't." *And neither did you, you feckless and importunate little shit of a housebreaker.* He had for sure been in the house. How many times? No matter. If he did it once he could do it a thousand times. Should he call him out now? Force his hand? No. Best to let things unfold as they would.

Caldwell ran his hand over the desk. "You know you should keep a dust sheet over this. Exposure to direct sun can dry out the wood."

That's all he needed. Dust sheets. Shrouds in the house of the dead. "Good idea. I'll get onto that."

At least the desk was empty. He had cleared it out years ago. None of Crane's Wisconsin hate pamphlets.

Caldwell was grinning again. He looked like the cat that got the cream and the early bird that caught the worm. Little Jack Horner with a plum up his bum and what a good boy was he. What was the stubby little prick grinning at now?

"Can I show you something Paul? Do you mind?"

"Ok. But what—?" Was he going to pull a rabbit out of the desk?

"Watch this." He leaned over and eased up the entire writing surface via some kind of hinge device. Paul stepped forward to look. He had no idea that it came up like that. Inside was an empty compartment. But Caldwell wasn't done. He bent down and reached underneath the raised surface to the back of the cabinet, sliding his hand around until he found whatever it was he was looking for. "Here it is."

Paul leaned forward and peered in. Caldwell slid back

a tiny panel to expose a hidden drawer. He pulled the drawer out, but then he suddenly moved to the side and obscured Paul's view. He leaned in further for a moment, then shut the drawer and slid the panel back. He lowered the writing surface and straightened up. "Pretty clever, don't you think?"

"I didn't know about it. I cleared the desk out years ago. We were never allowed to go near it. I guess all these old desks had special compartments." He was starting to feel warm again. Feeling the pulse rise in his ears.

"They were a kind of signature for the cabinet-maker. Each had their own way of personalizing their work. It was like a game—you come up with a hidden compartment that no one knew about unless they were shown. Was your dad—sorry, your stepdad onto it, I wonder?" He looked at Paul, a twinkle in his eye. "I guess we'll never know, right?"

He could see where this was heading. So let it happen. Make him do all the work. He was pretty sure the man had slipped something into the desk when he was playing around with the hidden drawer. He made it all too obvious he was up to something.

Now he was back in the living room, doing a running commentary on the oak wainscoting and the ash hardwood. But Paul should see to the creaks in the floorboards, he said. They had dried out after years of central heating, and some had come loose from the joists underneath. They could be reinforced, he said.

"You can buy a type of nail with no head, and hammer a bunch into the joists under the floor. Then you mix up some plastic wood, same colour as the boards, cap the perforations on the surface, and bingo—who's to know? Worth doing with hardwood like this. Maple floorboards, Paul, and look at the width of them. You should check for woodworm. Can we get at the floor joists from the basement? Do you mind if we take a look?"

"They were sealed up when the ceiling was paneled during the renovations."

"Paneled, not plastered? Lino squares I bet. That's what they used. 'Seventies or 'eighties, right? It would have to be a false ceiling to allow access to the pipes and wiring. Whatever they're made of, they can easily be removed. You just push them up and out. Can we have a look?"

Of course the ceiling squares were lino. Good guess Caldwell. But not a guess at all, was it. "Okay. Let me go first. The steps are narrow." He led the way into the basement and glanced across at the freezer chest.

Caldwell eyed the high ceiling and nodded. "Yeah, this'll be a breeze." He pulled a chair out from the table where years ago Sebastian had eaten his meals in silence.

He placed the chair in the middle of the carpet. "Can you hold this for me Paul? It's a little shaky." He took off his sandals and stood on the chair in his bare feet, then reached up and pushed a panel out of its frame exposing the underside of the floor above. "Just look at those beams. You don't get those anymore. Wow. They're thick."

Yes, the beams were very thick. Good, solid, weight-bearing beams.

"Got some woodworm in the joists though, Paul. You want to get that treated." He turned to survey the room.

"Great basement. Eleven foot ceiling. And hey, that's a cast furnace. Probably the original, given the size of it. Not very cost-efficient but reliable as hell," he said, missing the irony. "You want to see about that asbestos, though. Before you sell the place you have to remove the asbestos—or you can just replace the whole furnace. But you can't have asbestos any more."

"I'll look into that for sure. I keep the furnace on low in winter so the pipes don't freeze."

And at that moment as if on cue, as if it had been hanging on waiting to go public with its contents, the freezer kicked in.

"Hey you keep the freezer going?" He stepped down from the chair and made his way towards the humming appliance.

Paul followed. "I do. Just bags of ice inside. Better to keep a freezer running especially if you plan to use it again sometime. Doesn't cost anything to run because the ice does most of the work." A drop of cold sweat trickled down his stomach.

"I guess that's why you don't lock it, right? You've got a latch here but no lock. Funny. Never seen a freezer chest with a latch. Makes sense if you think about it though. You take a family with small kids. You hear about kids climbing into abandoned freezer chests. They make great hiding places. And then they can't get out. That's why they make you take the doors off a fridge or a freezer before you put it out on the curb for collection. So yeah, I guess a latch on a freezer makes sense when you think about it."

"Okay Caldwell, you've seen everything now and I appreciate the advice—asbestos, woodworm, all that. Can we go back upstairs? It's getting a little stuffy down here." He hoped he didn't sound like Norman Bates. *And here in the cellar if you look inside the freezer under all the ice, Mr. Caldwell, you'll find the well-preserved body of my stepfather. He was a dentist, you know. Have a look at those choppers.*

He followed Caldwell up the steps to the kitchen and turned to lock the basement door.

"I think I've seen everything I need to." He glanced upwards. "Four bedrooms on the second floor, right? My friend can see for himself if you decide to sell."

"Of course. And you can tell him I might be considering it after all."

"Seriously?"

He thought the man was going to lick his lips. "Seriously. I'll let you know. Meantime, I hope the tour has satisfied your craving for history."

"This'll fetch a million and a half anyway, I'm not kidding. And with the furniture? That desk? Wow. Anyways thanks for the tour Paul. I'll talk to you sometime." He went down the steps to the front walk. Paul watched him cross the road to his own house. No final wave this time.

Thanks for the tour Paul.

No. Thank you, Caldwell.

He returned to the study. His heart was pumping, or maybe he was just noticing it now. He slid back the top of the desk and pulled up the writing surface. Leaning inside he scrabbled for the movable panel at the back. He felt a tiny crescent indentation, grooved for a thumbnail, and slid back the panel. Inside, his fingers ran over a tiny knob. He pulled open a drawer. Slipping his hand into the drawer he felt something. He took out a tightly folded paper and examined it.

Cream vellum. Typed in black 12 point from an old Underwood. Crane's instructions. A carbon copy. In case Paul mislaid the original? Or did he intend them to be discovered? It didn't matter.

The paper was only the beginning of the rest of the story. All that mattered now was the rest of the story. Things were moving along nicely, he thought.

Caldwell knew everything. He had given an Oscar-winning performance of pretending to discover the hidden compartment with the document. He was a good housebreaker and an even better actor. The whole antique road show was an elaborate fiction, like his prospective buyer friend.

He closed the desk compartment and slid the panel back into place. No point in putting the document back now. It didn't matter now. It never mattered because the instructions hadn't fucking worked had they? He folded the paper and laid it on top of the desk, so Caldwell would see it when he came back.

Had Caldwell opened the freezer? The lock would never have stopped him. He must have looked inside the freezer, and probably shat his pants when he pushed aside the ice bags and saw what was underneath. He would have put back all the ice bags exactly as they were.

He'd be putting his two and two together now. Doing the math.

Nothing left to hide. That was a step. A twitch in a limp sail and, hopefully, a freshening breeze to follow.

He picked up his car keys. Nothing left to do here.

He locked the front door knowing Caldwell would

unlock it again when he went to check on the document. Paul had left it lying open on the desk. Let the games begin.

He climbed into the minivan and started the engine. As he pulled away from the curb he glanced at Caldwell's house in the rearview. No one on the porch. He would be inside watching from his window, just as old Mrs. Harrison had watched from her window all those years ago. After he checked things out he would dash off another of his semi-literate emails. It would arrive before Paul did. The guy would probably time his trip home. Put him on the clock. All part of the game now.

He stopped for gas on the way. And cigarettes. He smoked one in the van on the way home. Linda always knew if he'd had a cigarette in the van but she was in Winnipeg, and anyway he opened the windows while he smoked. Two hours later he pulled into his driveway.

In his study he sat at the desk for a moment and stared at his computer. But before he could go online the phone rang. He picked up. "Hello".

"Hey Paul. Caldwell here. I phoned earlier but you weren't back yet. I gave you an hour and a half, so I guess you stopped off somewhere. Not a lot of traffic this time of day—middle of a holiday weekend—anyway, glad you made it home safe and sound."

"How did you get my number?"

"White Pages, Paul. Not difficult. It's the information age, good buddy, or did no one inform you?"

Good buddy now. Paul said nothing.

"I know what you did with the old guy. Pretty simple plan all things considered."

"What do you want?"

"You know you can go to prison."

"What do you want, Caldwell?"

"It's a fascinating story. The house. The old man. The coming and going. All that. I filled in the gaps that old lady Harrison left because I was curious. I wondered about things from the beginning you know. You were kind of twitchy the first day we met. And then all that visiting and staying over. Clearing the eaves, mowing the lawn, window boxes in the summer, storm windows in the fall, you know, like someone's still living there. But no one's living there. Not actually living. Right? You listening?"

"I'm here." The man would have his say. He would want Paul to know what a clever snoop he was. So let him go on. Let him feel good about himself. Give him all the rope he wants.

"I know about antiques you see. I go to all these estate sales, especially out in the country. The city market's overrun with dealers. When old people die the family auctions off their things. Lots of bargains out there if you know your stuff."

Where was this going?

"So I look through the obits most days. See who's died and then follow up. I make a note and keep an eye out for the auctions, or just make a call and offer my services. But only after a time you understand, I'm not some kind of ghoul."

Pretty close, Caldwell.

"So just for the heck of it I went back through the obits from a decade ago. The newspapers here, and once out in Victoria. Old lady Harrison said that's where they took him to die. But here's the funny thing—there was no obituary. Nothing in *The Globe* or *The Star*, nothing in *The Sun* or *The Colonist* out west. Like, *nada.* So I checked out the Vital Stats office at Queens Park. No record of his death there because they don't officially record deaths in Ontario. Did you know that? I guess you did. You probably found out about all that stuff back then. They had his date of birth because he was born in Toronto. But no mention of Victoria, because he never lived there. He would have been ninety-five this year. Correct?"

"I guess." Paul hadn't kept track. What did it matter how old he would be now? "You've been a busy little beaver, haven't you?"

"Oh, but I didn't stop there. I checked out the estate court records, but got nothing there, so I guess you had power of attorney back then and you're estate trustee now. Right?"

Paul said nothing. He remembered how easy it had been to make his stepfather disappear. All those years. Until now.

"So I was curious. Here's you hanging on to a piece of prime real estate and an empty house with no record of the owner's death. All kind of curious. Like, how does someone just vanish into thin air?" He paused. "You still there?"

"Still here." Wishing Caldwell would vanish into thin air.

"So I had to see for myself. And I thought, who locks a freezer in a vacant house? That was a dead giveaway. What were you planning to do, thaw him out when they found a cure?" He laughed.

Dead giveaway. Good one. And did I ever tell you

about my highly-strung mother? "How did you get into the house?"

"You left the back door unlocked after one of your visits. I guess you got distracted before you left. But don't beat yourself up about it, good buddy. There's a dozen ways I could have got in. Anyways, I found your spare keys on the hook and got one copied. No alarm installed. These days that's irresponsible Paul. All those antiques? Are you kidding me?"

Not housebreaking then, just house entering, through an unlocked back door. There was something appropriate about the unlocked door. Like it was meant to happen. Ordained, maybe.

"The freezer was a piece of cake. I didn't need the combination. A paper clip was all it took."

He was enjoying himself. On a roll.

"And the desk?"

"Found that paper by accident. I was going through the desk of course. I do know about desks, so I'm looking for the hidden drawer. The signature thing I told you about. They all have one like I said."

Pretty clever device, he had said at the time. "So what do you want, Caldwell?"

"Well now what say we discuss this like civilized people. You're a good man, Paul, and I'd hate to see you get into trouble. I mean it's not like you did anything wrong is it? You helped the old guy ease his pain, die with some dignity, all that. Happens more and more these days, I'm told. Still it's against the law, right? The police would be interested in the disappearance of Doctor Crane do you think?"

Let him talk. He wasn't ready yet to say what he

wanted. And that was okay.

“Seriously Paul. What did you plan to do with him in the end? Or were you just going to keep him in there forever?”

“Don’t know. Never got that far.”

“A little weird, don’t you think? You go to all that trouble to make it like he never died, and all that time you’re stuck with a corpse you don’t know what to do with?”

Paul said nothing.

“Why didn’t you just stuff the body into a hockey bag or something, drive up north some night, load it up with breeze blocks and dump it in a lake?”

“Maybe I should have.” But he had never owned a hockey bag.

“Or freeze it, sure, like you did, but then saw it up into little pieces and bury them in a field somewhere. Or chuck ‘em in a dumpster.”

“Not the sort of thing I could have done I guess.”

“But to hang on to it all those years? Unbelievable. Stranger than fiction, as they say.”

There you go. But now it was time. “Listen Caldwell, I don’t feel like carrying on this conversation right now. I’m kind of at the end of my rope here and I need time to think. Tell me what you want and I’ll think it over. But don’t call me again okay? My family right now—they don’t know. So no more calls. I won’t answer. Just let me know what you want.” He hung up before the man could speak.

He went outside and smoked another cigarette. When he came back inside he opened a beer and sat down to watch a few innings of the Jays game. He didn't want dinner. Between innings he checked his messages.

When Caldwell's red flag finally appeared he opened the message and saved it without looking at it. He would read it in the morning. Everything could wait till the morning. There was no hurry.

He drank another beer and switched off the TV before the ball game finished. He wished he could have stayed awake because the Jays were winning this one. You never knew with baseball though.

Thirteen

The doorbell woke him next morning. At first he didn't move, thinking it must be early. Today was Sunday. The long weekend. Who would come to the door this early on a Sunday? Church people maybe? He rolled over and tried to drop off again.

Tomorrow was Monday. Canada Day. Dominion Day, once. The Dominion of Canada, the Red Ensign flying on Parliament Hill. Now Canada, and a flag that looked like a nosebleed, his stepfather said once during a rant about the conspiratorial decline and disintegration of imperial something or other.

He wouldn't go back to sleep now. He'd give the church people time to go away and then he'd get up.

The doorbell rang a second time and he looked at the clock. 10:49. The morning was nearly over. He stepped into his jeans and went down to the front door.

It was Magnus. He had half-turned away and was about to head down the steps when Paul appeared. He looked back and smiled. "Hey. I didn't waken you, did I?"

"Come in Magnus." He moved to the side of the doorway. "I can't believe I was still asleep. I'll make some coffee. Come through."

Magnus stepped into the hallway. "Thanks. I'm sorry I woke you. I was dropping Alison off at a friend's and I saw your van in the drive."

"Really, it's okay. I kind of wish you'd come a couple of hours ago. I've wasted the morning." He filled the coffee maker and switched it on. "How come you're not at the cottage?"

"We decided to stay here. Remember? I asked you

guys to come for dinner."

"Yes, of course." He had forgotten to reply to the message. "I'm so sorry, Magnus, I meant to tell you. Linda's away in Winnipeg at her parents'."

"Okay, but come anyway."

"Thanks, Magnus, but I have things to get done this weekend. Stuff to catch up on, you know?"

"Tell me about it. There's never time for anything during term. But, you know, if you change your mind we'd really like to see you."

"Thanks. I appreciate it. And sorry again for not calling you back."

"Don't worry about it, my friend. Just show up if you feel like it."

After he made the coffee they sat at the table by the French windows, looking out into the garden and the ravine beyond. Paul would like to have sat outside and had a cigarette with his coffee, but the morning was already hot, and Magnus didn't know he liked a smoke now and then.

"Jays win last night?"

Magnus shook his head. "Nope. Up 6-3 top of the ninth and Detroit bats straight through the order, so we're down 10-6. Bottom of the ninth, we go out one-two-three."

"Martinez?"

"Martinez. Twenty-two saves already and it's not even the All-Star break yet."

Paul smiled. What his father would have made of Detroit winning a game like that. He wondered if his father might have gone over to the Jays when they joined the league. Likely not. The Tigers were his team. Last night he would have hung on right through the ninth as he always did, until the final out, then gone to bed a happy man.

"So Linda's with her folks. Rachel with you?"

"No she's at a friend's." He didn't want to get into the business with Dan right now. That could wait.

"Rachel and her friend can come too. Alison's not at camp yet and Jeremy's just back from tree planting. They'd like to see her. They can all jump in the pool and cool off."

Paul stared out at the still garden and the trees beyond. They looked sapped in the heat, and it wasn't yet noon. "Thanks Magnus. Maybe in a couple of weeks if I'm around?"

Magnus set down his coffee mug. "You going somewhere?"

"I don't know yet. Everything's sort of up in the air right now but I'm working through it. I'll let you know. Linda wants to get together with you guys when she comes back."

His friend sat back and folded his arms. "You know, Paul, we haven't seen much of you these past weeks. Lately you just do what's needed at school and then you're gone. You missed the staff meeting and you didn't come to the year-end party. Are you sure everything's okay?"

"I'm just a little preoccupied right now. You know, with—everything."

"Family okay?"

He nodded.

"You've lost some weight."

"I could stand to lose a few." He was thinking maybe he should have gone to Magnus for counseling. Magnus who listened and didn't judge. All the kids at school trusted him. Paul felt like one of them now. In need of some counsel. Dr. P. had been a good listener, though.

And really, he was managing things—just by letting them manage themselves. He had saved Caldwell's message last night, already knowing what it said without reading it. He wasn't in any hurry to read it. The message would fall into place with everything else.

He looked at his friend sitting opposite. Magnus wouldn't ask more questions. He would wait for Paul to say more if he wanted. He would sit and allow things fall into place as they had done all his life. And if Paul didn't want to say anything Magnus wouldn't push him. He would stay until it was time for him to go. No one made Magnus do anything he didn't already want to do.

Paul felt he was acquiring the knack now. The two of them sitting in a sun-splashed lounge on a Sunday morning in control of the moment as much as it was possible to be. He supposed Magnus had no real regrets in his life, but he didn't envy him for that. Envy was negative; it could control you. Like the past could control. What you have to do with the past is let it go. An acquired skill, but he was getting there.

Now he would like to be a little clearer about the future. Maybe his friend would know something about that.

"What do you do when you've reached the end, Magnus? Can you tell me? Have you ever come to the end of something? I need to know what you do when you get there." He looked at him. Big, heavy-shouldered, broad-faced Magnus, who had lived in a diving bell fathoms below. Away from it all, under the sea. He seemed even to breathe more slowly than normal people, as if his diver experience had taught him to use as little oxygen as possible. A life skill in this humidity.

"Is it you and Linda?"

He shook his head. "Not any more. We're fixing that." He took a breath. "I've done something wrong, Magnus, and I have to put it right." He paused. The sound of his words pleased him. He liked their simplicity. Even saying the words was a step. They gave form to the thought. *I have to put it right.* Then the action would give substance to the words. First the words, then the action. That's how it went when you took control. He had spoken his own words and he had Caldwell's words now too. Taking control.

"Does Linda know?"

"I'm not sure what she knows. We haven't really talked about it. Not for a long time."

"What did you do? Can you tell me?"

Paul shook his head. "What I did isn't important. I can manage what I did. I just need to know what you do when you come to the end. Of anything, I mean." He kind of knew but he needed to hear his friend say it. Hear the words, so it was real. It was absurd to tell Magnus nothing about the problem and still ask him for the answer. But he would understand because he understood everything.

Magnus looked at him for a moment, like he was reading his thoughts. "I don't know. Walk away maybe? Or, if you're at the end and you can't just walk away how about starting all over again? Go to where you last felt good about yourself and take a different road. Better than beating your head against the wall, I've found. Let go of the bad stuff and begin again."

"Like Michael Finnegan."

Magnus stared.

"Michael Finnegan. It's a song. It goes on a loop.

There was an old man named Michael Finnegan,

He had whiskers on his chinnegan.

They fell out and then grew in again.

Poor old Michael Finnegan begin again."

Jennifer would sing it to Paul when he was going to sleep. Her father sang it to Jennifer before Paul was born. Paul sang it to Rachel when she was little. Generations on a loop too, like the song. The song was a place in his life where he felt good about himself. Go back to where you felt good about yourself, is what Magnus was telling him.

He grew fat and then grew thin again,

Then he died and had to begin again.

Poor old Michael Finnegan begin again.

Did Magnus wonder as he nodded with the blank expression on his broad face that maybe his good friend had just popped a final rivet? The meaning of life in a nursery rhyme? But that was the point—simplicity was entirely the point.

"You're a teacher Paul. You know about starting again. Every year. It starts all over when September comes. New faces. New books. Always a new start. It happens all the time."

Paul nodded. Outside at the edge of the ravine he could see some trees showing the first patches of rusty orange. There was still one day left in June, but soon enough it would be autumn, and the land would show off a coat of many colours.

Summers in Ontario passed quickly. Relentlessly. Maybe it was the sudden ferocity of heat that drove summer to make an early dash for autumn's cover. It had hardly begun and was already showing signs of its passing.

The students at Centennial were the same. They burned to be older when they were at school, desperate to leave and become adults in whatever it was they called the real world, and when they came back for their reunion five years later they already showed signs of a too-rapid aging. The boys had filled out, and some had receding hairlines. Others had grown thin beards and trendy goatees that aged them even more. And the girls were women already. Their beauty, sleek and tight when they were at school, had thickened somehow.

On homecoming weekend they stood on the sidelines to cheer on the teams where once in school colours they themselves had run like deer. Now, as though regretful, they came to retrieve what they had too quickly surrendered and too eagerly wished to be behind them. They were once too young to love the simple things—the green crayon tips of the maple buds and the tiny yellow flames of the new forsythia. Love the simple things as the poet can and forgiveness is possible, said Father McGrath.

Teachers like students aged as the maple trees did, each school year adding another precise ring. You could spend a lifetime just adding the rings. Counting them. The circles of memory intertwining and inseparable like the Olympic rings, each threading through another and another and then into itself again. It was time to stop counting the rings, time to untangle the circles and begin again, like Michael Finnegan. It was so absurdly simple.

Life was renewable. And love too. What else was reincarnation? *Ye must be born again.* Jesus Christ and Michael Finnegan. Both fictions, but no less true for that in the ways that mattered. He would tell Linda, but he would wait until she came home. She had asked him not to call while she was away. Except in an emergency. This could wait. This wasn't an emergency. Not now.

Magnus waited. He would wait till Paul was ready. He was a good listener—like Dr. P.

"I'm okay now." He stood. "Thanks Magnus. I'll call you. I might need you later today."

"We're here all weekend, like I said. And think about coming over, okay?"

He stood by his open car door in a way that reminded Paul of his father in the photograph with his brand new Kaiser Henry J. "Let me know. Anything I can do. Call me. Good luck, friend." He reversed out of the driveway and drove off, his arm raised outside the window in a last wave.

Paul went into the study and opened Caldwell's message from last night.

I dont know how much money you have Paul but you've got a nice piece of real estate here. sell me the house and everything inside and I mean everything including the stiff so you dont have any worries. a nominal price to make it a proper transaction. lets say a dollar. ill look after things from there. Guarantee you no police involvement.

Thank you Caldwell. Not such a clever-pants after all.

Hoist by his own petard. Like Tweedledum and Tweedledee, Hamlet's treacherous friends, also undone by a letter.

He clicked once and the message was saved. His now. So simple.

He typed out a note to Linda.

I'm not sure where I'll be when you read this but it won't be far. I'm dealing with everything now. I don't know how it will turn out but you and Rachel will be okay.

I wasn't the husband you thought you married. I wasn't the father Rachel needed. That's done with now. When all this is over I want to start again if you think we can do that. It's never too late to start again. I love you both. I hope Maureen and Jim are okay. Please tell them I'm thinking of them. Paul.

He read it over once and pressed Send. The words would already have broken up into whatever words break up into when they hurtle through cyberspace. Sentence fragments perhaps. Syllables. Letters. They would already be on Linda's laptop, beamed down faster than the speed of light, as words once more.

His message to Rachel was brief. *I'm sorry for everything but I'll make it up to you. I promise. I'm going to be out for a bit but I will call you. There's nothing to worry about. I love you. Dad.* He would send it just before he left the house.

He wrote to Jennifer in England. Only to say that he would tell her everything one day, but that he was fine. It was time that she came back for a visit.

Then he looked up the phone number. It was just after two o'clock when he dialed. A voice answered after one ring.

"Good afternoon. Niagara Police. Heritage Division. This is Alana. How may I connect you?"

"Good afternoon Alana. My name is Paul Thorne and I want to report a crime."

"Okay sir, but 9-1-1 would have been faster. Do you need assistance?"

"No. What I mean is I committed a crime and I want to report it."

A brief silence. "I don't think I understand."

"I want to speak to a member of the police—an inspector maybe—or a desk sergeant—so I can report my crime."

"Sir, I don't really know what department to connect you with. This isn't how we do things here."

"Can you put me through to the department that deals with criminal investigation? I mean someone who deals with, you know, crime? Felonies. Burglaries. Homicide. That type of thing?"

"I'll put you through to the desk sergeant in your precinct. Can I have your full name please?"

"Paul Daniel Thorne."

He was put on hold. Then a voice came through. "Yes hello, Mr. Thorne? Desk Sergeant Phillips here. Is this an emergency?"

"No it's not an emergency. Not now. It's all under control. I just want to report a crime that I committed."

There was a pause. "I'll transfer you to Inspector Fairchild. Hold for a second will you?"

It was more like a minute. He supposed Inspector Fairchild must be switching on a recording device of some kind. Or maybe looking for a pen and paper to write down the details. He didn't know how these things worked.

"Inspector Fairchild here, Mr. Thorne. So, what's this about a crime you think you've committed?"

He sounded casual, like he was asking him what he would like in his coffee. *Will you have crime with that, Mr. Thorne?*

"I enabled my stepfather to die and never reported his death."

The inspector cleared his throat. "When did this happen, sir?"

"Ten years ago. In Toronto. I want to report it now."

"His death was never reported?"

"Until now. That is correct."

"There was no coroner?"

"No coroner. No death certificate. Just a death."

A pause. "And you say this happened ten years ago?"

"Yes. In Toronto."

"Can I ask what you did with the body?"

"It's in a freezer. A chest freezer in the basement. My stepfather's house on Maple Street."

"Where are you calling from now, sir?"

"I'm calling from my home. I live at 253 Escarpment Drive, right here in Heritage."

"Do you have a lawyer sir? It's your lawyer who should have contacted us. Not yourself directly. You do have a lawyer, I presume?"

"No, but I can get one. I'll need to make another call first. I don't know any lawyers in town but I can get a number and call one." It was irksome to discover there was a right and wrong way of reporting your own crime. He hoped things wouldn't become complicated again when he wanted them simple. Simplicity was everything, and he hoped the police would cooperate on that. He was giving himself up, for heaven's sake. How could there be a protocol in surrendering to the police?

"Okay sir. I must ask you not to leave your house. We'll be bringing you down to the station for questioning. In the meantime, please contact your lawyer. I'm dispatching a cruiser right now and it'll be at your house shortly. I'm coming from the Falls, so I'll be there a few minutes later. Is there anyone in the house with you now, sir?"

He supposed the Inspector Fairbanks was worried he might do something desperate. Enable his *own* suicide perhaps before the police could get to him. He had thought once or twice about how he might do that—just out of curiosity, really—but none of the methods appealed to him. Anyway, he wasn't desperate. It was life he wanted now, not death. He wondered what his sentence would be. In the end of course he had done more than merely *enable* the old man's demise. He had suffocated him with plastic garbage bags. More than helped him on his way. But he'd leave all that to police procedure, and anyway his lawyer would advise him. Homicide was homicide with or without plastic bags. But it was a one-off, and by request, not like he was a serial killer or anything.

"Mr. Thorne?"

"Everything's fine here Inspector. I'm in the house on my own, but I'm okay. I won't do anything. I'll wait for your people arrive."

Why hadn't it occurred to him that he would need a lawyer? A lawyer had done their house purchase and land transfer, and more recently drafted their wills. But not criminal stuff. There was Gilpin all those years ago in Toronto, but he didn't really want to see Gilpin now. *You mean that friend you were telling me about was you all the time, Mr. Thorne? Seriously?*

He would phone Magnus. He should have asked Magnus that morning but it never occurred to him. No matter. He rang his number.

Magnus didn't ask questions, but gave him the number of a lawyer he knew. Sam Kershaw. Magnus told him to call back if he needed anything else. Paul thanked him and dialed Sam Kershaw, who was at home. He knew Kershaw would be home because with everything falling into place he wouldn't be anywhere but home, even though it was the holiday weekend and Kershaw no doubt owned a cottage in the Kawarthas. When he finished explaining his situation, Kershaw agreed to meet him at the police station. Such civility extended to a criminal. It was all running smoothly. The clues falling into place. Everything accounted for. Just like in a crossword clue. He sent off the message he had composed for Rachel. Then he went into the living room and dialed another number.

He watched the street through his front window as he listened to the ringing at the other end. He felt like Mrs. Harrison now, checking the neighbourhood, waiting for something to happen, like the police cruiser pulling up to the curb now.

"Hello. Bradley here."

"Hello Caldwell. Just a quick call to say I won't be making any deals with you."

There was a pause. “How did you get my number?”

“Call History. The information age. I thought you knew.”

He heard him chuckle. “Okay, snap. So, no deal, eh? I’m sorry to hear that Paul. I thought you were smarter. You leave me no choice now.”

“You’re right.”

“It won’t take much for the police to get a warrant to search the house.”

“You don’t want to speak to the police because I’ve already spoken to them. But there’s a cruiser outside my house right now if you insist. Hang on and I’ll put an officer on so you can explain your little scheme. Blackmail, it’s called. Oh, and your email. You’re really rather stupid when all’s said and done. Goodbye Caldwell. I don’t expect I’ll hear from you again.”

The line went dead.

Two uniformed officers, one a woman constable, were at the front door. He invited them into the living room. They didn’t want tea, but they thanked him anyway and then read him his rights.

Some minutes later a second cruiser pulled into the driveway. The neighbours would be at their windows now, the ones who hadn’t spoken to him in twenty years. A plain-clothes man and another uniformed officer got out of the car. One of the officers opened the front door to let them in. Paul introduced himself. Inspector Fairchild was civil just as he had been on the phone. He mentioned again that the situation was unusual because there should be a lawyer already present at the house when the police arrived. Paul told him that he had a lawyer now who would meet them at the station. Inspector

Fairchild seemed satisfied.

He wondered if Linda had read his email yet. Probably not, or she'd have called him straightaway. She would have to cut short her visit to her parents. He was sorry for that but it couldn't be helped. She would understand that some things had to shift around to allow everything to fall into place. Once procedures were under way at the police station he would ask Sam Kershaw to give Rachel a call. He knew he wouldn't be allowed to contact members of his own family and he was glad he had already sent off his message to Rachel.

She would wait for her mother to fly home. They would meet up first and then come down to the station together. All in good time. There was no hurry. Not like he would be going anywhere.

Inspector Fairchild was telling him that he would be cautioned and asked to make a statement. They would not make a formal arrest until after they had searched the premises on Maple Street. Paul told him not to bother with a warrant—he would give them the keys to the house. And they wouldn't need the freezer combination, because he hadn't secured the lock after his last visit. He said nothing to Inspector Fairchild about Caldwell. The man had done him a favour really, so he could have no hard feelings towards him now.

The inspector told him they would need a warrant regardless. Procedure again. Paul would be fingerprinted, and there would be photographs. Mug shots. Head on and profile, just like on TV. He would have to hold up a number for the photos, he supposed, or maybe that's not how they did it any more.

Fairchild continued. Once the details were sworn before a Justice Paul would be charged, remanded in custody and detained over the rest of the holiday weekend. There would be a bail hearing on Tuesday morning. Fairchild didn't think that would be a problem. A man who had turned himself in was not likely to go on the lam. Paul would have to provide security but he could manage that. He owned a healthy piece of real estate in Toronto. His frozen assets. But he didn't say that to the officers.

Inspector Fairchild outlined the procedures to him like a surgeon explaining a pre-op. If he were found guilty he would have a criminal record. There could be a jail sentence. He would lose his teaching job. Paul hoped there might be compassionate grounds when everything was known but he couldn't count on that. Justice would take its course. He expected nothing less.

Things would work out when he had done his time. He could do volunteer work. Community service. Private tutoring maybe. Life would go on.

He felt like he'd been anaesthetized.

He wondered again if Linda would leave him. He couldn't blame her if she did. He hadn't made her very happy. Rachel would escape to Malawi with Dan. Get away from it all for a while. Break out, be free, be youths without borders. He wondered how Linda would manage while he was serving time. She had her own income of course and he would arrange for the sale of Maple Street. Would her life be all that different with him locked up? Just in a different place this time, imprisoned in something larger than a nutshell, and without the bad dreams he hoped.

In the end they would survive. And it wouldn't be the end. They would begin again. It was never too late to do that. He was certain of it. Hopeful anyway.

He made sure the house was locked when they left, and then handed his keys to the inspector.

Fairchild's cruiser smelt of new upholstery. Paul climbed into the back behind the thick metal grille. Overkill in this case he thought. He was unlikely to go berserk—*go postal* as his students would say—and attack the officer in front of him. Not after he'd been so eager to give himself up, and anyway he would likely be granted bail. He was surprised all over again at how easily everything had gone and how right it all felt.

He wondered if he needed a cigarette now, recalling how he enjoyed a cigarette most when he was feeling relaxed and at peace with the world.

But he didn't want a cigarette right now. He was okay right now. Inspector Fairchild and his officers had kept their composure through it all, and so had Paul. Everyone was being civil to each other.

He didn't feel like a cigarette or even a criminal.

And they told him he had the right to remain silent. That was something.

Acknowledgements

Writing is a solitary activity, but I owe much to some kindred spirits who have supported me along the way.

Lee Gowan at the Banff Centre, David Bezmozgis at Humber College, Justen Ahren, Jack Soni and fellow scribes at the Noepe Residency in Martha's Vineyard. Pauline West, for her astute critiquing. Pauline Couture for her encouragement.

The Canadian Authors Association (St. Catharines, Ontario) and The Writers' Circle (Niagara-on-the-Lake).

The late Richard B. Wright, dear friend and colleague at Ridley College, who taught and wrote great books with passion, and from whom I learned that writing is primarily its own reward.

My daughter Catherine Rose, who edits with a sharp eye and who believed in this book from the start.

To friends who read an early draft, and encouraged me to carry on: Diane. Robert. Shelley. Harry and Michelle. Jewell-Ann. Michael and Marion. Rob. Ellen. My mother, Eunice, and my brother, Paul, who resembles my protagonist in nothing but name. By the way, all characters and events in this book are entirely fictional.

Finally, to Keith Abbott and Karolina Robinson at Michael Terence Publishing, for their encouragement and patience.

55179520R00177

Made in the USA
Middletown, DE
08 December 2017